Defending David

Barbara M. Britton

Defending David
COPYRIGHT 2021 by Barbara M. Britton

Contact Information: titleadmin@pelicanbookgroup.com

All scripture quotations, unless otherwise indicated, are taken from the Holy Bible, New International Version(R), NIV(R), Copyright 1973, 1978, 1984, 2011 by Biblica, Inc.™ Used by permission of Zondervan. All rights reserved worldwide. www.zondervan.com

Cover Art by *Nicola Martinez*

Harbourlight Books, a division of Pelican Ventures, LLC
www.pelicanbookgroup.com PO Box 1738 *Aztec, NM * 87410

Harbourlight Books sail and mast logo is a trademark of Pelican Ventures, LLC

Publishing History
First Harbourlight Edition, 2022
Paperback Edition ISBN 978-1-5223-0354-1
Electronic Edition ISBN 978-1-5223-0352-7
Published in the United States of America

What Readers Are Saying About "Defending David."

Ms. Britton drew me in on page one. Rimona's and Ittai's story of love, faith, and valor still lingers in my mind today. Defending David is definitely a jewel.

~ **Olivia Rae, award-winning author of the Secrets of the Queens series**

Barbara M. Britton's best yet! Readers will fall in love with loyal Ittai and strong Rimona as they work separately and together to support the anointed king of Israel and uphold the sovereignty of the Most High God in the midst of turmoil and unrest while also seeking shelter from their own enemies. Their story is intertwined with thorough Biblical research on the life and times of King David, and shows the complexities of his character as well as the faith that made him a man after God's own heart. Add suspense, wit, wisdom, and characters whose struggles are real and relatable even thousands of years after the historical events they experience, and you get a masterful and inspirational exploration of the events of Absalom's rebellion in II Samuel. *Defending David* turns the Psalms into battle cries, reveals the warrior within the psalmist, and reminds us all exactly where our help comes from in times of trouble.

~ **Jenna Van Mourik, author of *Jerusalem's Daughter*.**

Step back in time to the days of King David when

he's lost control of his family and a foreigner is his staunchest ally. Britton brings the Bible to life with strong characters, recognizable names, and the thrill of sharing a faith in the One True God.

~ **Terri Wangard, author of** *Roll Back the Clouds*

Dedication

For my family and friends who have been with me
through the ups and downs of life.

"A man of many companions may come to ruin, but
there is a friend who sticks closer than a brother."
Proverbs 18:24

Acknowledgements

This book would not have been possible without
the help of so many people. My family has been the
best cheering section throughout my publishing career.
I am blessed to have their love, encouragement, and
support.

A big thank you goes to my editor, Fay Lamb, who
helps to make my stories shine. I am blessed to have
Nicola Martinez in my publishing corner. She has
brought all my stories to light through her leadership
at Pelican Book Group.

My critique partners have encouraged me to finish
this story and see it through until the end. Thank you,
Denise Cychosz, Sandy Goldsworthy, and Kathy
Zdanowski for your wisdom and friendship. My
brainstorming group has kept me writing faithfully
each week. Thank you, Betsy Norman, Karen Miller,
Sandee Turriff, Jill Bevers, Alison Welli, and Christine
Welman.

I am blessed and honored to have the

endorsements of Olivia Rae, Jenna Van Mourik, and Terri Wangard for this story.

The author communities of ACFW, RWA, SCBWI, and Pelican Book Group, have been a huge support in my writing career.

My church family has kept me going during good times and stressful times. What a blessing to have their loving support.

And last, but not least, the Lord God Almighty, for giving me the gift of creativity and breath each day to write these stories. I am a cancer survivor, and not a day goes by that I don't praise the Lord for his healing. To God be the glory.

Books by Barbara M. Britton

Tribes of Israel Series

Providence: Hannah's Journey
Building Benjamin: Naomi's Journey
Jerusalem Rising: Adah's Journey
Defending David: Ittai's Journey

Daughters of Zelophehad

Lioness: Mahlah's Journey
Heavenly Lights: Noah's Journey
Claiming Canaan: Milcah's Journey

The Children of Jesse noted in
I Chronicles 2:13-17:

Sons:
Eliab
Abinadab
Shimea
Nethanel
Raddai
Ozem
David

Daughters:
Zeruiah
Abigail

The notorious sons of Zeruiah; David's
nephews:

Abishai
Joab
Asahel (deceased at the time of this story)

Prologue

Ziklag, a Philistine town

Ittai calculated every footfall so as not to spook the piglet. The young animal chewed leaves off of a bramble bush oblivious to its stalker. Ittai had seen older boys wrestle livestock, and if he and his mother were to eat this day, he would need to be quick to subdue the runt. His hands grew slick, but he would not wipe them on his tunic and chance missing a meal.

The piglet ravaged another branch. How could the animal be hungry? The Hebrew warrior David and his men had conquered many villages before the sun thought to grow tired. Surely, the owner had slopped pens earlier this morning. Ittai hadn't been slopped in two days.

Below him, along the slope of the rolling hills, men drank and boasted of their spoils. No one mentioned a missing sow or her babe.

His prey chewed, and chewed some more, heedless to the noise all around and to the rumblings of Ittai's belly.

Nearer and nearer he prowled using other bushes

for cover. He may not have fought with the Hebrews, but he would fight this pig and bring his mother some meat.

His heartbeat surged as he drew closer. The pound echoed through his bones and filled his throat. His nostrils feasted on the dank of the pig's hide. One swift lunge, and he and his mother would sup for days.

Ready, and—

"You're a Gittite." A deep voice spooked the pig and Ittai's feast fled.

Ittai whirled around, fire racing though his veins. A Hebrew man smirked at him. Ittai would bet the man's belly was stuffed full. Why did the stranger have to speak before Ittai caught his food? He fisted his hands in case the foreigner wanted some sport. A boy may not win a battle, but he could kick and bite.

Straightening to his full height, Ittai glared at the man's waist and lifted his chin higher. His mouth stung making it hard to swallow, let alone answer the stranger. Someone owed Ittai a pig even if it wasn't fully grown.

"You—"

"Of course, he's a Gittite. Why would any of our men chase unclean animals?" A second warrior approached and laughed, but not like an enemy. He laughed as a friend, as friendly as one could be after slaying a town. "The battle is over, Joab."

Ittai had heard of this second man and glimpsed him from a distance. He had slayed tens of thousands, or so the women sang. If their songs were true, one day this man would be a king of the neighboring land. All the women whispered about David, son of Jesse, camped in Ziklag, far from his own people, but not far from Ittai's hut. Would this David have food to share?

Swallowing, Ittai coughed as saliva clogged his throat.

Joab bent and glared at him.

Now, Ittai had become the small animal being hunted.

"He's a spy." Joab crossed his thick arms. "I'll wager on it."

Ittai's stomach cramped. How would he explain where he lived? He understood Hebrew better than he could speak the dialect.

"You've lost your gold," David said. "If he's a spy, he'd be whispering to his king at the moment. The boy is still with us and not in the northern foothills with Achish."

Nodding, Ittai agreed with the man in the songs.

"Why isn't he fighting with his father?" Joab pushed Ittai closer to the bush. "Answer me. Did your voice take off with that pig?"

Pressing down a remark that may get him whipped or beaten, Ittai remembered his upbringing. He was a Philistine. An enemy of the Hebrews until recently. Until King Achish allowed the man, David, to settle in Ziklag.

Ignoring the mean warrior, Ittai focused on David. "Mm...my father is dead." Ittai's temples pulsed with his confession. "And my king doesn't always win. You do." That was the truth. Truth he would never say to his king. Not if he cared to live.

"What makes you think I always win?" David swaggered toward the bramble bush and twisted a leaf clean off a spindly branch.

David's companion jabbed a finger into Ittai's chest. "Spy, he's waiting for your wisdom?"

Ittai shrugged and tried to ease the sting of the Hebrew's poke. Puffing out his chest, he dipped his head in a show of respect to David and spoke the tale he had heard since he was old enough to understand why he and his mother were alone. "My mother saw you. You killed our fiercest fighter. When you were young. Like me." He pointed to himself. "She said you killed Goliath...with a stone. No sword or arrow."

David's gaze became like that of a swooping hawk. "That Philistine Goliath made a mistake no man should make if he desires to live."

Should I ask? Ittai's heart boomed louder than the raucous army camped below. Curiosity bubbled on his lips. He wanted to learn to fight well so his mother would always have enough to eat. From the looks of the men celebrating in the valley, David provided for his men, unlike the King of Gath who left Ittai's family to starve. What could the men take from him now? His pig had fled. He didn't have any coin or even a blade. "Tell me, lord. Tell me how not to be foolish like Goliath so I can become a great warrior like you."

David knelt in the dirt, barely a footfall from Ittai. A slight breeze brought a waft of David's breath to Ittai's nostrils. The warrior's breath held a hint of cloves and honey. The Hebrew commander had filled his belly. If it were any other warrior, Ittai would have sprinted into the bramble bushes, but something, something about this man, held him fast like a curse. David's smile was as big as Ittai's mother's when her oil jar overflowed.

"Uncle." The mean man sighed. "Send the boy home. We have battle plans to make ready."

"In time, Joab." David untied a satchel on his belt and took out a piece of bread. A big piece. He held it out. "It's not as big as the piglet."

Ittai almost fainted. His belly roared as he took the bread. He hid some in his palm for his mother and bit into the food. He almost swallowed his bite whole. The bread was the best he'd ever tasted.

David grinned. His eyes creased on the sides. "Goliath mocked my God. The God of my forefathers. That is why I fought him. For his offense."

"My father is dead. He fought against Hebrews." Ittai didn't know why he shared this truth, but the truth burst forth with some spittle. He stared at the wide brown eyes beholding him. "Your king gave the order. Now, you're here. Hiding."

"Saul won't harm us." Joab stroked the hilt of his sword. "Not as long as I have breath and a weapon."

Ittai wished the scar-faced young man would leave. He didn't mind David though. On his hip, Ittai placed the fist holding his mother's bread and pushed inward, protruding a tiny bump of flesh. "I will kill your Saul."

"Do not speak of such." David furrowed his brow at Ittai and regarded Joab with the same scowl. "No one will harm Saul. He is God's anointed king. He was anointed long before I was."

Joab shrugged and gave a slight nod. His lips pressed thin as if he agreed with David's answer, but his nose wrinkled like an empty sack.

"I'm s-s-sorry." Ittai's words stuck to his tongue. "Is that why you are here? Instead of in your land?" He stuffed another piece of bread in his mouth.

"I'm here for a time," David said. "I'm waiting on God."

"Your God?" Would he be struck for not knowing the Hebrew God?

At the mention of his God, David's shoulders fell, and the lines vanished from his forehead.

"The One True God. Though, he is not solely my God." David laid his hand on Ittai's shoulder. "Remember that, son."

Son. He couldn't remember anyone calling him son. He couldn't remember his father's voice. Or for that matter, his father's face. Tears welled in Ittai's eyes.

"What is your name?" David rose and, with sunlight sparking in his brown eyes, beheld Ittai.

"It-tai." His teeth chattered on a name he had spoken for years.

The man that women sang about squeezed Ittai's shoulder. "Ittai the Gittite. That is a name to be proud of." David released Ittai's tunic and strode down the slope toward his men. Turning, he said, "Do you know where the mules are tied, Ittai the Gittite?"

Ittai nodded. "I filled waterskins before."

"Good." David smiled like Ittai's mother again.

"Tell the tall, bushy haired man that his commander has awarded you a dressed lamb. If he squawks like a hen, tell him he can find me near the washing basin." The future king untied the satchel from his waist and tossed it in the air. The bag landed at Ittai's feet in a puff of dust. "Have him fill that with more bread. Go in peace Ittai the Gittite. And do not speak about our raids."

"I won't." His voice squeaked as if he had caught the piglet. Ittai took a step backward and gripped the soft leather satchel in his hand. David's words echoed in his head. Go in peace? How could a warrior go anywhere in peace?

Someday, he hoped to be half the warrior David had become. He'd be strong and have lots of gold. He might even be a man about whom women sang.

1

Thirty years later

Beersheba, south of Hebron, in the land of Judah

Rimona clutched the tunic of her elderly neighbor and nearly ripped the embroidered cloth. "Let me stay with you, Leah. I will gut fish, bring you water, anything you see fit for me to do."

"You know I cannot take you into my household when you have kin," her friend's voice quivered, but she did not remove Rimona's fingers from her garment.

Welcoming the old woman's callused-hand caress, Rimona leaned against the small stone home she had shared with her mother for twenty-four years before her mother had passed away. Rimona cradled her confidante's hand close. "Why didn't my uncle come to mourn his sister? He could have claimed me after her burial." Rimona's lungs became as tiny as an unopened bud. Thirty days was not long enough to mourn a mother. Or mourn the loss of the life she knew.

"I would beg you to stay if there was no other," Leah whispered. "Your mother's brother will welcome you to Jerusalem. Think about your life in a palace. You will not have to work so hard every day." Leah's eyes grew wide, but they held no hint of glee. She shook her head. "Be brave. It is not safe for you here without a protector. The elders have arranged an escort for you. Jerusalem is only a few days' ride." Leah stepped away from the wall and pulled gently on Rimona's arms. "Come along now."

What choice did an unmarried orphan have? Shuffling her sandals, Rimona followed her neighbor away from the familiarity of her home and into the trampled dirt road. Jerusalem may be only a few days' ride, but the ride was one Leah, a widow, could hardly manage at her age. This was another burial. A farewell to a woman who had become like a beloved aunt.

Tears welled in Rimona's eyes.

Leah leaned closer. "Your escort awaits. If he keeps pacing, he will dig a ravine with his feet."

"Eglon is always impatient." Rimona swept her grief from her face. "I hope the collection of coins bestowed by the elders was sufficient, or he will complain at every hoofbeat." Why couldn't she have a kinsman closer in blood than Eglon?

"Do not mind him. You are going to the king's palace. Your mother would be pleased to see you in the City of David." Leah rested her head against Rimona's shoulder.

The scent of wisdom and wildflowers comforted Rimona's angst.

"Seek out a scribe or a nobleman to wed while you are there."

"I am too weary to seek out a man. A quiet room with food that I do not have to roast would be a blessing." Rimona relished the warmth and bony stature of the woman who had loved her since she was born. She avoided the scowl of the escort who balked at her tardiness.

"Hurry, woman. You are wasting daylight." Eglon whistled, spooking Rimona's donkey tethered to an acacia tree.

Rimona dutifully bobbed her head, making sure her curls did not spring forth from beneath her head covering. As the day grew warmer, her ringlets would grow tighter. "The road should offer us some speed." A three-day ride with Eglon was punishment fitting a criminal. But Eglon had sailed with her father, when she had a father, so she withheld her complaints.

Leah embraced her and gave a forceful kiss. "Remember me, but only until you find another home and a husband."

How could she let go of this woman whom she knew in her heart she would never lay eyes on again. She prayed the soft, yet withered feel of Leah's lips would never fade from her memory. "Please, let me celebrate one more Sabbath here." Her request was wispy and barely spoken aloud, but it reached Leah's ears.

Leah's chest shook. "I hope there is an opening in the palace courts for you. You never tire of arguing." Covering her face with her veil, Leah said, "Go now. Sing to God in the flatlands. I will pray a blessing on your journey."

As Leah rushed toward her dwelling, Rimona ambled toward her mount. She wouldn't look back.

She couldn't glance at the stone threshold where her mother's image would always remain. She had her memories tucked away deep in her heart, and those pieces of her past would travel with her to Jerusalem.

At a full stomp, and coming face-to-face with her, Eglon muttered, "Get on that mount. Murderers wait in the dark. You're not worthy of my life." He grasped her arm, pinching her flesh.

No scream fled from her lips. She met his narrow-eyed scowl. "Release me. I am your kin and a recent orphan. Didn't you receive payment from the elders?" Her voice rose in defiance of his touch.

Eglon released his hold with one last twist of her skin.

She would not give him the satisfaction of a flinch.

When she was reunited with her uncle, she would recount Eglon's insults and serenade anyone who cared to listen. After her confession, Eglon had better flee from the City of David, or he would spend the night in prison. Some privilege had to come with being the niece of a royal official even if her uncle had shut himself in the palace and forgotten his family.

Before mounting her donkey, she rubbed the leather satchel covering its haunches. The satchel held her mother's striped veil and a single golden earring embedded with three emeralds. Her father had brought the gems from one of his voyages. Over the years, one earring had been lost. Rimona treasured the bold green stones. A series of three jewels, one for a mother, a father, and an only daughter.

With every clop of her donkey's hooves, she bid

farewell to Beersheba. Her heart couldn't bear glimpsing her home one last time. Ghosts lived there now. Memories of loved ones buried in the hills. She scanned the road ahead of her small caravan. Her new life loomed before her.

Traveling with Eglon had one benefit: the man wasted few words on her. She and her escort plodded north toward Jerusalem. The northern route through the mountains bustled with lines of camels and merchants who were intent on selling goods and bedding down at towns along the way.

Under the midday heat, her veil soaked and weighed heavy upon her curls. When moisture trickled down her face, it seemed each ringlet of hair grew tighter like a possessed vine. Later, as the sun began to set, no village came into view.

Halting his mount, Eglon pointed at some caves located west of the next incline. "We will camp in the crags for the night."

"Would it not be safer to sleep within city walls?" Rimona glanced at the foreign landscape. Burlap brown hills. No waves or water. No gulls squawking overhead. Her nostrils itched from the day's dust.

"An inn will cost me, and the elders were not as generous as you seem to believe."

"Surely, the innkeeper would be respectful of my uncle's position at the palace?" Any mundane chore she would be called upon to perform for a wage would be preferable to resting out in the open with Eglon.

"We are a fair distance from Hebron. What is one night for a fisherman's daughter? Pretend you are on a boat."

Throwing you overboard. How did her father ever work alongside this fool? She dismounted and gave her donkey a drink from the half-empty waterskin. No doubt, the animal thirsted from her escort's stingy stops.

Movement on the trail caught her attention. Eglon turned from atop his donkey.

A stranger approached. He trotted his mount closer.

From where had the man come? Most people found shelter when the shadows of darkness dimmed their route. No caravan followed this lone traveler. She did not remember passing him earlier in the day.

The stranger nodded to Eglon. "Where are you headed?"

"Jerusalem. But we will camp for the night." Eglon indicated the covered caves. "Ahead."

"Perhaps we could join together. I've had a long trip from Lachish."

Lachish? Sweat did not stain this man's tunic. If he'd come this far east, he should glow like an ember.

Eglon kicked his mount and trotted forward. "Come along if you like."

"No." Her refusal rose toward the vanishing sunset. She sprinted to catch up with her escort and blocked his path. "We have not been properly introduced to this traveler. How do we know a band of raiders does not hide in those hills?" She indicated the ominous caves that Eglon embraced with delight.

"Hah. Do not be troubled." The stranger lifted a

golden emblem hidden beneath his collar. "Does a bandit wear such wealth? If I have faith in you to show you my medallion, you can trust me to cause you no harm."

Was this man more of a fool than Eglon? Who wore gold without an army of servants to protect his wealth? A rich man surely had slaves to carry his load. Only one saddlebag and two small skins hung on the back of the man's donkey.

"I don't—"

"Follow me." Eglon motioned toward the crags. "I am in need of food and drink."

Passing by her, the traveler bowed his head. "I am in your debt."

Her stomach fluttered as if it contained a startled pigeon. Their visitor seemed too sure of his welcome. Her escort was eager to eat, but what about his duty to protect, not only her, but their mounts?

Squinting toward the north, she tried to spy the lamps of Hebron. Could she make it to the town on her own? Not in the dark. A few missteps and her donkey could pull up lame. Pressure mounted behind her eyes like an afternoon squall. Why did You send me from my home, Lord? Why couldn't I stay with Leah? What welcome did an estranged uncle offer?

"Girl, our friend has wine," Eglon called as he trotted his donkey toward the caves. "Come and fix us a meal from his provisions."

Friend? What had happened to Eglon's grumbling spirit?

She led her donkey toward the crags and secured

her mount next to the others. She made sure the animals were far enough away from the ledge and a steep drop to the flatlands. The poor beasts needed straw as much as she needed nourishment, so she gave them some of what Eglon had stored for the journey. A jut between the caves made for a nice trough.

Eglon whistled. "We grow faint."

Why should she hurry to feed her guide? He treated her like a slave. *O' Jerusalem, you will be a haven.*

"I will see to our meal, but we do not want to walk to Jerusalem leading sick livestock."

She made a stone fire pit and prepared a meager stew in a small pot.

Her kinsman approached and placed a wineskin at her feet.

"Drink. You look as sour as the grapes." The scent of fermented fruit hung in the air.

She shooed Eglon away. "Let me work in peace, and then I will drink." She gave a nod to their guest who lounged against a large rock. "After such a long ride, we shall not sup on burned food."

The stranger chuckled, but his gaze lingered too long for her liking.

Her flesh pimpled under her robe. Would Eglon be steadfast in his protection of her? Do not delay sunrise.

"What is one swallow? Join us." Eglon would not be deterred.

Grabbing the wineskin, she feigned a sip. The tangy liquid did not wet her throat. She would keep her wits under the starlight.

"Shhhh." Eglon pointed to a lizard perched atop a rock. "An unclean guest comes to steal our warmth."

"Thief." The prominent traveler hurled a rock at the curious skink.

The lizard scurried away.

Eglon flung a pebble at their guest and laughed. "Your aim was never any good, Nalib."

"And yours is better?" The traveler held his palms close together. "I was not far off."

Rimona stilled. Eglon knew this man? So, why had he acted as if the man were a passerby? Her hands shook as she stirred the stew. *Think.* Were they plotting a scheme? Here in the hills or in Jerusalem? The night air became a heavy drape suffocating her breaths. If these men were plotting evil this eve, she needed to be near her mount so she could charge the road and race toward Hebron.

She picked up the wineskin and feigned another sip. Her teeth blocked the fermented juice, but she was sure they carried a stain as if she imbibed. Positioning the food between the two men, she offered them bread to dip and backed away toward the other side of the campfire.

"I am tired of traveling." She stretched her arms to the stars and yawned, displaying her violet teeth. "I will rest my head on a blanket and let the breeze cool my body." Fanning her face with her hand, she pretended to stumble her way toward a cave beneath the cliffs. Her mount waited nearby, tied, and slumbering with a full belly.

God, watch over me this night.

Slipping between the donkeys, she untethered her mount in case she needed to flee.

Sandals scuffed behind her.

"What are you doing?" the traveler asked.

Her heart rallied against her chest. For a moment, she forgot to breathe. Turning, she gave a giddy smile. "I am checking on the animals. They must be rested so we can be on our way in the morning to see my uncle."

"We will be on our way." Eglon slurred his affirmation.

"Toward Jerusalem," she added.

"We will go north." Nalib stepped too close. "But not to see your uncle."

Heat flooded her face. A high-pitched hum wailed in her ears, drowning out his lie. "Eglon promised the religious leaders he would take me to Jerusalem. To the palace."

"That is what Eglon promised. I did not give my word to the elders." Nalib leered like a mad man. "Your father owed me money. And you will be sold to pay his debt."

"Liar." She fisted her hands. "That isn't true. I would know of such a debt. I shall testify against your lie." Spittle chased her furious words.

Nalib unsheathed a long thin blade from his belt.

Rimona's heartbeat boomed to her temples. She attempted to shift away from Nalib, but her sandals and feet seemed to be floating above the ground.

"That is why we shall cut out your tongue. Slave masters don't read Hebrew."

The darkness became a dream that captured all her

senses. She forced words passed her lips, but her lips had become boulders, unmovable and heavy.

"Wa-wait." She forced a swallow. The smoke from the campfire choked her plea. "Don't you fear God?"

Nalib drew closer. "Which one?"

He and Eglon blocked her path toward the main road. Donkeys on each side of her hemmed her in tight. Her only escape was down a steep hill. But how high had she climbed? She was intent on the safety of her donkey, not on assessing the height she trekked.

She glanced ever so briefly at the ledge. Unknown terrain waited below. What could be worse at the bottom than what she faced at the top?

"My uncle can pay... more...."

"And he can have the palace guards arrest us at your testimony." Eglon jerked his head in her direction.

"I won't speak one word." Her throat clicked with her confession.

"Exactly." The lust for blood in Nalib's grin sent a chill rippling over her flesh. "The blade is sharp. The pain will be swift."

Her stomach heaved. She needed a distraction. If only she hadn't left Leah and her village. Leah.

Finding her footing, Rimona forced a gleeful smile and fluttered an arm in the direction of the campfire behind the men. "Leah, you came."

Eglon and Nalib turned around at her screech.

She pivoted, ducked under her donkey's jaw, and raced over the rocky ledge.

2

East of Hebron

Ittai perched his sandal on a rock jutting heavenward from the hill. The sparse lights of Hebron flickered in the distance like obscure outposts. In two days, he would face a warrior king he had not seen in decades. Not since he was a boy. Would David remember his allegiance? Or would the Philistine kneeling at David's throne be struck down in earnest.

Gazing at the drape of black sky overhead, He prayed. *God of David, I defied my own king because of You. Go before me to Your servant David. Spare the lives of my men. If blood needs to be shed, let it be mine, and mine alone.*

The lithe form of Hamuran, his fiercest and most loyal warrior, settled a breath from his left shoulder. "You should rest and let a few of us stand guard. Do you think the men of Hebron know we are waiting behind this hill?" Hamuran words were barely audible, but Ittai knew every nuance of his companion's voice.

"If they suspected we were here, the town would be ablaze with torches," Ittai whispered. "The women and children will sleep soundly tonight."

"Will you? We are not on the coast protecting

Philistia anymore." Hamuran edged forward without the sound of a scuff. Ittai swore his fellow warrior hovered above the dirt when he marched.

"Blame the king of Gath." Blood pulsed through Ittai's veins. At least his lifeblood wasn't pooling on palace stones in Philistia. "Exile is better than a beheading."

"What about in Jerusalem?" Hamuran crouched as if welcoming one of his sons. If Ittai didn't have thirty pounds and a few inches on his friend, he could prance around like a lynx, too. "You're sure King David will welcome us?" The flash of moonlight in Hamuran's eyes spoke of uncertainty or the thirst for a fight.

"I will be soon." Ittai fingered the hilt of his sword. "Do not fret. I will not accept anything less than a celebratory kiss of welcome from our future sovereign. We will dance like virgins on the stone streets of David's city."

"I would pay thick coin to see you dance." Hamuran strutted toward the crest of the hill and cocked his head. "Shall I get rid of the spies?"

"No spy shouts curses." Ittai assessed the movement on the slope below.

"Merchants then?"

Ittai dipped his head at the shadows. "Our closest visitor breathes like a storm gust. I will send him on his way. I'm sure you could persuade the other travelers to settle elsewhere. I do not desire to spill Hebrew blood. I desire to live among them."

Hamuran nodded. "I'll be less of a fright than the six hundred men you have camped in the valley."

"We might need a judge to decide that my friend."

Grinning, Hamuran turned and disappeared down the side of the slope. Those caravan deserters were in for a shock when Hamuran emerged with his weapon drawn.

Stifling a laugh, Ittai surveyed the approach of the closest stranger. Why was anyone traipsing over rock and crevices in the dark when sunlight wasn't far off? Some men had no sense. How many fools had he encountered in battle? Too many and they were dead.

Crouching near a tower of rocks and a spindly sapling, Ittai unsheathed his blade. He breathed in cool air untainted with kicked-up camel dust. His eyes overcame the darkness to rest on a form breeching the top of the hill.

Sandal slaps. Wheezing. One fool had made it to the crest. Hamuran would cut off the others.

Nearer and nearer the climber came. Ittai swallowed. The sour taste of bile pulled his jaw tight.

Lord, give me victory.

The man stumbled over a rock and whimpered.

Ittai lunged.

He grabbed the stranger and pulled the thin frame taut to his chest. His knife rested against the flesh of the prowler's neck.

"Stay silent, or I will send your head thumping to the dirt."

His captive turned to stone. Trembling stone.

A swell of breast rose and fell beneath Ittai's arm. No stench of sweat or body odor offended his nose. This quivering climber smelled of scented soap even after a trek up a hill. An abundance of soft curls tickled his chin.

He'd caught a woman.

What was a woman doing out at night? In the wilderness? In his arms?

He eased his blade from her neck. "I mean you no harm. I am not a foe. I will release you if you keep your voice low."

She nodded ever so slightly. A tiny whine escaped from her lips as if she were agreeing to his demand in earnest.

He loosened his hold but kept her upright with a commanding grasp of her arm. A crazed or enraged woman could do harm. He had learned that in the most difficult of ways. He gave her enough slack to turn and face him in the shadows.

"Help me," the woman rasped. "Men are chasing me."

Securing his weapon, he kept his gaze centered on the gleam in her dark eyes.

"They mean to cut out my tongue." Her chest rose and sunk like the sea. "And sell me as a slave. My father is not a thief."

The woman's eyes blinked without rest. He had only seen someone so undone under two circumstances—when he told his mother he was going off to war, or in war, when a man was pleading for his life. His mind became a fog of memories. His calm, tranquil night had been set ablaze.

"Take me to Jerusalem." She whipped around and gazed at the crest of the hill. "My uncle is an official in the palace. He will welcome you. Welcome us."

"The palace?" Ittai released his hold until only his fingertips lingered on the threads of her garment.

"Of King David." Bending, she braced her hands on her knees. "My uncle will pay you handsomely."

If he had pulled lots, what were the odds he would capture a woman with ties to the king? His gaze darted around the rocky landscape almost expecting to see a messenger from God. How could he make battle plans this night when strangers were stumbling upon his camp?

He glanced at the path she had traipsed. "Is one of the men a husband?" He did not need a clan of Hebrews accusing him of kidnapping a man's wife, or worse. "I have companions that are intercepting them."

She shook her head. Strands of wayward ringlets stuck to her face. "No. One is a distant relative. I hardly know him." Her eyes bulged as though she had spoken a long-held secret. "Please. Eglon was to take me to Jerusalem. Nothing more. The elders paid him for his escort. Now he believes me worth more as a slave."

"I am not a judge in Israel." If she only knew how far from the truth that statement was. "But I will protect you and take you to Jerusalem. That is where I am headed."

"Praise God. I petitioned for His help this night." She hobbled toward a boulder and sat. "Toda raba. I don't know what would have happened to me if you were not on this hilltop." She inspected her bloodied foot and winced.

Her sturdiness, the wildness of her hair, the way

she moved from panic to calm, brought back images of his mother. He missed her. But oh how she would have wept at his exile. Death spared her more heartache and scandal.

"And my pursuers? What will you do to them?"

"Hmm." Ittai scanned his surroundings. A lapse in control could cost him his life.

"Will you kill them?" She glanced at his sword and beheld him with those captivating eyes.

"One of my men is persuading your Eglon and will coax him to venture in another direction."

She nibbled her lip. "Only one? Will he need help?"

Was the woman challenging his decision? How bold of her. Ittai crossed his arms. "My friend can take care of himself." He was surprised Eglon's screams hadn't split the night air, but then no one hears Hamuran arrive. "He may have taken a scout or two."

"Scout? What are you scouting?" She squinted at him and then turned and stared into the valley. Her head rotated, taking in the expanse of tents camped in the shadows. Whipping around, she almost fell off her perch.

His heart stuttered. More like flinched. Could his future become any more uncertain?

With her eyes rivaling a harvest moon and her mouth round and slack-jawed, he knew, he just knew, that he had another explanation to confess.

"You. You're attacking Israel!"

So much for another peaceful night on his journey.

3

Rimona attempted to rise, but the pain in her foot streaked into her ankle and then into her calf. Unsteady, she collapsed onto the large flat-topped rock. How could she flee from this giant of a man? She should have known something was amiss. He was too quick with a blade and too unshaken by her circumstances. Never once did he seem to fear her pursuers. From his size and the dialect, she should have placed him as a filthy Philistine straightaway. Now, she had everything to fear. She may not be sold as a slave to Egyptians, but this foreigner was likely to keep her for his own servant, or worse.

She leaned forward and tried to ease the cramping in her stomach. Her lips trembled. In her mind, she assailed God. Why O Lord did You take my father, and now my mother? I should be sleeping in the warmth of a home in Beersheba, not in the wilderness near Hebron. Save me from this heathen.

Wrapping her arms around her waist, she fought to control a wail. "What you are…going do…to me?" Her words were as jumbled as a pile of threads. She had nothing with which to bribe this man, and her bones could not scramble over one more treacherous slope. "All that I own was left behind." She flapped her hand in the direction of the path. "Some cave." Covering her mouth with her palm, she tasted, soil, grit, and salt. She cursed the jagged hillside. And Eglon. He'd made her flee and abandon her treasures. Waves of regret pulsed behind her eyes. *Don't cry and show weakness.*

Her enormous captor stepped closer.

She fisted her hands and held them in defiance. Why did they have to quiver?

The warrior held out his hands. Steady as a fisherman's footing, they were. He hadn't fled Eglon in the dark of night, and from the number of campfires in the valley, he had plenty of swords to come to his aid.

"Do not worry. I will take you to Jerusalem." He scrubbed a palm over his jaw and steadied a hand on his hip, above his blade, but not in a position to impale.

Should she believe him? She eased back on her large sitting stone and glimpsed the valley. Only a fool would travel to Jerusalem with an army of Philistines. Her breaths hitched as she turned her attention to the warrior stationed before her.

"I did not lie earlier." The gruff in his voice sharpened. If it got anymore sharp, she would bleed. "I mean to keep you safe and deliver you to the City of David."

"With an army in tow?" A crazed laugh bubbled on her lips. Would her uncle, or the king, believe her to be a traitor? She had nothing to escape her captivity. No mount to ride. No emeralds to tempt. No strength to fight. "You could send me off in the morning. With a donkey and a waterskin. I wouldn't speak of your presence."

"I have plenty of donkeys. But unlike your kin, I don't send women into the wilderness alone." He met her gaze with an intensity that could slay a man's, or woman's, heart. "You will stay in our tents tonight and set out with us at first light."

"Us?" She assessed him to be a Philistine, but were there other peoples among his men? And under whose tent would she sleep? Could this man assure her safety in his camp? She shook her head to stop a leak of tears.

The large Philistine beheld her with a look that mirrored her father's when she was a girl. At least it was an expression she remembered her father having. One of compassion. This soldier did not sneer or slither his sights all over her body.

"You have my protection. My word is respected among my men."

"But who sends you into battle?" Disdain filled her voice. She breathed in the night air. The aroma of campfires and ash tickled her throat. "What king craves a portion of the lands of Judah? We are at peace."

"I don't serve a king at the moment." He smirked and pinched his stubbled chin with fat fingers. "And I do not seek a battle or to conquer your land."

How could a man who killed to stay alive be so hospitable? The tension in her shoulders eased, but only a half jerk.

"I am traveling to Jerusalem to see a boyhood friend." He quirked a brow as if challenging her wits. "Your king kept my mother and me alive with his kindness. We knew him as David, son of Jesse."

What was this warrior thinking? "King David won't welcome your fighting men." Her forehead pounded. She would be caught in a blood bath. Her captor didn't look or speak like a fool. Truly, he had a plan. "Have you sent messengers? Word of your coming?"

"Soon." He came even closer, close enough that she could kick him if her toes weren't already screaming from her sprint over jagged rocks. Her toenails couldn't damage the thick leather protecting his shins. His chiseled greaves filled the air with the scent of livestock. "I do not believe God would spare my life in Gath and send me to Jerusalem to die."

"You're a Philistine warrior." *Heathen.*

He nodded.

"What God do you believe spared you?" She straightened. The hard stone beneath her dug into her thighs.

"Your God." He dipped his head and crossed his thick forearms as if this conversation was ordinary. Nothing about this night had been ordinary. Her forehead pulsed with an ache that made her feel faint.

"My God is not your God." She blew out a breath of disgust. Was this foreigner insulting her? Lying to her? Or both? "I serve the God of Abraham, Isaac, and Jacob. You do not. You are an uncircumcised pagan in His sight." She clenched her teeth and stopped any more insults of his honor. He was an expert at bringing forth that blade.

Stifling a smirk, he said, "How do you know who I

serve or if I have undergone circumcision?"

"Uh." She didn't know. Her cheeks heated hotter than those valley fires. Burying her face in her sleeve, she attempted to hide her embarrassment, her confusion, and everything about her being. The cloth smelled of dirt and desperation. Gone was the lingering scent of hyssop when she cared for her mother. Gone was the faint hint of jasmine oil that Leah wore to the market. Gone was the sweet air of Beersheba. All gone.

Sniffling, she held her head high and faced the foreigner. "Why would the God of Abraham spare your life?"

"Because I have asked Him to spare it. And the lives of my men." He paced toward the edge of the hill overlooking the flickering campsites below. "I learned of your God from your king. When he was in exile outside of Gath." The Philistine hesitated. His fierce gaze impaled her. "Why can't I ask for victory or mercy like King David?"

An answer caught in her parched throat. Before she could swallow and form a response, the Philistine raised his arms toward the stars.

"Elohim, Adonai. Love the Lord your God with all your heart..."

Couldn't be. Her captor was speaking Hebrew and praising the One True God. Her God. She stared at this mountain of a man, a Philistine fighter, relaying the truths of God given by Moses to her people. Her mouth gaped, shut, and then brought forth words.

"With all your strength." She finished the well-known prayer with her rescuer. Tilting her head, she asked, "What is your name?"

Another man bounded to her side. Her heart catapulted to her throat. She struggled to breathe. A stench of sour body odor wafted her direction. She covered her lips with calloused hands. Now, she had another heathen to appease.

"Ittai, the men—"

Their intruder halted and gawked.

Hand to her heart, she reclaimed her countenance, and pointed a finger at the man who had moments before been praising her God and whose name rung in her ears.

"You are named Ittai? From Gath?" She blinked at the two men beholding her as a ghost.

Ittai nodded. "And I expect the men who were chasing you are traveling in a different direction."

"With an escort." The messenger indicated her presence with the slightest of movement. "To make sure they do not double back."

Ittai gave a silent, stoic, side-eyed command to their latest guest. "We will see this woman safely to Jerusalem. And we will leave before dawn." Ittai lumbered toward his soldier and clamped a hand on the man's shoulder. "Hamuran has a wife and family you can stay with until we break camp."

"I—I do."

"Toda raba." She nodded to the tall, lanky messenger. Hadn't she asked God to watch over her this night? Who would have guessed a Philistine convert would have rescued her from her own kin? "I will pray we have safe travels to the City of David. I am in your debt for your kindness, Ittai." She acknowledged the fighting man. "And Hamuran."

"My men call me Ittai the Gittite." Somehow in his dark, chiseled features, she thought she saw the tug of a smile. Perhaps he was gleeful to be done with her for a few hours. He cocked his shoulder-length mane of hair. "I will accept your prayers." His brow furrowed. "Though, I do not know your name."

"Rimona." She pitched forward on her stone seat. "Of Beersheba." Placing weight on her feet, she winced. "My kinsman was going to take me to Jerusalem. And now my belongings are lost on a hill. My mount—"

"Do not worry. Rest now, Rimona of Beersheba. Tomorrow we head toward Jerusalem. Soon, you will be walking the palace steps."

She wished she could be as confident as Ittai that successfully accompanying an army of Philistines to David's palace could be accomplished with only a few prayers.

The *whoosh* of his cloak caused a gust of wind to bathe her face. She blinked, and before she knew what was happening, her body lifted into the air and into Ittai the Gittite's arms. She squealed. Was she lying on a felled tree? His arms were as solid as mature branches. What would the elders of her tribe say if they witnessed his forcefulness? Or his swathed touching.

I said rest, Rimona." His chuckled rumbled in her ear. "You are wound tighter than a rolled rug."

One thing she knew this night. Ittai the Gittite

didn't lie.

4

Ittai held Rimona loosely, but not too loose lest she topple out of his arms. Her stiff frame screamed of her unease. Buried beneath the folds of his cloak, her dark-lashed eyes never met his gaze. He could feel her elbow gently thumping against his chest like a rabbit burrowing into its hole. He stifled a bark of a laugh from the tickle as he trotted, half slid, down the slope of the hill. Disturbing his fighting men and their families with his chuckle would draw questions or fright. As their commander, he didn't have to explain his actions, and he had no time for idle conversation with dawn nipping at his greaves.

When was the last time he had held a woman? He had carried his mother when she had been too ill to walk. He needed but one arm to support the hollowness of his mother's bones. Rimona required more strength to uphold. Any robust woman would, but he was not in the habit of carrying women. No wife filled his tent. Warring for the King of Gath had left him alone. He had seen enough battles in his thirty-six years to rest on his accomplishments as a commander. He had no experience at being a husband, and he did not have the distractions that came with being bound to a wife. He had been free to search out wars without worrying what his death would leave behind.

Traipsing through the broad tents that held his fighting men, he hurried toward the inner circle of tent tops filled by wives and children. Fire pits did not burn as bright in this part of camp. Security gave way to peaceful slumber. The sweet aroma of oak embers and washed bodies enlivened his soul. For a moment. Only for a moment. He could not grasp even the shadow of a thought that David and his men might slaughter these innocents. His chest constricted tighter than tent seams. His people needed refuge, not war.

"How much longer?" Rimona's words reverberated through the cloth barrier between their bodies. Her head shook and dislodged her head covering. Her hair stuck out like a bramble bush.

Haunting eyes filled his vision. Helpless eyes. Eyes too wide awake for this long into the evening. What if she had stumbled onto a caravan of lustful merchants? A hint of a shiver bathed his skin. He tamped down the fear of a boy entrusted with the burden to hide his mother from scavengers. A burden too lofty for a boy but not for a brawny young man. A man taught to be skilled with the sword. It was David who had given him a small sword among the skins of milk and loaves of bread all those years ago. The blade became a treasure from a man who was destined to be a king.

"Ittai?" Wisps of hair blew in the breeze as Rimona beheld him. How long had his mind been distracted? "Surely, your arms grow weary. What if someone sees us?"

"Hamuran's wife lives ahead. At the end of this

path." He cleared his throat and adjusted his hold on Rimona. "I don't anticipate a charge against me. This is my command." Dirt nestled between his toes from the temporary trail. Not even the desert trade winds could cool the warmth radiating from Rimona's body. "I trust Parveda to tend to you."

Rightfully, any woman would watch over Rimona at his order, but Parveda was like a sister, or at least what he expected a sister to be. Loyal and forthright.

Dipping her chin, Rimona cast her vision at her sandals, battered, dirty, and dangling in the darkness. "You seem like a fine commander and fighter. Why would a king allow you and your men to leave?"

Is that why she'd remained quiet. Had she been pondering her rescue by an outcast?

"I find kings do not want the stones of their cities stained with blood that a thousand servants could not scrub clean."

"You have seen that before?" Her eyes held a hint of disbelief. Or was the shine from the moon playing tricks on him?

"Every disciplined commander has." He slowed his gait a short distance from Parveda's dwelling. He desired to wipe out any doubt in Rimona's beliefs that his men would do harm to King David. The streets of Jerusalem would not be bathed in blood. "What does the One True God say about serving other gods?"

She flinched in his arms. "There are no other gods."

"You speak the truth, but kings can come to believe that they are a god. Or as powerful as one." In the shadows of camp, he waited to see understanding in her brown eyes. "And kings demand loyalty."

"Yours let you go with hundreds of his men?"

"He let me leave with men who would never honor him or at least, would cause dissension in his ranks."

"Truly." She nodded. A simple nod, but it made his posture broaden. "I needed you on that hill. Praise God the king let you go."

Stifling a grin, he said, "Yes, praise God."

"Perhaps your king believes you will return one day." Her words sounded hopeful. This Israelite woman did like to talk.

"I doubt I will ever return to Gath. There is no place for me there." The welcome of his mother was long buried. "I'm in search of a new place to live. A peaceful place."

"What about your family?" Her tone was wistful yet filled with concern. Little good her kin did her this night.

"My mother and father are gone." He sped his pace. Reminiscing weighed upon his bones more than this woman.

Rimona blew out a short breath. "As well, my mother and father are gone." Her eyelids blinked.

O God, do not have this woman weep on me tonight.

A sniffle.

Quick glance.

No tears.

Her inquisitive eyes beheld him anew. "I believe you to be a good man, Ittai the Gittite. You left your

home so that others might live. A commandei
for power might have betrayed the king and ki
advisors."

He could not accept her praise. She meant
but she hadn't lived by violence.

His throat sputtered a cough. "There are m.
ghosts who would say that I am not a good man."

A faint grin plumped her cheeks. "I do not kno
those ghosts."

"I do." In his gut and in the marrow of his bones,
he vanquished any thoughts about past battles where
he had killed upon order of a king. Emotions were best
bestowed on the living.

Parveda's tent stood before him. His oversight of
Rimona was complete for a few hours.

Slowly, and with as much gentleness possessed by
his thick arms, he lowered her to the ground and
reclaimed his cloak. As he removed the garment that
was the barrier between their bodies, her hair caressed
his hand. The sensation lingered like a calming aloe.
Woe that his flesh was ridged and calloused, and
nothing like a soothing balm. His touch was more like
the sting of a burr.

He rubbed his tingling fingers along his jawbone.
"I never thought I would disobey my king and seek
refuge with yours." His boyhood allegiance ran too
deep to confess.

Rimona faced him, fully. Her lips parted to speak.

The tent flap opened wide.

"I thought I heard your voice." Hand on her hip
and with a quick toe to breast assessment of Rimona,

'arveda bobbed her head while quirking a brow at ιttai. "Go get at least a snore of a rest, would you? My husband's life is under your command. I can take care of your guest." Parveda grasped Rimona's arm before she could shuffle away. "Poor girl couldn't even run from you with those battered feet."

"She wasn't fleeing from me." How was he going to explain his trap?

Flapping her hand like a disgruntled goose, Parveda cut off his babble. "I'm sure the woman can speak and tell me of her trials. Now, go get some sleep."

Rimona's gaze darted between him and Parveda, but she did not flee the bold wife.

Had Rimona found comfort in the protection he offered? He nodded toward Rimona. "I will return at first light."

"Send my husband or a younger man," Parveda answered. "Shut your eyes for a moment. You have to lead us safely to Jerusalem."

Parveda had voiced his task well. The families sleeping all around in tents were depending on his relationship with David to keep them alive. And if David refused him or decided to fight, Ittai would need a miracle to honor his pledge of survival to his followers. He hadn't lost a battle yet, and now he had the One True God on his side. But so did David.

Growing to his full height, he acknowledged Rimona and offered her some peace. "Shalom."

"Shalom," she said, looking in as much peace as a Hebrew woman would inside a Philistine camp. "And,

Commander, I do not know what would have become of me had you not been on that hill tonight."

"We will never know, Rimona of Beersheba." He would not give the poor outcomes another thought.

"I will pray we have a successful journey." She bobbed her head and allowed Parveda to lead her into the tent.

Had Rimona run out of words, or would Parveda receive an earful?

He turned and breathed in the sweet air of night. He needed all the peace the One True God could bestow on a warrior seeking to avoid war with a king lauded for slaying tens of thousands.

5

Rimona clenched her teeth as Parveda stroked a rag over Rimona's feet. The basin darkened in the low lamplight. Blood and dirt tainted the water. The stench of a wounded animal wafted to Rimona's senses. She tamped down any tears at her predicament. Why had God allowed Eglon's deception? She had lost everything. Her family. Her possessions. Her pride. She prayed Jerusalem would be a new home where she could come alongside her uncle as she had done with her mother.

Gripping the sides of a wooden stool, Rimona bent forward toward the tall, dark-haired Philistine woman. Why did Philistines have to be so big? Rimona cleared her throat. "You are too kind to care for my feet. I can clean myself. You must be tired from your journey." Rimona would catch her rest in the City of David. In the household of her uncle. Did he have servants? Would she? She doubted she could run through the halls of a palace as she ran in the hills surrounding Beersheba. Gone were the days when she felt like she could run right into the clouds.

Parveda slowed her caretaking and glanced at Rimona with eyes awake as midday. "You are a guest in my tent. It is not every day Ittai delivers a woman to my home." Parveda grinned. "Ittai and I have an understanding. As long as he keeps my husband alive, I will help him manage this camp." Parveda wrung out the rag and let the water dribble into the basin. "You are no trouble."

A young girl sat on a bed mat and stretched her arms. Two boys slept soundly at her side. The smallest child emitted a rumbling snore. How peaceful they were amongst all the uncertainty of David's welcome.

Hunched and covered by a blanket, the girl approached. Her straight black hair cascaded down her arms She looked to be about ten years old. "Can I help?"

Rimona's heart grew heavy. How many nights had she asked the same thing of her own mother?

After glancing at Rimona's feet, the girl rummaged through a basket near the basin. "I will tear some cloth for bandages."

Grateful as she was, Rimona indicated the sleeping boys. "Won't you wake your brothers? My bleeding has stopped."

"Barely stopped." Parveda patted Rimona's right foot dry. She addressed the girl. "You may assist, but I do not want to hear any complaining about being tired when you are leading our donkeys." Parveda applied pressure to Rimona's ankle. "You have a bad gash here. We will wrap it. You do not want to be walking into Jerusalem like a cripple."

"No, I do not, but you are too kind. I can bandage my foot. I have interrupted your sleep and disturbed your home." Rimona shook her mass of untamed hair.

Home. She was a homeless Hebrew thrust upon a Philistine woman in the middle of a camp of Philistine fighters. She clamped her eyes shut to stem a leak of tears. What had her life become?

"Hey, you are no trouble." Parveda lightly snapped her fingers. "Lana, hand me the cassia balm."

The girl brought forth a small jar from the basket and held it in front of Rimona as if she were offering a gift.

"Breathe deeply." Parveda caressed Rimona's arm. "Your eyes are sinking into your cheek bones. The spice will bring you back to me, so you do not fall into my arms. I am not as strong as Ittai." Parveda finished her careful drying of Rimona's feet.

"Mother makes me smell it sometimes." Lana lifted the stopper on the jar. She breathed deep and circled the small container in front of Rimona's nose.

The sharp scent of cloves and cinnamon filled Rimona's nostrils and relaxed her muscles. She released her grasp on the stool and her knuckles nearly floated to the tent top.

Here she was in the outskirts of Hebron in the middle of a Philistine camp, and she could have wrapped herself in Lana's blanket and slumbered 'til dawn.

"Did our commander bring you here?" Lana tilted her head.

So, she had heard her mother mention Ittai.

"Your commander is an honorable man." Rimona placed her dried feet on a woven mat. A scarlet streak on her ankle throbbed and itched. She would take the

42

bruising ache instead of a broken bone. Rock-strewn hills in the dark of night were a formidable enemy. "Ittai rescued me from a wicked kinsman and another thief. I don't know what I would have done if he were not standing on the hill. I couldn't have run all night."

Parveda wrapped Rimona's feet and halted her labors. The tiniest of weight squeezed Rimona's toes as Parveda leaned forward. "He has rescued us as well. I would crawl on my hands and knees to Jerusalem if Ittai asked it of me. Because of him, I have my husband and children."

"He had a disagreement with your king."

"Disagreement." Parveda arched a brow. "When Ittai went into battle for Philistia, it was as if the Living God was on his shoulder. No one ever defeated Ittai. Our king ate the victories like a fatted ram. Everyone was to bow to the king and worship his wealth."

"We didn't bow." Lana stared at her mother.

The innocence in her stare made Rimona's gut clench. What if Eglon had sold Rimona to a pagan? Would she have been forced to bow before an idol? And what happens to a woman who doesn't obey? Rimona shivered while Parveda bandaged her ankle.

"Ittai didn't worship your king. He told me so," Rimona said.

"He said God would not allow it." The fire in Parveda's voice could have singed the bandage. "Ittai offered his life so his men could live. He said he had ordered every man to serve the God of David. And that they had taken an oath before God on his orders."

"But the king let you leave." Banishing them to an

uncertain fate.

Lana shifted closer to Rimona. The girl clutched the cassia balm, but after this conversation, Rimona's battered feet were a distant memory.

"The king of Gath is no fool. If he had murdered Ittai, there would have been a riot. He sent us on our way so David could...." Parveda halted her speech. Discreetly, she drew an imaginary blade across her throat.

Rimona would not think about Ittai's demise. Or the deaths of this caretaker and her young children. Woman-to-woman, she said, "I am headed to the palace where my uncle is an official. I will sing praises about Ittai's protection and your kindness. My uncle owes you a debt. As do I." Rimona rested her cheek against Lana's soft hair. Hadn't she sat by her own mother and listened to stories about the history of her people. This small tent was a home to children and a family that served the One True God. For whatever reason God had seen fit to place her among foreigners, and she would speak of their allegiance and their hospitality to all of the palace officials. If she had to crawl across the palace steps and beg at the feet of King David, she would do it for Ittai and Parveda. With the hint of morning's light peeking under the tent, it seemed she would get her chance to testify sooner rather than later.

~*~

Rimona squinted at the rising sun. Her arms held

the tied bed mats of Parveda's children. A cart waited nearby to accept the provisions from the neighboring tents. Her feet throbbed, but Parveda's bandages and balm had taken the pain from a wave to a trickle. When she had started her journey, she never would have believed that she would spend the night in an enemy's tent.

A young man charged toward her pulling a hesitant donkey. Banging against the man's shoulder was a leather satchel. Could it be? Yes! Her satchel. A satchel with frayed stitching and a stain on the front pouch. Her spirit soared as though she were dancing in the streets of Beersheba. Ittai's men had found her donkey. She couldn't remember if she had mentioned her mount. Her babble was a blur. *Toda raba, Adonai.* God had remembered her petitions. And, apparently, so had Ittai. Perhaps the road ahead would be less troublesome than the one she had left behind. A soul could hope.

"You must be the Hebrew," the man said through rushed breaths.

"Yes, I am." She set the mats on the ground to receive her satchel. "You have my belongings. Thank you."

"Our commander found them." He handed her the satchel before securing her donkey to the tent lead.

Immediately, through the soft leather, she felt for the bump of her mother's veil. Tension fled her tight shoulders. Opening the satchel, she saw that the fold of the cloth had not been ravaged. Her emerald earring remained secure. Hope blossomed in her heart that this day would bring her safe travels to Jerusalem. Even if she was surrounded by Philistines.

Parveda rounded the cart. "Off with you, young man. Tell my husband I will watch over the Hebrew woman."

Rimona stifled a laugh. She had no doubt in Parveda's proclamation.

6

Three hours north of Hebron, Ittai slowed his donkey and swiped the sweat from his forehead. His headdress could no longer dispel the heat from the sun, neither could the rolling hills to the east that led to a wilderness. Soon, his men would need to rest and water the livestock. The afternoon heat would take a toll on the children and babes. With as badly as Rimona's feet were battered, he prayed she had found a level cart to set upon. Parveda would see to Rimona's comforts. Hamuran's wife made sure everyone was content and heard. If they could make it to the outskirts of Etam, they would be halfway to Jerusalem. Except for a few wide-eyed camel traders and an Egyptian's harem, no one had taken an interest in his soldiers. No threat had arisen from the men of Hebron. God had bestowed His favor on a Philistine convert and an army of believers.

He unclenched his palms and let the leather reins fall upon his mount's mane. The scent of warm leather calmed his nerves. A day, maybe two, remained before he could banish a skirmish with zealous Hebrews from his conscience.

May You go before us to Jerusalem, Lord. Where else can I take these men and women who call upon

Your name?

From the flatlands, donkeys at a full trot headed Ittai's direction. The storm of dirt they amassed foretold of their distress. His scouts had returned, and they were in a frenzy.

Hamuran joined him immediately. "Has word gotten to Jerusalem about us?"

Ittai reclaimed his reins. He patted his mount to calm its bucking head. "We shall soon hear if it is so."

Two scouts blocked Ittai's donkey with their mounts.

"Commander," Banak, his accomplished sentry began, "a chariot is moving this way. In the plains. Around Etam." Banak's words rushed forth, clipped and precise. No greetings or random reports rang out.

Chariots were a rarity in Israel. "How many men?"

"We count about two hundred." Banak spit in the dirt and tried to control his breathing.

"That is more than a raiding party." Hamuran leaned forward. His companion never backed down from a threat.

"But not enough men for victory if they have spied our six hundred." *Lord, give me wisdom.*

Banak shifted his mount closer. "Who would travel with such a force?"

"Did you see who was driving the chariot?" Hamuran gripped the hilt of his sword. "Our men are much larger than the Hebrews."

Shrugging, Banak cast a side-eyed glance at his cohort. "I do not know who he is, but I have never seen so much unbound hair on a man. At first, I believed a harlot drove the chariot. The driver's hair is dark and thick with curl."

"Could it be King David?" the younger sentry offered.

Ittai scoffed. He knew enough about King David's prowess to know the description wasn't his old friend. Ittai's guttural rebuke echoed off the hillside. "David never had flowing hair. It is a hindrance in battle. I doubt his hair would make such a display even after living in peace for many years."

"What are the other men riding?" Hamuran squinted at the valley. "Are there more chariots."

"No. Only one. Some men are on mules. A few are marching alongside." Banak rubbed his brow. "They aren't in a hurry either."

Hamuran stretched tall to scan the horizon. "Who do you think it is?"

Ittai considered who would be strolling through the valley in a show of authority?

"Only princes or commanders ride chariots in Israel. Since David rules over a peaceable kingdom, I would venture it is a son. I have never seen David in a chariot nor on a horse. Stallions are a rarity in this land." With all the fidgeting his men were doing, they weren't amused by this noble procession. He swallowed hard. "I do not know the sons of David. They were born after David left Ziklag." He arched his back. "But I will meet this one and announce my presence, before he can trumpet for reinforcements."

"What if it's a trap?" Banak licked his lips. He

fingered the sword resting against his thigh.

"He's in the flatlands," Ittai said. "And—"

"Who could ride a chariot over the craggy hills," Banak's eager companion offered.

"Flatlands leave no hiding places for slingers or archers." Ittai's retort shut his young sentry's lips. "If I were laying a trap, I would not travel in the middle of a plain."

"How many men do you want to accompany you?" Hamuran had his mount ready to head down the road and count off fighting men.

"You mean how many men do I need? We have a prince with only a few battle-ready men." He glanced at Banak. His trusted sentry nodded in agreement. "There is no landscape for a surprise attack. And I have hundreds who can ride to my aid." Ittai observed his sentries and then focused on Hamuran. "Fifty."

"Will that be enough?" His youngest sentry's eyes widened and then he bobbed his head. "Fifty it is."

"We do not want to threaten the king's family. I need to reestablish my ties to David, not burn an alliance by spooking his son into battle." Ittai arched his back. "Make sure our fifty drink their fill and eat a honey cake. I want my men on alert. This heat is no friend to those chariot runners."

"Shall I assemble your mightiest?" Hamuran asked.

Ittai breathed in the stale air seasoned with body odor and a hint of soured breath. "My mightiest and those who stay calmest before we clash swords." Ittai grinned. "An army of men like you."

"There are no others like me, but I will do my best to gather forty-nine more." Hamuran guided his mount away from the hillside and down the road.

"Wait," Ittai said.

Hamuran halted his donkey.

Ittai unfastened his sword and held the blade out to Hamuran.

"You aren't taking a weapon with only fifty men?" His friend did not immediately accept the sword.

Hairs on Ittai's skin rose and stayed on alert. "I seek refuge for my men and their families." *Lord, may You carry this burden with me.* He held his loyal friend's stare until his gaze did not settle upon anything else. "I cannot risk inciting a riot. If a prince rides in the chariot, his hold on the reins will keep him from drawing his blade. He will rely on his men to protect him as I will rely upon you." Ittai jabbed his sword at Hamuran anew. "I do not know why God has brought these men into our path, but we will meet them. May God go before us and protect the innocent."

"May God go before you and every man in your command." Hamuran accepted the suspended sword. "You had better be alive to accept this later on."

"God will have mercy on me. I do not desire to hear your bickering and insults on our way to the heavens."

"Who said we will be able to talk or complain?" Hamuran kicked his mount and trotted down the road. Dust clouded the trail. His second-in-command bellowed orders. Men raised their weapons and waterskins in a show of allegiance.

Lord, spare my men and their families.

Banak bobbed his head. "What will you have us do?"

"Set up ranks on the road. Have two hundred men ready to aid us if swords are drawn. Leave the rest of the men in file to protect the families."

"Where would we go if there is bloodshed, and we are not welcomed by the Hebrews?" Banak swallowed and eyed his fellow sentry.

"That is a question I have been asking myself since we left Gath. There are no other kings that worship the One True God." Ittai's stomach clenched tighter than his grip on a sturdy sword. "If we do not find peace this day in the flatlands, thousands of Hebrews will amass for revenge. We ride between two strongholds of Judah. Hebron and Jerusalem."

"So we shall—"

"Pray, Banak. We should all pray that this chariot driver is out for a stroll in the sun."

~*~

Ittai had ridden into many a battle. But those battles were to be won by killing the men on the opposing ravine or field. He had never faced an enemy with armed fighting men while praying for peace. His leather breastplate clung to his chest as though it were made of wet cotton. The sun showed no mercy as he advanced toward the chariot. His headdress was folded in his satchel and a band of leather secured his hair and kept his vision clear. He swept his tongue over his teeth and dislodged the remaining grit of his hastily eaten honey cake. Bits of sweet honeycomb could not overpower the tart pull of his saliva.

After he and his first line of men had become visible to the chariot-led forces, the Hebrews had halted. The Hebrews fortunate enough to have mounts formed a barrier in front of the chariot. Blades drawn, men surrounded the cart and their official.

Banak's assessment of the chariot driver had been precise. His sentry's eyes were like those of a starving vulture. The driver's waist-long curls blew in the breeze. His robe was woven with designs and colors only seen on Egyptian nobles. No wise commander would wear such bright colors into battle. The opulence would attract every enemy arrow. Gold bands around the driver's ears reflected the sunlight. The glisten begged to be a target. If this was a son of David, he hadn't gained battle skills from his father.

God give me the words to avoid conflict.

Ittai raised his hand in greeting and to halt the progress of his men. His foes would see he had no blade.

"I come as a follower of your God. As a friend of the household of David."

Mutterings hushed as his greeting was received.

"We seek refuge in your lands. Our loyalty lies with your God and your king. That is why we journey to Jerusalem." Ittai made sure the driver knew of their allegiance, and that he and his men were relying on this official to grant safe passage to the City of David.

"You are Philistines? Why not settle in your own

lands?" Mumbling accompanied the driver's question. "Who dares bring an army into the lands of the tribes of Israel?"

Ittai loosened his grip on his donkey's reins. The leather had grown slick as freshly pressed olive oil.

"I am Ittai the Gittite." Laughter rippled through the crowd of Hebrews. He tamped down the ire rising from his gut. "I'm a friend of your king's when he sought refuge in Ziklag."

"That was before my time." Muscles bulged as the driver controlled his jittery horse. "My father has never mentioned a Philistine named Ittai." The son smirked as he elongated the foreign name. "Does anyone remember this man?" Locks of hair draped over the driver's robe as he consulted his riders. Heads shook as if Ittai had spoken a lie. Not a single voice aligned with Ittai's truth.

God ease his disbelief.

"I was a boy, and your father showed me kindness." He met the assessments of the closest Hebrews. The officials with swords.

"Of course, you were. You are not past your days of battle like my father." The driver cast a glance at Ittai's men. "If you lived in Ziklag, then you are acquainted with my uncle, Joab."

Ah, a trap. One slip of the tongue, or a brief lapse in memory, and his men would face swords. "I believe Joab is your cousin. A nephew to King David and foul of mood most days." An honest recount.

"He is my most favored cousin," the driver shouted.

A drip of sweat trickled between Ittai's shoulder blades. "Then you have never tried to sneak one of his raisin cakes or his wineskin."

Silence.

Hebrew gazes glanced at their leader.

"Your words hold a truth a stranger would not know." The driver grinned and motioned for a runner to take the reins of the chariot. In a bounce of curls, the driver rounded the end of the cart and approached Ittai, halting a few feet away. "Come on down from your mount, Philistine."

A bold move for an heir, even if this was David's son. "Who is willing to greet an exile from Gath? I do not know your name or your command."

Laughter.

Arms open wide as if for an embrace, the driver stepped closer. "I am Absalom. David's heir." Absalom motioned for Ittai to join him on the hardened ground. "You will not find a more sought-after judge in all of Israel."

Wasn't the king the final judge in a kingdom? Insulting a prince would not be prudent. He needed all the alliances he could muster. Dismounting, Ittai approached David's son. Should he bow? Kneel on one knee? What would his men think if he showed weakness to a prince with fewer men at his command? To avoid an offense, Ittai acknowledged the prince with a steady bob of his brow.

Absalom's gaze swept over Ittai's men. "You have an allegiance to my father then? You and your fighting men."

"Our allegiance is to God. Where else can we go and worship the God of Abraham, Isaac, and Jacob? I will not bow to an idol." He stepped nearer the heir. Ittai's shoulders were a hand above Absalom's, but the prince stood as a fortress before him. "You might say that was the folly that sent a band of Philistines over the border. I could not worship a king as the One True God."

"And you shouldn't." Absalom cast a glance at Ittai's hip. "You do not carry a sword?"

"I prayed I would not need one. I do not seek a war or bloodshed." Addressing the men stationed behind Absalom, he said, "I have come to settle in this land and worship the God of David. Wherever I am needed, I will serve."

"His men have swords," one of Absalom's runners shouted.

Opening his hands to show he didn't hold a dagger, Ittai said, "I could not talk them out of their weapons. We are outnumbered. And we lack a chariot." He dipped his head in the direction of the exquisitely crafted cart.

"You like my chariot? Hah!" Absalom howled. He clapped a hand on Ittai's shoulder.

Ittai curled his toes and stood as solid as a stump. He forced a glee-filled laugh from his chest. If Absalom sunk a knife into his side, Ittai would die laughing and allow time for his men to attack. "I've come with nothing as bold and grand as you. My mount is not as fair as your chariot." Acknowledging Absalom, he cracked a grin. Up close, the prince's hair resembled a mass of wild grapevines, but his features were as smooth and beguiling as a virgin's. "My men are not as handsome or obliging either. I doubt I could convince them to chase me on foot."

Absalom shook his mane. "I like you, Gittite. You're plain spoken." The prince's breath reeked of cloves. Had he eaten his fill of honey cakes, too? "My father did flee to Ziklag to escape the hand of Saul. King Achish kept my father alive, and I stand before you this day because of a Philistine's loyalty."

"Lord, Absalom." A man bowed and hurried forward. The sheen on his sword caused Ittai's eyes to burn. "This could be a plot by our enemies to hem us in. Do not let him pass."

Who was this man to mock his motives? Ittai's forces had come from Hebron. He had no forces advancing from Jerusalem. Why was this confidant questioning Ittai's moves? Retreat, fool.

Absalom secured his mass of hair behind his ears. He motioned toward Ittai's men. "How can you say these Philistines are a threat when they have a woman joining their ranks."

A woman?

Ittai turned. His belly swirled like a pool at bathing time. There she was. Rimona. His Hebrew runner was seated on a donkey, trotting closer, and covered with a veil of vibrant stripes fit for a queen. She almost outshone Absalom in his fine wares. "That rider is not from Gath. She hails from Beersheba. We rescued her outside of Hebron. Her own kinsman was trying to sell her as a slave."

Hamuran's mouth gaped and then shut as Rimona passed by on her mount. She traveled between the opposing forces as if she were a mother coming to chastise her sons. Her feet were still bandaged and hung limp over her donkey's ribs. The stale breeze exploded with the scent of cassia and lilies as her mount halted by his side. She came alongside him, the foreigner, and not her prince.

His heart did a tiny flutter as he met Rimona's wide-eyed glimpse. He knew those captivating brown eyes. He had admired them in the moonlight when he caught her on the hill. Her eyes held a hint of fear, an emotion he remembered seeing in his mother's eyes. If only a widow's life didn't contain so much hardship and worry. His brief nod acknowledged Rimona's arrival.

Beholding David's heir from her perch, she bowed her head. "Shalom, my lord." Rimona's voice rang out as a noblewoman's, sturdy though with a slight quiver. She swallowed with an audible click that Ittai ignored. "I have words to speak."

Indeed, knowing Rimona, she had words in abundance.

7

Rimona repositioned herself on her mount, sitting as tall as one of her stature could, and tried not to tremble among so many warriors. Parveda had not thwarted her decision to leave and speak on Ittai's behalf. Rimona hoped, and Parveda agreed, that the presence of a Hebrew woman giving testimony in favor of Philistine fighting men might ease tensions on the plain. A young sentry on the road had assessed her direction of travel, but he did not order her to rejoin the women. Perhaps the sentry welcomed the sight of a Hebrew who could pay tribute to his commander. And pay tribute she would, for Ittai had rescued her from the horrors of slavery. She prayed her words would prevent a war and bloodshed.

The sculpted-browed chariot driver scrutinized her with eyes awake and astute. Had she plodded into a miraculous vision? This man was more beautiful than most women, or at least the ones she had known in Beersheba. His skin was without mole or scar. His cheekbones were bold and thick. Even his lips were fuller and deeper-hued than her own.

Surely, he was royalty. Gold ornaments hung from his robe and loyal followers surrounded his chariot. Her cheeks warmed from the attention of the crowd and the presence of the chariot driver beholding her with a sultry gleam in his eyes. She did not turn away from his intimidating presence but stared into the rich brown pools of his eyes, willing her words to rest upon his soul. On this day, no one was going to die.

She cleared her dry throat. "My lord, I've come to testify on behalf of these foreigners. This man" —she indicated Ittai— "he saved my life and offered me protection. I would be a slave in Egypt if he had not scared off my pursuers. He has allowed me to join him in his travels to Jerusalem. I go to the city to see my uncle who serves in the palace." She swept her tongue over her teeth to moisten her mouth, but her saliva had evaporated.

"Well, my child. Do not be afraid. I hear you hail from Beersheba." The beauty of a man strolled toward her mount. He did not bring the stench of the sun, but the aroma of a concubine's perfume. With his fingertips, he brushed the mane of her donkey. "I lament that I was not there to hear your grievances and see you safely to Jerusalem. I have spent many a day judging among my people."

Managing a nod to confirm her birthplace was all she could muster. The authority with which the driver spoke, and the compassion that he genuinely offered, befuddled her senses.

The chariot driver pursed his perfect lips. "Let me carry your burden and assure you that injustice will not be tolerated in our lands." He stroked higher on the mane. A breath of a caress touched her fingers. "I can protect you now."

He must have misjudged his proximity to her hand. His touch was brief. Only a foolish woman would start a quarrel about a misguided tap. She stilled as if the sun overhead had baked her bones and created a helpless idol. Who was this man with skin as soft as cream? Surely, the son of a king if he was judging among her people. Hadn't she heard a tale of a prince going into the countryside to silence quarrels?

"Toda raba. You are too kind." Her praise came forth on one breath. "I am anxious to see my uncle." She cast a glance at Ittai whose gaze appraised the prince. Her Philistine commander didn't seem to be relinquishing her to the prince's oversight easily. When had she ever had two strong men at odds over her? Never. Dipping her chin, she said, "May I be so bold as to ask for safe passage for these men who have cared for my wounds and escorted me closer to my home?" Instinctively, she flexed her bandaged foot. Her ankle throbbed under the wrapped cloth.

"They have spoken of their loyalty to my father." Was it possible for this man's eyes to gather more fire? He stepped away from her mount. A slight grin enlivened his jaw. "What have they shared about their loyalty with you?"

What had Ittai said? Their conversations had vanished from her mind. Was it from lack of sleep, or this heat, or this gorgeous nobleman standing before her, that her words failed to be brought forth? "I believe" —she blinked at the mounting interest in her answer from a legion of sword-toting fighters— "their loyalty lies with our God. They were exiled for their beliefs. One of their women also told me of their commander's allegiance to our God." Truly, Ittai would know she spoke of Parveda. "I have offered prayers to God with them."

"Absalom, how do we know she speaks the truth," a man yelled from near the chariot.

This was David's heir? Conversing as if she belonged to his household? Smiling, her whole body became giddy with the honor of speaking to an exalted and beloved prince.

Holding his hand high, Absalom silenced the scoffer and then rested his palm on the hilt of his sword. "Who do you seek in Jerusalem?" His tone sharpened. Gone was the balm in his voice when he had welcomed her. She had to convince him she wasn't a traitor. Even though she had only been traveling with Ittai and his men for hours, she cared about their plight.

Like a baby bird at feeding time, she stretched her neck and squared her shoulders, facing this inquisition like a woman with blood from the tribe of Judah coursing through her veins. "Shamar ben Ehud, my mother's brother." Her voice grew louder so that everyone in this tense assembly could hear her reply. "I've only met him once. When I was a young girl. He sings like no other and he plays the lyre. My uncle is my nearest kin...since" —her gaze drifted to Absalom in hope that the concern he showed earlier was authentic— "my mother died a little over a month ago. My father has been lost for years." Tears pooled in her eyes. Why did her mother have to be taken from her?

From this world? Here on this dusty plain, strangers were judging her truthfulness and her sorrow. "You do know of my uncle? Of his music, don't you?" *God, I need Your help.*

Absalom laughed, heartily.

Had he not seen her sorrow?

Hamuran's donkey bucked its head. To her right, Ittai skillfully shifted his footing as if he expected an attack.

"I know of him. My wife enjoys his music as does my father. I do not have much skill with a lyre." Absalom waved for his men to give him a wide berth. A path formed to the cart of the chariot.

"Nor do I sing or play anything worthy of listening." Inwardly, she praised the musical passions of a woman and a king whom she had never met. Rimona's chest sank as Absalom's inquisition disappeared.

Absalom turned and addressed Ittai. "Did my father summon you?" The prince secured a stray ringlet behind his gold-banded ear, and pierced Ittai with a wily glare.

A high-pitched hum reverberated in Rimona's ear. Hadn't her testimony brought peace? Absalom had been chuckling a moment ago. Why would King David seek Ittai after all these years?

Ittai's features crinkled into the dreadful scowl she had glimpsed on the hilltop when he thought her a foe.

"Your father doesn't know I am coming. My plan is to send messengers when we are nearer the city." Ittai rolled his shoulders.

Did he grow weary of these questions?

"Praise God, no one has bothered us so far. I have tried to avoid a skirmish in your land."

"You are wise, Ittai the Gittite, though you do not need an artful plan. Wait in the hills before the valley. I will return to the city shortly, and we can celebrate your arrival. Are we not recently acquainted?" Absalom grinned showing flawless alabaster teeth. "You have followed the law in Judah and saved an orphan from harm, which is precisely what I would have done as judge." He cocked his head in her direction. "I would be honored to offer these Philistines refuge when I return to Jerusalem. Your uncle can arrange the music for the festivities."

Rimona's spirit flew like a dove toward the heavens. Her friends would not be slain before her eyes. Better yet, they would have a home outside of the city. "Toda raba, my lord." Rimona bowed her head. "May God bless your generosity."

"You aren't returning to Jerusalem with us?" Ittai rubbed his stubbled chin. Where was his glee at being offered refuge and avoiding a battle?

A few men *tsked* at Ittai's question.

"We are on our way to Hebron." Absalom swept his arm to indicate the chariot followers. "I made an oath to the Lord that I would worship him there. Though, I will not be far behind you, Gittite. While I expect Shamar's niece to be delivered to the palace safely, you must wait for me so I can accompany you into the city."

Ittai nodded. "Peace be with you." He raised his

arm toward the men surrounding Absalom's chariot. "May God go before you and grant you safe travels, so we can speak again soon."

Only a few men accepted Ittai's greeting with a head bob.

Absalom beheld her anew. How blessed she had been to have the ear of David's heir.

"I will see you in the palace, Rimona of Beersheba. You spoke forthright today." Sunlight sparkled in his dark brown eyes. "Not many women would have been brave enough to face a chariot and its runners." He bounded toward his cart. "I trust I will see you in Jerusalem."

For a moment, a brief moment, lilies bloomed in her belly, but then chills tamped down their budding. Absalom, though handsome and powerful, had a wife.

Prince Absalom cracked the reins on his horse, splitting the calm of the balmy afternoon. With a jerk and a bellow, he was off again to Hebron. Men and donkeys chased his cart. Dust shrouded the view of the distant flatlands.

Ittai coughed, long and guttural.

She cast a glance in his direction and met the gazes of many a Philistine. Ittai assessed her with his fiery commander stare. A shiver cooled her heated skin.

"If they meant to slay us, I would be saving your life again." Ittai crossed his thick arms and puffed out his formidable chest. "You should have stayed with the women. They are safe with my men."

"Absalom is a Hebrew and heir to the kingdom. His men are from the tribe of Judah. They're my people." She folded her arms to mirror his stance. Shouldn't he be afraid of offending her? After all, Absalom extended concern for her well-being. "Absalom did not seem set on war."

"You could be a traitor. Paid handsomely for your deception. Although,"—he pointed at her bandaged feet—"most spies would hide an injury that shows weakness."

She wiggled her throbbing toes. "I believe I brought a calm to the situation." A little praise would be welcomed.

"You did?" Ittai chuckled.

Was he agreeing with her? Or was he questioning her?

Hamuran dismounted and joined Ittai near her donkey.

"Doesn't the son of the king have everything he needs for worship in Jerusalem? Why would he drive a chariot to Hebron?"

Ittai squinted at Absalom's retreat as though he were in a trance. "David was king in Hebron for years before moving the Ark of God, and his throne, to Jerusalem. But that was early in his reign. After he left Ziklag."

"Hebron was our city of worship before Jerusalem." Rimona secured her striped veil. Her tribal history was not unknown to her. It still seemed strange that a Philistine knew it so well. "That was many years ago before our tribes were united, and we had peace."

Ittai mounted his donkey and returned to her side. "We best be on the move. You and I both have people waiting for us in Jerusalem."

Hamuran returned Ittai's sword. "You might have need of this."

"You are going into the city?" Rimona's mind whirled. "Absalom gave you his blessing to settle in this land. He asked you to wait outside in the valley." A few of Ittai's men turned their heads at her rising voice. Or was it at her hint of chastisement?

"My concern is not for Absalom. I began this journey to seek David. And seek him, I will." Ittai fastened his weapon. He acted as if the conversation was over. Well, it wasn't.

"Absalom offered to escort you into Jerusalem." She swallowed the tart saliva pulling at the sides of her mouth. "Why would you disregard his offer. The offer of a prince?" Didn't Ittai realize the power Absalom had in Judah? In all of Israel?

Ittai rubbed his chin. His brow grooved deep like the carvings on the chariot. Was he recalling the encounter? He glanced at Hamuran and then turned his attention back to her. "Why does Absalom need to honor a vow to God in Hebron when God's Ark is in Jerusalem?"

"I don't know what you mean." She blinked, again and again. All these men galloping through the flatlands had stirred up the soil. "Why would Absalom lie about honoring an oath?" Suspicion must be in a warrior's blood.

"If he is honoring a personal oath, why does he need hundreds of men to accompany him?" Ittai cocked his head. "What foe is a match for a chariot at full speed? He could travel to Hebron straightaway on his own. Isn't an oath between a person and God private? Why the onlookers?"

She bit her lip and contemplated Ittai's response. This was folly. Ittai was correct in that few men, almost none, if she were honest, could face a chariot and claim victory. Though, a prince didn't travel like most people. Ittai should understand. Weariness weighed upon her bones. The pain in her ankle didn't help her state of mind either. "We are leaving Etam unharmed. Can't we give thanks for that blessing? None of us knows the mind of a prince. Save God."

Leaning forward on his mount, Ittai's broad form shaded her face. To meet him in battle would melt her bones.

"Absalom has an abundance of wealth and stature as his father's heir. That is true." His authoritative tone softened. "But an heir doesn't rule the kingdom. How can Absalom offer me anything of value without his father's blessing? How will David feel if I align with someone whom I barely know instead of the man who gave me bread and acceptance as a boy?"

"So, you are going to march into the city?" She wrapped her veil tight around her neck.

"My allegiance is to David."

"What will Absalom say when he returns?"

Shaking his head, Ittai unnerved her with the intensity of his stubbornness. "If David accepts me into his kingdom, Absalom is the least of my worries in the palace." His eyes held a hint of remembrance. "Some men fight well. I have no doubt Absalom can win a battle. Other men claim victory by deceit. Their blade will pierce your belly before you can bow."

Was someone waiting for revenge in Jerusalem? Rimona straightened the wrap of her head covering. The soft linen of her mother's veil soothed the fear rising in her heart. Her journey to Jerusalem was supposed to be uneventful and safe. Hah! Trickery, schemes, and the whispers of war abounded in the hours since she left Hebron.

"The boundary lines have fallen for me in pleasant places," Ittai said. "Surely, I have a delightful inheritance."

What was Ittai reciting? Something from Gath or Philistia?

"Is that what you believe?" Rimona shooed a pesky fly. "That David will give you a delightful inheritance?"

"Those are his words. Spoken in Ziklag years and years ago." Ittai straightened. "Look how God has blessed David. I have to place my trust in his God. The God of the man that fed me as a boy and gave me livestock to sell to keep my mother alive. I do not believe David's generosity toward me has waned."

She had lost the will to fight Ittai. Or anyone for that matter. She needed to rest in her new home. A home that did not fold onto a camel or a Philistine cart.

Couldn't warriors see the heart of a man? Be grateful for peace? A bead of sweat snaked down her hairline. "Absalom has power at his fingertips. He is a Hebrew prince."

"True." Ittai scanned the terrain as if seeking

another enemy. His donkey shuffled its hooves trying to join the men returning to the road. Ittai held the reins fast. "A son's inheritance comes when his father dies. Or is dethroned."

"Or killed in battle." Hamuran urged Ittai to follow him with a nod toward his retreating warriors.

"Do not speak of such." She guided her donkey around Ittai's mount. "We have been at peace for many years. Our king has seen to it." Why was Hamuran mentioning war? Did all men seek a fight? At least Parveda would sing praises that no swords were drawn this day. Rimona had done her duty and voiced a good opinion of Ittai and his men to her prince. The Philistines were alive and had the promise of land, even if the stubborn commander chose to ignore the offer.

"I have repaid my debt today." She glanced at Hamuran and avoided looking directly into Ittai's brooding features. A hawk floated in the wind over Ittai's banded hair. Squinting, she followed the bird's flight. "I spoke in favor of you and your men. We have rescued each other in times of need. I will rejoin the women and leave you to lead us where you will. I only need to go as far as the palace steps." She bobbed her head, briefly and trotted her donkey toward the road. Ittai did not call her name. Neither praise nor a farewell left his lips. Did she desire his commendation? Somewhat. How many women would ride into a conflict?

She and Parveda had designed the best battle plan for the day and won. When her uncle welcomed her to the palace, she wouldn't need to see Ittai the Gittite again. He and his men could settle as far from the city as they pleased. Her boundary lines had already fallen into place. Until they all reached Jerusalem, she would avoid the commander and help Parveda with her children. Her plan made sense.

So why did her heart feel like a sliver of wood had burrowed into its flesh?

~*~

Hamuran scuffed Ittai's arm with his palm. "You need to be quick with your praise. Women do not care about the details of a decision. They want to hear flattery with their name attached."

"Hmmm." The damp fur of Hamuran's donkey brushed the side of Ittai's leg. The stench of wet hide and regurgitated hay filled the air as Rimona rode away. He would talk to her later, say something to settle her worry. She didn't understand the horrors of war or the bond he had with David in Ziklag or the wiles of a powerful prince. For now, Ittai turned his attention to his companion who understood conflict. He needed to test Hamuran's skills. Exile had not been granted, yet. "How would we hem in Absalom and his men for a battle?"

"I was speaking about our Hebrew guest." Hamuran shoved a thumb in the direction Rimona had ridden.

"I'm inquiring about the other beauty on the plain. The one who could summon an army and double back."

Sober-faced, Hamuran said, "To trap the chariot, we would need to have fighting men hailing from Jerusalem. Or from another northern city as we flank the south."

"We don't have forces in Jerusalem. David would have to bring men from the north to hem in his son." Ittai waited, giving his friend a side-eyed challenge. Had Hamuran gleaned the warning from Absalom's runner, or had he been distracted by the prince and Rimona?

"A son fleeing the army of his father would bring more than two-hundred men to protect him." Hamuran's jaw flared. "Though, a trusted soldier would never call battle plans to his commander in ear shot of his enemy." Cocking his hand, Hamuran held back a grin.

"Your wits still amaze me, my friend."

Hamuran sat tall on his mount. "Some of Absalom's men weren't soldiers. They were nobles or wealthy officials."

Thank You, Lord, for the cunning you have given my confidant. Ittai clapped a hand on Hamuran's sun-warmed shoulder.

"And those can be the most dangerous of enemies."

8

Hours later, outside of the Hinnom Valley, Ittai halted his mount and his men. Donkeys and families needed rest, water, and food. He dismounted and led his donkey under the shade of an olive tree. He broke off a thin leaf and rolled it between his fingers. The airy sweetness of the juices brightened his senses like honey. During this time of refreshment, he needed to find Rimona and take Hamuran's advice. Flattery wasn't ripe on his tongue, but he could offer his thanks for her presence on the plain. She meant well, meant to save him and his men from war, but she didn't realize the weight her attendance would have placed on his soul if swords had been drawn. He had vowed to protect her life, not watch it end. Tomorrow, he would escort her to her uncle and to safety. Along with relief, a hint of emptiness took root as he envisioned her boldness in her new home.

A young boy ran toward him with a bucket in one hand and a waterskin in the other. The boy reminded Ittai of when he'd run to refresh David when the future king returned from raiding. That was a long time ago, yet it seemed like a breath ago.

Hamuran rode toward Ittai. His donkey's mouth snarled as if it wanted to suck water from the boy's bucket.

"We could make Jerusalem by dark." Hamuran spied the landscape in the distance. "The valley has plenty of groves to hide our arrival."

"We could arrive at sundown, but I find the dark frightens men too easily. I will ride into the city in the morning when the gates open."

Hamuran's mount nudged the boy's shoulder as the boy poured water from the skin into the bucket. "You will enter by yourself. Unannounced?"

"I will ride with Rimona and an appropriate escort."

"That's not what I meant." Hamuran slid from his donkey and joined Ittai in the shade. "We could send a messenger to King David. You could meet an advisor at the city gate. Determine David's mood." Hamuran swiped a hand over his chin. "Your memory may be long forgotten in David's mind." His friend spoke forthright. More than likely, he echoed what others feared.

Ittai tossed the rolled leaf onto the ground. The scent of life still lingered. He needed the refreshment. Leading his men into exile and into a relationship with the One True God was harder than leading them into battle. He could never truly explain his bond with David to anyone who hadn't experienced the acceptance and kindness of the then-future king. He prayed David held fast to that bond as well.

"I know some of the men may be uneasy camping so close to Jerusalem." Ittai squinted at some approaching carts. "The One True God has spared all of our lives. We have traipsed across the plains of Judah with barely a notice. Today, when we encountered a prince, he offered us land."

His friend nodded. "I do not doubt God, and I don't believe I have ever doubted you."

The admiration Hamuran showed strengthened Ittai's resolve, but it also rested like a stone tower upon his shoulders. *God grant me wisdom where my men are concerned.* "I will not let any of my men give into fear where my relationship with David is concerned." Ittai's words were accompanied by the lapping sounds of thirsty mounts. "We must trust in God, and we must trust in the king He has chosen. You, my friend, must trust in me once again."

Removing his headdress, Hamuran dried the sweat on his brow. "Haven't I always trusted in you? And added advice when I thought you needed it?" His companion grasped a leafy olive branch. His shoulders relaxed as the limb held his weight. "It was a miracle King Achish allowed us to leave. God must have a reason to send us on this journey."

"Other than to save a Hebrew woman?" Rimona sauntered toward him with a tender gait. Gone was the bold striped veil she wore in Absalom's presence. Her plain veil had returned. The one she'd been wearing when she'd fled into his arms. Some of her ire from that night had returned along with the grooves in her forehead. Her improved stride pleased him.

Parveda drove a cart closer to the olive tree. Her children huddled in the back among sacks and wares. Lana waved as if this was a joyous gathering.

Ittai opened his arms to receive the women. "Would you like a drink? We have a waterskin." Although his words did not ring out in praise of Rimona, he had made a hospitable offer of drink.

Pursed lips and sour faces received his hospitality.

"I have seen to our needs," Parveda said, her head covering blowing in the breeze. "I have come to make sure you and my husband eat. You have barely tasted a fig." Halting her donkey's progression, Parveda came down from her perch on the cart. "You may give Rimona some water. I will prepare the food. Lana can assist me." Parveda's head moved ever so slightly toward the tree. Who was giving commands now?

Hamuran joined his wife and family. Out of the corner of his eye, Ittai glimpsed Parveda's hand flapping, keeping hungry boys away from her delicacies.

How did a man fall on his dagger and offer amends when people milled about? He motioned for Rimona to join him under the tree away from the wide-bellied mounts. "It is cooler in the shade." *Of course, it is, you fool.*

Rimona did not shift a sandal. "There wasn't any shade on the plain." She crossed her arms and nestled them against her hips.

"And you were dripping and scarlet-faced."

Her mouth gaped.

Flattery.

"Yet…yet you were stunning. The prince could not keep his eyes off of you." *Or his fingers.* Ittai forced a smile as his stomach coiled tight.

Hamuran's torso shook as he popped a date into his mouth. Was he laughing? His advice was to say kind words.

Tugging on her head covering, Rimona strolled closer. She blinked, gazing everywhere but at him. "My mother's covering must have caught your eye. The stripes and the colors are bold." Shade covered her face. "I didn't believe I would need to wear it. Not until Jerusalem. And even there, I would need a reason. A celebration, or a—"

"We should have a celebration of your bravery." *Much better praise.* His breathing eased. "I have never seen a woman ride into battle." *Make it about her.* "You spoke forcefully. I am in your debt."

Her lips opened and then closed.

Rimona speechless? Had he finally said something of worth?

"I believe I will take that drink." She smiled, and her cheeks turned a sweet shade of scarlet even protected from the late-afternoon sun. Her tantalizing aroma of newly budded lilies overpowered the sweetness of the olive leaf he had plucked earlier.

Ittai raised his hand to catch Parveda's attention. "Do you have cups to spare?"

Lana bounced off the cart and gathered a basket and some cups. The girl grasped a blanket and stumbled toward the tree.

"If we are eating so near the valley, does that mean we are waiting for Absalom to return?" Rimona tilted her head and smiled at him as if he were the glorious Absalom. "I can stay in the valley for a few days. You do not have to rush into the city on my account. My uncle will delight in my delay."

Ittai's flattery was going to become a dung heap. He placed a hand against the trunk of the olive tree, but the smooth bark might as well have been quills. His skin prickled where his hand rested.

"My men will wait for Absalom in the valley. As you suggested. But we will enter the city. If I do not return, they can receive the prince's offer of land. It's not because of you that I need to go into Jerusalem." *It's for me.* "And I doubt your uncle frets about your arrival."

"I wish that were true." Rimona fingered the cloth covering her ear. Her features lost all expression. "So, you're delivering me like a message or a bundle of sticks." The ache in Rimona's voice settled in his ears like the buzz of a biting horsefly.

Lana traipsed between them juggling a basket while freeing her sandals from the drape of a woven blanket.

"Let me help." Rimona grabbed the blanket and settled it on the ground. Bending over, she took the food from Lana while the girl secured the cups.

He stood over the blanket as big and silent as the olive tree. *Say something.* "I will still protect you, Rimona. We will have an escort, and I will remain with you until your uncle arrives to greet us."

"How many men then?" Rimona took a sip of water. "Fifty like before?"

"Riding into Jerusalem with fifty Philistines will draw more attention than if I ride into the city with you and a companion." His forehead ached. His fighting men did not question every statement he made. They followed orders without contempt.

"Can I go with you and Rimona?" Lana swiped her hands. Breadcrumbs sprayed into the air. "The guards will think we are a family."

A family. Leading armies, appeasing a king, and fighting battles hadn't left much time for wooing a woman and beginning a family. "I haven't assigned an escort."

Rimona slumped on the blanket and reached for a piece of flat bread. She nibbled it, but he did not see her swallow. Was she ignoring him and Lana?

"Lana, will you see if your mother has goat cheese for the bread." He wiggled his brows and motioned for the girl to leave them alone.

The girl followed orders as precisely as her father. Stifling a smile, she hurried toward her mother who was serving food from the cart.

How blessed Ittai was to be in a peaceful land, for as he sat bent-legged and facing Rimona on the blanket, he left his back vulnerable to an assault. Hopefully, the water boy was on alert. How could he share his boyhood memories in only a moment and convince Rimona he had pondered the best course of action for her, his men, and for himself?

"I owe David everything. I owe him my life, and I owe him for sharing his faith with me."

Rimona ate a piece of bread, but her beautiful eyes studied him.

"I bragged as a boy that I could provide for myself

and my mother, but everything I brought home was due to David's generosity. Maybe he took pity on a son without a father. I believe he actually cared about me." Ittai bit into a strip of dried mutton and let the salt refresh his tongue. "You might say it's because of David that I'm sitting here with you. Had he not shared about your God, how God had rescued him from the hand of your King Saul, I would have worshiped King Achish and the gods of Gath."

Rimona sipped from her cup as if he were babbling to the donkeys tied nearby.

"Ah, you are hungry and thirsty, and I am remembering days long ago."

"Has it crossed your mind that you remember David more fondly than he remembers you?"

Her barb was placed solidly between his ribs. How many nights had he banished that lie from his mind?

"It has, though it won't change my mind about entering the city with you at my side. If a prince I've never met offers me land, how much more of a blessing will come from a king who shares my past? I have to trust my decision. Why would God lead me astray? God placed David in Ziklag, and God placed David in my life." He drank some water wishing it were wine. At times, his mind traveled the hills of Ziklag. "I'm not related by blood, but there's a bond between us that's never been broken."

Rimona held her cup in her hands and moved it closer to her chest. She inspected the rim as if the wood had splintered.

It had not.

"I'm glad you shared your reasoning with me. I can be stubborn, and, well, it is hard to listen when one talks a lot." The edge of her smile did not reach her cheeks. "My mother and father are gone as are yours. I'd like to believe if something happened to my uncle that I could go home to Beersheba and be welcomed. I have a friend there, Leah. She brought food when my mother was ill. My mother was ill for a long time."

"I am sorry to hear about your mother's sickness." Ittai finished his bread and braced his weight against his arm as he stretched out on the blanket.

Rimona still cradled her cup. "The night I fled Eglon, I pretended Leah had come to bring me home. I must have portrayed a desperate woman well, for Eglon and his friend turned to explain their scheme to the ghost of my neighbor."

"If someone called out David's name right now, a herd of chariot-pulling stallions couldn't stop me from turning around," Ittai said.

She smiled this time, big and beguiling.

He sobered at her beauty and her acceptance of his past. "If you need me in the city, I will help you."

She shifted on the blanket, wafting her fresh enticing scent his direction.

"You are a loyal man, Ittai." She took an interest in her cup again. "I believe we have shared enough time together that if someone called out my name, you would whirl around."

"I believe we have, Rimona." Assurance fled from his lips. His words were not flattery; it stunned him to realize how much truth he had spoken.

Lana halted at his side. "I have your goat cheese, Commander."

He rose to receive the food.

Rimona stood and bent to collect her plate. Her head covering gaped.

"Your earring is pretty, but I think you have lost one." Lana patted the blanket around where Rimona had lounged.

Against Rimona's veil, a gold and emerald earring shone. He hadn't noticed the jewels before. The gems had been hidden by a wrap of cloth. Her one ear was indeed bare.

Ittai stooped. The least he could do was search for the gemstones.

"It is fine." Rimona halted Lana's hunt. "I only have one earring. The other was lost years ago. They belonged to my mother. She said the three stones reminded her of our family. My father, my mother, and me." Rimona tightened the cloth around her face. "All I have are memories now." Her glistening gaze met his.

"Maybe it is a sign, Commander? To enter the city as a family." Lana voice rose too loud for a warrior's ears. The boy watering the donkeys, her parents, and a few men gawked at Lana addressing him with earnest. "Rimona doesn't look like a Philistine, and I haven't grown to my full height." Lana's head whipped around toward her mother. "You'll let me go into Jerusalem with Rimona? Won't you mother? I can be an escort, but the merchants will believe I am her daughter. I can tend to her tomorrow like you did last night."

"I have not agreed to this plan." Ittai calmed his voice. Was anyone listening to him? His command was being challenged by another woman and this one was still a girl.

"I didn't approve it, either." Rimona chewed her lip.

"You know my daughter is right." Parveda shook her head and offered a piece of bread to her youngest son. "How did I birth such a shrewd daughter? She turns my own actions against me."

"On your own, you may be noticed." Hand on his hip, Hamuran surveyed the groves in the distance before taking a drink from his cup. "Who seeks a fight with their wife and daughter at their side?"

"I give you my word." Rimona hurried to Parveda's side. "I won't let any harm come to Lana."

Ittai pinched the cleft in his chin. Plans had already been etched into hard rock. By Lana, by Parveda, and by Rimona, no less.

If the boundary lines had fallen for him in pleasant places, why did he meet a woman's question or scorn around every turn? He bit into a succulent raisin cake and let the sweet tartness pleasure his tongue. This evening he would disperse his men among the groves of the valley. In the morning, he would deliver Rimona to the palace as he had promised. And during the night, he would pray that David would remember the boy he had rescued from servitude and starvation. For no matter what Ittai faced in Jerusalem, he would protect Rimona and Lana as if they were his true family.

9

Rimona's backside ached from riding the wide girth of her mount. The donkey plodded toward Jerusalem without a concern to its welcome. A pulse of tears strained against Rimona's eyes as she remembered her farewell to Parveda. When would she see her Philistine friend again? If King David did indeed give land to Ittai and his men to manage, would it be close to the city, or farther into the hillsides? She took a deep breath and commanded herself to remain strong. Seeing tears would only cause Ittai and Lana to worry.

The incline on the road to Jerusalem's southernmost gate tested her donkey's fortitude.

In the distance, the stone wall grew taller with every hoof stomp. The grandeur of the hilltop fortress made Ittai's towering form wither by comparison.

Hen-flesh beaded on her arms as an image haunted her thoughts. How many stones had she climbed over to escape from Eglon? If not for Ittai and his men, she would be a speechless slave languishing in Egypt and not the niece of a palace official entering the city. She would use all of her influence to make sure Ittai received a word with the king. Her debt to him would be repaid in abundance. For truly, her uncle had some relationship with the King after years of loyal service.

Clusters of merchants with carts, wagons, and load-bearing camels traveled on the side of the road traipsing to a brisk marketplace. A few of the men regarded Ittai with concern. The width of two traders could fit inside Ittai's tunic. So far, no one dared to call out a bargain or a taunt. Her prayers for a safe journey had been answered.

"There are so many travelers," Lana said, her gaze inspecting the wrapped wares and baskets of produce waiting for coin in the markets.

Rimona's chest tightened beneath her sashed robe. Why couldn't eagerness and anticipation well inside of her body as she trod toward a new home?

"That is in our favor." Rimona drew closer to Lana's mount. Shade from the city wall tempered the warmth of the morning sun. "And it's why the commander dispersed his men and their families this morning. People travel from all over to barter and trade in Jerusalem. The valleys afford ample waiting room." She winked at her young escort and captured the image of the girl's tooth-filled smile to remember in the months ahead.

Voices, men's voices, grew louder than the mutterings heard along the roadside. Ittai stiffened, growing foreboding like the city wall.

Her heart rate rallied. Perhaps she had sung praises too soon. Had someone alerted guards to a Philistine's presence?

Ahead at the gate, shouting continued.

"Stay here." Ittai motioned for her and Lana to rest under the protection of a terebinth tree.

"No," she and Lana chorused.

"We are going with you." Rimona exchanged a glance with the girl. "What Lana said yesterday was true. Together, others will think we are a family. You have already caught the eye of some merchants. Their curiosity may cause you trouble." She bobbed her head. Once, but boldly.

"Are you prepared to be caught in a scuffle?" Ittai said.

"I spoke in front of a prince. I can speak to whomever is yelling at the city gate. My uncle's position gives me standing above a dove keeper." She flapped her hand. "Or a spice seller."

Ittai's dark stare was as unyielding as the cut stones "I will speak at the city gate. Men will be conducting business. I may be a foreigner, but I am a man."

Her stomach hollowed and sank to her knees. How could she argue with those words? Or the hurt in his eyes that pierced her quicker than his sword. In Beersheba, she had to care for her ailing mother and take on responsibilities in her father's absence. Here and now, she had a protector in the flesh. Her mother would have scolded her for insulting Ittai's leadership.

She dipped her chin. "We will follow your lead. You are accustomed to fighting with men." Such a skill was not one she wanted to acquire. But she was a Hebrew, and he was not. This was her land and soon she hoped it would be his home, too. It couldn't hurt to be ready to come to Ittai's defense.

Nearing the gate, she spied a few men lined up by the massive wooden beam. The traveler at the head of the line flailed his arms. His words accosted anyone who passed by the small crowd. An older man dressed in a woven robe with embroidered trim, held his hands in a manner to rebuff any curses.

"My brother and I have waited for two days," the troublemaker shouted. "Where is our judge? Shall we wait here while our families go hungry? My livestock is being stolen as we speak."

The older man grabbed his gray beard as if to yank the hairs from his chin.

"Your grievances will be heard, but I cannot search the city and countryside for the king's son. Absalom is not in Jerusalem at the moment."

Rimona envisioned her meeting with Absalom on the plain. The prince had taken time out of his travels to speak to a woman and a Philistine. These men desired the prince's attention as well.

Ittai kicked his mount and came alongside the arguers. He halted between the men heavy with burden and the besieged elder.

She and Lana followed but positioned their donkeys in the center of the road behind Ittai and with the irate travelers on their right. A few merchants refused to pass by the confrontation, preferring to linger and listen to the argument.

"This elder is correct. The prince you seek is not in the city." Ittai spoke as if ordering a charge. Voices hushed. Footsteps slowed. "I met Prince Absalom on the plains outside of Etam yesterday afternoon."

Her lips pressed thin, halting an assertion of "I did, too."

"He was heading to Hebron." Ittai's donkey side-stepped, giving her a better view of the befuddled travelers.

"We have waited two days." The line leader held up two fingers and shook them at anyone in his sight. "When will the prince return? We need someone who has the king's ear." The man's gaze shifted between Ittai and the elder.

"I have no knowledge of his plans," Ittai said, dismissing anymore conversation. "Although he will return. The prince asked me to wait in the valley so he could grant me some land."

"What? I have not heard of this allotment." The elder secured his headdress and fixed his gaze on the men clustered by the gate. "You can wait for the prince or return home and come back after the Sabbath. The king's son should be in the city by then."

"Three days? Isn't there anyone else who could judge among us?" a traveler shouted.

"The prince was here yesterday morning," the elder sputtered. "If he does not return shortly, I will find someone to hear your complaints."

"What good does it do us if no one wants to listen?" The leader spat on the dirt road.

"Let me find an official who can stand this heat." Huffing, the elder scanned the main street.

"Will it be a prince?" Enthusiasm riddled the leader's question.

"Shall I concern the palace about a disputed goat, and upset Absalom's standing?" The elder's tone sharpened.

"I'll wait for Prince Absalom. He has always been fair."

Grumbling accompanied the men as they retreated into the shade to retrieve their mounts.

Was Absalom the only official who decided disputes? Shouldn't King David be concerned about his people and providing justice in the land? She would mention the need for more overseers when she got settled with her uncle.

Ittai and his mount filled the space vacated by the men. She and Lana maneuvered their donkeys closer.

With a roving assessment of Ittai, the elder stroked his beard instead of yanking on its length.

"How did you speak with Absalom? He left in a chariot riding faster than an arrow." The elder glanced at guards stationed near the gate. "You are a Philistine and a fright of a man at that. What business do you have in Jerusalem?"

Rimona rocked forward on her donkey and bit her lip. She had a mouthful to spill on her flight into the hills and on Ittai and his rescue.

"I am a friend of your king." Ittai's statement was as confident as his posture.

"Hah." The elder's head bucked like a frustrated donkey. "The king has no friends in Gath."

Ittai's shoulders rolled like a crashing wave. "Did he not seek refuge in Ziklag when his life was in peril?"

Was Ittai going to tell this elder about David's life? They would all be puddles of water by the time David's history was discussed. She kicked her mount and trotted beside Ittai.

"Shalom, elder. My uncle is an official in the palace. This man rescued me from bandits. He speaks truthfully about our meeting with the prince and—"

"Who is your uncle?" The elder crossed his arms and squinted.

"Shamar ben Ehud. He is in charge of the—"

"I know what he does. Do you sing?"

Lana raced to her side. "I would like to hear her sing." The girl batted her eyelashes and looked upon the older man with glee. "The king will rejoice in her singing."

"I cannot stand this heat any longer." The elder rubbed his forehead. "Follow me, Philistine. I will announce your arrival and the arrival of Shamar's niece to the king. I'm sure my lord will be interested in this gift of land his son has given you." With a wave of his hand, the elder beckoned their group to follow. A soldier broke off from guarding the gate and strode with the gray-haired elder.

"May I remind you, Gittite," the flushed official said, "we have been living in peace with our enemies."

"He knows." Rimona was ready with her defense. Lana bobbed her head in agreement. "He knows all about the peace in our land. He is the king's friend from many years ago in Ziklag."

"No one speaks of Ziklag anymore." Dismissing her with a click of his tongue, the elder plodded onward. His sandals scuffed against the packed soil. "The king hasn't had to seek refuge in years."

With the scowl Ittai bestowed on her, she may have to seek refuge right now.

10

Ittai guided his mount along the main road that sliced through the center of Jerusalem. Stone houses lined the street with their thresholds swept clean. Glare from the sun reflected off of sand-colored stone, causing him to squint and make sure Rimona and Lana kept pace with the eager elder. The man strutted toward the palace like a defiant rooster.

The City of David was a jewel in comparison to Gath. High on a hill, with a pristine calmness as if God settled upon each rooftop, the city called to Ittai's soul. He breathed in the air. Gone was the salt spray from the pagan towns along the sea. Here, with the winds of Judah in his lungs, he had freedom to worship God in the presence of God's anointed king.

When they reached the palace steps, the elder motioned to the guards. "They will make sure your donkeys are watered and have shelter from the heat. We don't need waste in front of the steps."

Relinquishing his lead, Ittai nodded to the guard who returned his appreciation with a stern stare. Rimona removed her satchel and flung it over her shoulder. Of course, she would cling to her possessions, they were all she had to remind her of Beersheba. He did not have treasures from Gath buried in a cart. Not a single one. His treasure was the loyalty of his men, and he would do anything to protect their lives and deliver Rimona safely to her uncle. If David's men sought his life, he would plead with his former mentor to spill his blood when Rimona and Lana had been lured away to Shamar's portion of the palace. Since Israel and Philistia had enjoyed years of peace, he doubted David would be cruel.

He halved his stride so the women stayed close. Higher and higher they climbed to a stone arch with intricately set tiles adorning the mortar.

Swiping sweat from his brow, he ducked slightly and entered an oasis. An oval pool took center ground in a courtyard with ferns and palm trees bringing life to its wall of alabaster stones. The breeze high above the city was like a misting rain on a march through the desert.

Lana ran toward the low-lying wall. His throat seized. Before he could move a sandal, Rimona stood beside the girl.

"Look." Lana pointed to rows of dwellings filling the city. "You can see everything from this courtyard. I can even see our donkeys."

"We will have plenty of time to see the city." Rimona turned Lana away from the wall. "We do not want to fly after you if you fall."

"I'm not my brothers." Lana pouted. "I won't fall."

"That is good to know." Rimona touched her heart and smiled, pulling Lana close for an embrace. Rimona's motherly gaze met Ittai's as long twisting curls slipped from her veil.

Ittai squeezed his hand into a fist. When had he ever seen Rimona with a carefree smile? His whole being became refreshed as if he were a tender green tendril unfurling in this oasis. Rimona's happiness and establishing her new home in this palace is what he would remember about his trek to Jerusalem. Her glorious smile is what he would treasure when they parted.

"Come along." The elder shuffled across the courtyard. "I have spent time enough in this heat." He hurried under another splendidly crafted archway.

Gathering his small band, Ittai strode into a large chamber. A roof banished the sun, while high windows let in enough light for comfortable viewing. A throne and stone chairs perched a few steps above the floor. Would David come to greet his guests? Or would David come to judge the Philistine who had brought an army to his gates? Perhaps, David would not come at all. In his heart, Ittai knew there were plenty of officials who could oversee his request for exile and receive the niece of a musician. Even a prince expected him to wait in the valley like a beggar.

Lord, may You go before us to David and soften his heart. If my boundary lines end here, then so be it. May Rimona and Lana be welcomed.

"Wait here. I will see what business needs the king's attention." The elder shook his head as he headed toward a door near the seats of honor. "I should have lounged in my room this day. Runaway princes. Giants at the gate." His mutterings ended with the *thunk* of a cedar door.

Ittai scanned the chamber for other doorways. None existed. But then who could escape from a palace rising above a walled city? He turned to speak with Rimona. She stood straight-backed and unmoving as if she were mortared into place.

The door opened.

Two guards flanked the frame. The left guard's dagger hung securely from his belt. On the right, the soldier's sword almost gouged the floor. Ittai had not brought a weapon. What would be the use? Except…

"Are you frightened?" Rimona whispered. Her dark eyes blinked in his direction.

He did not need Rimona to worry after him, but deep down in his gut, he was touched that she cared about his well-being. With her uncle having a position at the palace, he had fulfilled his promise of protection, for no harm would come to a daughter of Judah in David's house.

"I have to trust in the God Who brought us safely to Jerusalem." He cast a glance at Lana who gazed at him as though he ruled this ceremonial room. "I knew David when I was a boy. He was kind to me then, and I pray he is kind to me now."

"I have been praying." Rimona drew her veil tighter across her shoulders and secured it under her satchel. The aroma of her tantalizing perfume bolstered his strength.

"I haven't stopped praying since the shouting at the gate." Lana blinked as she scanned the height of the guards standing on each side of the door.

"Then we should be fine. I know hundreds of men

and women who are praying for us." *God spare Your people.*

Footsteps echoed from beyond the cedar door.

Ittai straightened, shoulders broad as if King Achish was inspecting his armor. The boom of Ittai's heart filled his ears. He cleared his throat and summoned a regal plea.

A guard opened the door.

There he was. There was David, approaching in haste with hair possessing subtle streaks of gray. Gone were the brown locks of a young exile. His waist was thicker, no doubt from eating the best food in Israel. His stare, the one that saw both truth and lie, held fast to Ittai's face, though the daring, and sometimes mischievous spark in David's gaze had faded. Would the brash raider of old remember the boy who tripped over his every order?

The king of legend sniffed the air, loudly, like a choosy man hungry for a meal. He paraded farther into the chamber and halted a foot from where Ittai stood. His robe flooded at his feet. Needing a polish, his simple crown tilted to the side.

"I thought I smelled the stench of a Philistine." The King's voice was familiar, yet it lashed like an oiled whip. "Did Hushai let this animal in here?"

For the first time in his adult life, Ittai's toes trembled.

~*~

David lunged. The King of Israel was upon him.

David's soft hands held Ittai's face firmly while he inspected every scratch and battle scar. Ittai relaxed his jaw and allowed David to swivel his head and sweep hair from Ittai's forehead.

Ittai's limbs turned to stone. His scalp tingled. He did not move one sandal but allowed the king to examine his brow and tried not to blink at the king's touch. The scent of the outdoors, grassy hills, and running streams that were once the home to this raider of Ziklag filled Ittai's nostrils, transporting him to his childhood and the times he kept watch over David's livestock under the starlight.

Silence reigned in the chamber.

David squinted.

I trust in You, God.

"Hah!" The King's exclamation echoed in Ittai's ears.

The guards flinched. Ittai did not.

King David loosened his hold and stepped backward. "I can still see where Joab struck you with that rock." Royal hands rested heavy upon Ittai's shoulders. The affirming grip calmed the hiccup of worry surfacing in Ittai's mind.

Laughter. Glorious laughter consumed the chamber. Laughter Ittai remembered ringing out over the hills of Ziklag.

"For one so young, you didn't cry."

"I believe I was in shock." Raising an eyebrow, Ittai grinned. He glanced at Rimona and Lana. They huddled together with gazes shifting from the king and back.

"Oh, to be in Ziklag again. I have thought of you from time to time. Especially, when my sons were boys." David grasped Ittai's hand. The coolness of a gold band pressed against Ittai's fingers. "I regret that I did not bring you with me when I left."

So, he had thought of bringing me to Hebron. Ittai swallowed any regret. "My mother wouldn't leave the ground under which my father was buried. And—"

"And you would never leave your mother." The king shook his long gray-streaked curls. "Your loyalty was born at an early age."

Rimona sniffled. Was she mourning her own mother? Or his?

Ittai turned.

"Ah, who is this lovely young woman." The king dipped his bearded chin and beheld Rimona. "You brought a wife to Jerusalem?"

"My lord." Rimona bowed, shaking her head, and clutching her satchel tight. "He is not my husband."

Her quick denial pinched Ittai's heart. "We are not married," he offered. Part of him wished he had a wife to parade before the king. "Rimona has traveled from Beersheba."

David sauntered in front of the women as if he were inspecting his fighting men.

"And the girl?"

Lana dipped her head and shifted closer to Rimona.

Now or never, the truth that an army hid in the valley would be spilled on mosaic tile.

"She is the daughter of my second-in-command."

"You have men under your command?" David's eyes brightened as if the sun rose within them. Ittai knew he had aroused the king's cunning.

Ittai nodded and met his mentor's perusal.

"Here? In the city?" David's head swept the chamber as though he had missed a procession of Philistine fighters. David's skill would never have missed such a threat.

Rimona's and Lana's eyes grew as round as the courtyard pool.

Ittai's jaw pulled tight. "I have six-hundred men stationed in the valley among the groves. Some have families with them." He indicated Lana. "They are loyal to me, and they are loyal to you. Above all, we are loyal to the One True God whose praises you sang to me every time I tended your donkey or brought you food when you were in exile."

David pinched Ittai's chin and wagged his finger in the air as he did to his commanders long ago when he was planning a raid. "You mean to tell me that you marched hundreds of Philistines into the Valley of Hinnom without being challenged?" The king cast a glance at his guards. "Battle ready Philistines lounge beyond our city gates, and we rest as babes? We have grown careless with the gift of peace."

"I can scarcely believe it myself. You taught me well. I have prayed to God with nearly every step to spare my men from war and to carry us safely to Jerusalem. I prayed you would see that my allegiance to you has not changed." Ittai would mention his meeting with Absalom when they were alone. Best to reestablish his ties to the father first.

David crossed his arms and settled them over his expanded waistline. "King Achish is not a fool. I cannot believe he allowed a commander to leave with hundreds of warriors." David stiffened. "Do you mean to warn me of an attack?"

"No, my lord. There is no battle forthcoming." Ittai placed a fist over his heart. "I am in exile. I refused to worship King Achish and call him a god. I explained my belief in the God of Abraham and that the laws of Moses forbid me to worship a man as the One True God. Even a king."

"And you lived?"

"Only because you explained about your God. And we all know how spirited you are when you are praising God. I will never forget that passion." Pressure built behind Ittai's eyes. Memories of his childhood, delights, and deaths, raced through his mind. "Our God can do the impossible." God always had. "God prevented a band of raiders from being discovered years ago, and He can protect Philistines who call upon His name when their lives are in peril."

"Oh, Ittai." The king's breath rushed forth like a wind. "If only we were still in Ziklag singing to God and dancing in the grass."

Ittai lowered to one knee. "I have men lounging in the grass of the valley needing land and a home. We will do whatever you tell us to do."

Grasping Ittai's arm, David pulled Ittai to his feet. The king exhaled a small grunt.

Ittai contained a tease. The boy who served a

future king was a wisp of weight compared to the stature of the thirty-six-year-old fighter kneeling in a palace.

"I have plenty of hillsides to house your men." David rubbed his palms together as if deciding on the exact stretch of land. "If God saw fit to bring you safely to Jerusalem, then who am I that I should thwart His plans. His protection is better than mine. I should know. I have been blessed by God's protection all of my life."

"Speaking of protection." Ittai cleared his throat. "Rimona is the niece of one of your officials. I offered to see her safely to the palace after she escaped into our stronghold. I thought she was a spy when I captured her in the dark of night."

David patted Ittai's shoulder. "You had a woman run into your arms. My, our God has shown His favor to you in many ways." The king's laughter shot to the ceiling reminding Ittai of when David sang loudly to the clouds when he lounged on hillsides.

"He has blessed me, hasn't He?" Ittai glanced at Rimona. She had joined his band of men and their Philistine families with ease. Insults hadn't left her tongue, and the praises she sung before Absalom impressed the prince. Or had Rimona impressed the man? Shaking his head, he decided not to think about the chariot driver. "Rimona is the niece of Shamar ben Ehud. We heard he is a musician."

"One of the finest." David clasped his hands as if in prayer. "It has been too long since I sat and listened to songs of praise. We should have him play at a feast to celebrate your arrival and to celebrate the days when I waited to wear this crown." Fingering his simple gold crown, David righted it upon his head. "You must bring fifty of your mightiest men to the feast. I want to hear about you, my friend, about your exploits as a leader." The king's eyes glistened. "I made a difference, did I not? Fighting for God and teaching my men about Him when I could?"

"Of course, my lord." How could David doubt his prowess and legacy? Women sang about his battles and his God-fearing heart. "Everyone listened to your wisdom. And I remember the laughter that startled a drunk or two."

"You must join in the festivities tomorrow night." David addressed Rimona as if she had grown to womanhood in the halls of the palace. "Shamar will not be swift in getting you settled. He has been alone far too long. Like someone else in this chamber." David grinned broader than a giddy bridegroom then sobered as he continued to address Rimona. "A guard will take you and the girl to the music room."

Was this the last time Ittai would see Rimona? Until when? His stomach twinged at the loss of her company. Her boldness was a refreshing elixir he wished to drink from again. His mouth gaped. Could he change the plans of the king?

David slapped Ittai's arm and held on tight. "After I find out how you traipsed through Judah, I will have you brought to meet Shamar. Surely, he will want to thank you for your oversight of his niece."

"I...ugh...I would like to discuss my travels." His

command-giving voice faltered. "And to meet your official."

"Me too?" Lana's lips puckered.

Ittai nodded and stifled a chuckle. *Thank You, Lord.* What other God could have marched hundreds of warriors across Israel without a skirmish, saved a spirited woman from slavery, and provided the grant of exile by a king and a prince. Only the God of Abraham, Isaac, and Jacob. The God, once a mystery to a boy, was now the counselor to a foreign commander.

Ittai should have been leaping and dancing as David did as a younger man, but that thought nagged at his conscience. The vigor David possessed in Ziklag had diminished and had been bestowed on his son. A son whose absence did not sit well with the travelers at the gate or with a Philistine exile waiting for land.

11

Rimona followed the palace guard through the cedar door her king had recently used to enter and greet Ittai. The planked wood glistened as if it held more oil than a lamp. She grasped Lana's hand for comfort as they traipsed lower through hallways and stairwells. Balancing the satchel on her shoulder, she let her free hand brush the stone walls. The rock was cool and sleek compared to the warm softness of Lana's skin.

How had her quiet ride to Jerusalem become a startling adventure? She had believed Ittai when he told her of his closeness with the king, but seeing David's sly reaction at first, she almost vomited on the indigo and mustard tile. For a moment, she believed the king had forgotten his young servant and might slay the foreigner. She praised God for Ittai's strong bond with David. If only she could hear their reminiscing.

Her heart tightened in her chest as she navigated the palace corridors. Would Ittai have come to say farewell to her if Lana was not at her side and the king had not suggested it? Surely, he would want to hear the praise of her uncle. She prayed for a cordial reunion and that the silence from many years apart might be filled with pleasantries.

Their escort pushed through a door. Ahead, daylight prowled around the seam of another doorframe.

Where did musicians practice in the spacious residence of the king? And did her uncle even know she was here in the palace? Had the officials informed him of her arrival? Questions swirled in her mind, though answers were absent. Soon she would greet the uncle who was a faintly drawn ghost in her memory and build a relationship with her sole remaining family member. The thought was more daunting than meeting the king.

"Will your uncle have a waterskin?" Lana's head bobbed as she kept pace with their guard. "I am thirsty."

"I should have brought our skin instead of leaving it with the donkeys." Rimona's main focus had been her satchel and belongings, not a drink. But now, inside her mouth, a thin sour paste had formed. "Everything here is new to me. I guess I thought cups would be waiting in every room. There has to be a hospitable servant somewhere in this palace."

The guard slowed his steps. "Shamar should have a waterskin to quench your thirst." The guard opened a wide door. Sunlight brightened the hallway. "This courtyard can be seen from the king's personal balcony. Any music played here rises to the king's ears and onto the heavens, to God himself."

Rimona thanked the guard for his guidance and squinted at a vast courtyard, rounder and fatter than the one set high above the city. Circled by a stone wall with a smooth slab on top of the stone, the courtyard could fit Absalom's chariot and all his men. From a distant building, a serenade of harps enlivened the air. Innocent melodies transported her soul to happier times. Times when love abounded in her home in Beersheba. Was that her uncle playing? Strumming with another musician, or teaching the song?

"A host of players and guests could fit in this courtyard," Rimona said, taking in the peacefulness of the private area set among the busyness of Jerusalem.

"Yes, at times." The guard grinned. "Your uncle must have students." Was the man's demeanor improving because of the serenade? Lana pranced across the courtyard, twirling toward the buildings on the other side of the stone seating.

"I didn't know my uncle taught lessons." Should she have known? So much about her uncle was cloaked in secrets. Whenever her mother spoke of him, her gaze would become distant and a mist would shroud the usual kindness in her eyes.

"Shamar teaches the sons of Levites and the children of the palace." The guard's eyebrows quirked. Did he believe her to be an imposter?

Her cheeks heated and not from the unrelenting sun. "Oh," was all she managed to say.

"Maybe he'll teach you?" Lana rested on a ledge of smooth rock.

"Or you." Rimona touched Lana's nose playfully. Rimona's elation dissipated with the harp notes. If the land set aside for Ittai and his men was far from

Jerusalem, she wouldn't see her young friend for a time.

"Woman." Their escort stood before cedar planks taller than his height, and a door wide enough to parade a small town through. An overhang shaded his face. "I will leave you with your kin." He pushed open the door and allowed the emboldened tones of the harps to bathe her body.

"Toda raba." She dipped her chin and stepped forward into her new home. A home near a grand courtyard, in sight of the king's balcony, and brimming with song. As soon as she and Lana entered the room, the heavy door closed behind them, banishing the sunshine. Didn't the guard care to address her uncle?

Sunlight entered the building from brick-sized windows near the ceiling. Lower, larger windows facing the courtyard were covered with strung reeds. Two young men, about her age, continued plucking harps, their arms stroking the strings as if they were caressing a newborn babe. Her uncle, white-haired and with a long, tapered beard, hunched over the farthest harpist. Shamar balanced on a cane.

The musician facing the door glanced at her briefly. His throat bobbed as if he had committed a grievance.

Tap. Tap. Tap. Her uncle's sandaled foot maintained a rhythm while his hand swept back and forth. He did not hesitate or acknowledged his visitors.

She closed her eyes and prayed. Was she to be alone even in a room full of musicians? *I am not alone, am I, Lord?*

Opening her eyes, she adjusted her satchel and drew Lana close. What had Ittai said about boundary lines? The Lord had brought her here, safely. He would not abandon her among the instruments. Shifting farther from the players, she leaned against a long table with cloths stacked at the end. The scent of olives wafted from the rags. The whole room smelled of cedar, oakwood, and oil. Along the wall behind the table, were harps lined according to their height. A few lyres that resembled upside down goat legs with strings attached rested on a shelf above the harps. All the instruments glistened, beckoning someone to come and play a lyric.

Lana motioned to a waterskin propped against a wall. A row of stools was positioned nearby. The farthest chair held cups.

Rimona set her satchel on the floor and grasped the waterskin. The feel of the liquid inside the skin made Rimona's jaw seize in want of refreshment. Lana readied two cups.

"What are you doing?" a voice barked.

The music halted. A lone string protested the stoppage.

Heart racing, Rimona set down the skin. She did not want to invoke the wrath of her uncle.

Sandals scuffed across the floor. The staccato beat of a cane pounded the same ground.

Her uncle approached, mouth huffing, with eyes that looked like they wanted to hang her from the wall. A greeting failed to emerge from his lips.

"No one is allowed to drink in here. Only in the

courtyard. These instruments are gifts given to the king. Moisture will ruin their tone." Her uncle's white hair assailed his shoulders. He jabbed a finger at the table. "What if a scroll was present? You would damage a psalm written by our king for a drip of water? Such foolishness won't be tolerated."

Silence.

How dare this relative treat her like an idiot. She bit down a rebuke. *Keep the peace.*

"Forgive us." Rimona straightened at the insult of a guest being yelled at like a thief. She took the cups from Lana and replaced them on the proper stool. Returning to Lana's side, she stroked the girl's arm to provide some comfort. Who would provide comfort for her? A slight tremble in her fingers snagged in Lana's hair.

"Do you know who I am?" Rimona's words warbled instead of showing her indignation.

"I knew the moment I glimpsed you at the threshold. You resemble her."

Rimona had heard that truth most of her life. She would accept his assessment as praise.

"Do you limp?" His nose crinkled as he studied her legs. "Your mother was afflicted. Infirmity keeps men away. I'm sure you know that well." Rounding toward the door, he stilled. "Where is our kin? Eglon escorted you, did he not? I expect him to pry more silver from my pouch."

"He's not here." Answers to all her uncle's questions scrambled in her head. She swallowed and tried to force a sentence from her parched mouth.

"Eglon attempted to run off with the money and sell me into slavery for more coins. I had to flee into the night. God showed me mercy and spared my life." Her heart was running faster than her words. "Praise the Lord I am here now."

"Mm-hm." Her uncle balanced on his cane. "You must have done something to anger Eglon. He is not a rash man."

Ire pulsed through Rimona's veins. "I did nothing but ride a donkey."

"Though you still arrived." Shamar nodded toward the rear of the building. "I have a room assigned to me by the king. I cleaned out a closet where you can sleep." His gaze fell to Lana. "Is she yours? Did you have a husband?"

"Uh, no—"

"Prostituted yourself to a man of the sea like your mother." His accusation lashed her flesh.

The awkward pluck of a few harp strings filled the room.

"That's a lie. My mother and father were married. How dare you mock the dead and your only sister." Rimona's body shook. She released her hold on Lana and now, it was her turn to stab a finger at her uncle, yet not as forcefully. Even for peace, she could not let a scandalous falsehood linger.

"My father was lost at sea. He would have returned to us if he could." Her defense was raging inside her like a stoked fire. "I cared for my mother until her dying day even after your father died—a burial you refused to attend. Just like you refused to care for your own sister."

A blast of light filled her vision. The harp players stood.

Stoic and idle like a lyre waiting to be tuned, her uncle gazed at her. "The girl is not yours?" he finally asked.

"I took care of your sister and your household. I've never married." She folded her arms. Somehow, they did not cooperate in finding a comfortable ledge with the heave of her chest. "And I do not have any children."

"The girl is with me." Ittai spoke in a voice that challenged anyone to deny his claim.

She turned.

In the doorway, he stood, his hand braced against the frame, allowing a slice of sunlight to brighten the room.

Not a single man in the music room called Ittai a liar.

Half of her wanted to flee through the path of light emanating from the solid door. The other half of her desired to flee to Ittai. He understood what it was to love a mother so much that you would never abandon her.

Her uncle gasped. "Are you acquainted with this pagan?" He jabbed his oakwood cane at Ittai.

Bruised by her uncle's accusations, all she could do was nod her head.

Lana emerged from Rimona's side. The girl didn't seem afraid with her commander defending the doorway. A tiny amount of fear drained from Rimona as well.

"Teacher." Lana blinked at the old man stooped before her. "If you must know, Rimona doesn't limp."

12

Ittai widened his stance and assessed the music room. Two harpists retreated toward the far wall with their instruments held as shields. Rimona's uncle remained steadfast and continued to point his cane in Ittai's direction. Not one word of welcome fumbled from his lips. David had bestowed gifts and food upon Ittai, yet a musician treated him like a diseased dog. The echo of blood pounding through Ittai's temples drowned out the lingering melodies from the harps. Before he returned to his fighting men in the valley, he would make sure Rimona was safe and accepted by her relation.

"I am Ittai the Gittite." He strode toward Rimona's uncle and halted close enough that if the cane jerked his direction again, it would be caught and snapped into pieces. "I am a friend of King David. The young girl belongs to one of my commanders. My men gave your niece safe passage from Hebron to Jerusalem."

"You're a Philistine." Shamar scowled. "Why would the King of Israel speak to you? A pagan. This is foolishness."

"Uncle, all of it is true." Rimona stationed herself by Ittai's side as if they were battling a line of adversaries. She beheld everyone in the room, head bobbing. "Ittai saved my life. He escorted me safely to the palace. I do not know what I would have done if he had not been in the outskirts of Hebron. Eglon chased me in the dark of night. I could barely hold my footing among the rocks."

"Hah." Shamar swatted his hand.

Ittai had half a mind to hold it hostage.

"I am too old to listen to this babble. This Philistine invaded our lands and you are praising his deeds? I do not know of any Philistine who has abandoned his idols." Shamar swiveled toward his students.

A harpist, tall and lean, took a few steps away from the wall. "I reside near the tabernacle far from Philistine lands, but God is sovereign. A conversion could be possible." His affirmation faltered.

The other harpist inspected the strings on his instrument without offering a word. His hair curled every which way like a broken string. If he were a Philistine soldier, Ittai would have shaken a response from his lips. Coward.

"Ittai believes in the God of Abraham, Isaac, and Jacob. Our king witnessed to him when Ittai was a boy. I saw them embrace." Rimona's voice grew terse. A hint of defiance lingered in her remarks. He remembered that confidence from the plains outside of Etam. She indicated Lana who was clinging to the nearby table. "Even the young believe in our God and our laws."

Shamar snapped his fingers. "I have heard enough of your boasts. Sing a psalm of David and prove your allegiance to our God. If you know David as you claim, then you will remember his songs." The old man clunked his cane against the floor as he traipsed toward the harpists. "Ahimaaz and Jonathan, start a hymn of praise."

The young men resumed strumming their harps.

Ittai rocked on his heels. Was the old man calling him a liar? How dare he insult Ittai's truth. In front of witnesses no less. His hand hovered at his hip. If his sword had hung there, it would have been drawn and the tip would have grazed Shamar's neck. He glanced at Rimona. She beheld him, wide-eyed and speechless. Being in the presence of her uncle had already dampened her fire.

He forced a grin. His lips barely parted. "I do not sing."

Shamar dismissed him with that annoying wave of his hand. "Then you do not know our God. Your lies were meant to soften the will of my niece. I have no doubt that on a longer journey, she would have been mired in disgrace."

"Uncle!" Rimona shouted. She loosened her head covering and fanned her face with her hand. Her emerald earring sparked a green fire under the faded brown cloth. "Ittai rescued me from slavery."

The pounding echo in Ittai's ears rivaled a raging river. Rimona's uncle should protect her reputation, not disparage her morals.

Rimona drew close and turned her back on her uncle and his musicians.

"You do not have to stay and listen to these

insults. I have seen how you love God with your actions and your words." Her voice was soft and gentle as if they were resting on the blanket under the olive tree outside of Etam. "You have nothing to prove to my uncle. You have proven your faith to me."

Sinking into the brown depths of her eyes, glistening with life amidst her hardship, his resolve strengthened. He couldn't leave her with Shamar's lies ringing in men's heads. But sing?

"We can speak it." Lana hurried over and grasped his hand. His palm engulfed her slim fingers. "In camp we recite praises all day long," Lana said. "My brothers sing songs before they sleep." Lana's eagerness drew him into the challenge at hand. How long had he been drinking in the loveliness and honesty in Rimona's gaze?

Ittai inhaled a deep breath and summoned his voice that would lead a charge. "Anytime is a good time to recognize the faithfulness of our God." His profession rang out above the melody of Shamar's harpists. He would disperse any doubt cast on him and on Rimona's reputation.

Clearing his throat, Ittai strode to the waterskin. "I need a drink. Your king and I shared too many stories." He lifted the skin. Two cups rested on the table. "Lana, we need one more cup."

The girl skipped toward a stool and brought him his request.

A harp string plinked, scattering a few foul notes.

Head down, Rimona joined him and accepted a cup from Lana. The girl drank in an instant. He gulped the tepid liquid and returned the waterskin to the floor.

"Shamar, this pagan is ready to praise the God of Abraham." Ittai marched over to where the musicians practiced and flapped his hand as if he were the master teacher. "Feel free to add your accompaniment."

The young men hunched over their harps as if Ittai would reach out and crush the wood. Lana bounced on tiptoes and joined him. Rimona stayed near the stools. Her chin rested on clasped hands as if she anticipated a glorious chorus. A Philistine would shatter Shamar's suspicions by aiming Hebrew psalms at the old man's rounded back.

"My eyes are lifted to the hills. Where does my help come from?" Ittai nodded toward Lana. Only two verses and his mouth soured liked unsweetened citrus.

"Our help comes from the Lord." Lana's smile rode the sweep of the harpist's fingers. Sweet, stern melodies rose to the roof. "He is the maker of the heavens and the earth." Lana's exuberance almost made him miss his entrance.

"The Lord will not let your foot slip." He glanced at Rimona. Her gash still healed from her race into the darkness. "The Lord who watches over us will not slumber. Truly He who watches over Israel will never sleep nor slumber." Relaxing his fists so that his veins fell flush with his flesh, he continued. "The Lord watches over us." His trek from Gath was a testament to his words.

Rimona nodded. Her eyes pooled with tears. Was she remembering her flight into the hills?

Lana jumped in with her song. "The Lord is the shade at your right hand." She added hand motions. Ittai would have to praise Parveda and Hamuran for their daughter's memory and boldness. "The sun will not harm you by day, nor the moon at night." Hair in disarray, Lana shifted her head covering with her hands, and feigned sleeping. Music from the harps softened until it soothed every one of his taut muscles.

Shamar toddled around his cane, stepping on his long robe. His grayish-white hair barely moved as he fluttered his hand. "Enough. At least you can speak our language well enough."

"My heart is singing." Rimona sauntered over and beamed at Lana. Sniffling, she hugged the girl. "I wish I could hear you and your brothers sing in the evening."

"Everyone can hear us," Lana said.

Ittai's irritation at Rimona's uncle waned. The teacher was old and set in his ways. Praising God reminded Ittai of his safe journey. He had arrived in Jerusalem without bloodshed, and Rimona had been received, albeit not as hospitable as he would have liked, into her new home.

The taller student leaned his harp against the wall and stood. "I am Jonathan ben Abiathar, and this is Ahimaaz ben Zadok." He indicated the other musician. "We serve at the house of God. I do not know of any priest who can say that he has heard a Philistine recite praise to our God with such surety. We have been blessed to hear such praise from your mouth." Jonathan bowed to his teacher but still towered over

Rimona's uncle. "We must be going, or we will be late for prayer."

Ahimaaz set his harp to the side. "I will remember this lesson." His head bobbed bouncing his curls. "Welcome to Jerusalem."

"Shalom," Ittai and Rimona said in unison.

"Return tomorrow, Jonathan." Shamar hobbled toward the instruments. "You need more practice."

Was this a game? Ask the foreigner to sing and humiliate himself and then ignore him?

Ittai's leather armlets grew tight. "About your niece, Shamar."

"More talking?" Shamar inspected the strings, plucking them at random.

Biting the inside of his mouth so he wouldn't reprimand Rimona's uncle and cause her trouble, Ittai folded his arms. "I will return tomorrow to escort Rimona to a banquet with the king."

Rimona's eyes grew wide as she rocked forward onto her toes.

Shamar shrugged. "Some have to feed the stomach while others serenade to feed the soul." The old man didn't face Ittai. A sliver of praise never slipped from Shamar's wrinkled lips. He remained hunched over one of his beloved harps.

"I will see you to the courtyard." Rimona glimpsed her uncle.

Her relation remained stiff as a corpse.

Rimona led Ittai and Lana toward the courtyard.

"Please forgive my uncle's rudeness." She smiled as if she had escaped a music-filled dungeon. "Though

I don't think I will ever forget your and Lana's Hebrew lesson."

"I'm going to miss you." Lana hugged Rimona, wrapping her thin arms tight around Rimona's waist.

Rimona embraced the girl with abandon. "Do not cry. I believe our paths will cross again. God would not allow you to enter my life and then banish you from it. I'm sure your father and Ittai will be traipsing through the city at times. It seems I will see them again at a banquet."

Ittai shaded his eyes and surveyed the palace. The aroma of burning cloves tainted the fresh air. He could not speak to Rimona's promise. Only God knew the future.

"David and I have only begun to get acquainted. I'm sure I will be back in the city. And now we know where to find Rimona, don't we?" He motioned for Lana to join him and met Rimona's teary gaze. "Wear your striped veil tomorrow. I will be looking for you among the guests."

"I will." She rubbed her arms even though sunlight abounded overhead. "May the Lord bless you—"

"And keep you." He held her gaze, for he understood what it was like to be alone in the world without the support of a family. Rimona had been hurt enough by her kin. He prayed Shamar would embrace the gift of his niece's arrival. Ittai turned and guided Lana through the courtyard, and ultimately toward the palace.

He did not face the music room one last time to see

if Rimona watched their leaving. He did not give a final wave, nor dip his head. A pressure built somewhere behind his eyes in a place he knew no tears would fall. A place he had sealed off after his mother died. That place had been a desolate cavern for over a decade. Rimona's kindred spirit had fearlessly chipped away at his seal. There would be no more assaults after the banquet.

Lana's footsteps clamored behind him as he charged through a side alley toward the palace steps.

Caravans of mules and camels waited for him. Gifts from David were packed on humps and haunches. A servant packed robes on a camel.

"Take that embroidered gown to Shamar's niece." Ittai pointed at cloth the color of malachite. The hue would be fainter than Rimona's emeralds and only he would know she wore the gems. "Do you know where he lives?"

The servant nodded.

Another man arrived with the donkeys he and Lana had ridden into the city. Lana headed over to her mount. Her eyes and cheeks glowed scarlet.

"So, it's true." The bellow startled a nearby donkey. "The Philistine piglet returns."

Ittai rounded, his gaze darting in the direction of the insult, waiting for any swift movement or strike. "Joab." One word was all he needed to say. Heat consumed his body as if a blacksmith had unleashed a gale into his forge. Ittai would never forget Joab's abuse during their time in Ziklag.

"Why are you here?" The stench of wine soured

Joab's breath. "I don't need any help protecting my uncle. I believe I made that clear years ago. I didn't want you around then, and I don't need you around now."

"Your uncle can welcome anyone he chooses into his home." Ittai met Joab's stare. The sun had not been kind to the Hebrew commander. Grooves, scars, and a jagged birthmark etched his face. "The king has invited me to a banquet tomorrow night to celebrate my arrival."

A slight sneer curled Joab's lips. His arm jerked.

Metal flashed in Ittai's sight.

Catch the weapon. Hold it steady.

Ittai captured Joab's wrist.

Arm trembling, Ittai denied Joab's blade the satisfaction of gutting him like a pig.

"Hah." Joab laughed over and over. Sunlight sparked off the dagger. "You are stronger than I remember, Gittite." Joab eased backward.

Ittai released Joab's fist and anticipated another strike. None came.

Joab sheathed his weapon. He turned to a worried servant. "It was only a test among warriors." When his gaze returned it was as welcoming as a shallow grave. "Men that rule with their hearts will die a painful death, Gittite."

"Men that rule with a heart for God will never die." Ittai knew better than to turn his back on Joab. Drunk or sober.

"Keep believing that Gittite." Joab poked a fat finger at Ittai's chest. "But that way, you must die in order to live." He spat at Ittai's feet before sauntering toward the palace steps.

The king's nephew didn't need to worry about a lethal strike. Lifting a hand against him would bring a death sentence.

David's words from long ago swept through Ittai's brain, yet he had heard the same caution from the king this very day. Joab is a man of blood.

Ittai had delivered Rimona to the palace, to her uncle. She was safe beyond the courtyard, wasn't she? A chill crept over Ittai's arms raising the thick hair to attention. Joab had no fear in murdering the king's guest on the palace steps. Even Shamar dismissed Ittai's relationship with the king. What had happened to the raider David? God's anointed king? The man who leveled towns and became the victor of song and legend? No one would have dared to spurn David's orders years ago.

Where had God's boundary lines taken Rimona?

And where had God's boundary lines taken a Philistine exile?

13

On Rimona's hand, the warmth of Lana's skin lingered. Rimona could not ponder the uncertainty of never seeing the exuberant girl again. Even at ten years of age, Lana had become a friend. Hopefully, God would reunite them someday when her parents, Parveda or Hamuran, visited the city. She grabbed hold of the certainty that she would see Ittai one last time at the banquet, even if it may be from across a room filled with officials and noblemen.

Turning to face her uncle's dwelling, her shoulder muscles grew taut. A large, brooding warrior did not tread in her wake to speak, or sing, or intimidate. Her mouth twitched at the image of Ittai singing. Could prayer, over time, soften her uncle's demeanor toward Ittai, or his own niece? Ittai and Lana had tried to appease her uncle's suspicions about Ittai's faith and intentions. In moments, she would face her uncle's disdain and questions alone. She prayed for acceptance from her sole remaining blood relation, for her future lay behind these alien walls of mortared stone.

She entered the dim music room. The aroma of burning cloves assaulted her senses. Twirling wisps of smoke rose from three pots of incense centered on the long table. Her nostrils tingled from the bold odor.

Her uncle plucked at a harp. Gone were the ethereal melodies provided by Ahimaaz and Jonathan. Staccato tones disturbed the peace. "How dare you bring a Philistine to my shelter." Her uncle's voice was drawn like a harp string ready for release. He did not give her the courtesy of his attention. "That murderer touched the waterskin. It is unclean along with the cups. Do you remember which is yours?"

Rimona halted a tongue-lashing retort. She waited feet away from her uncle with her insides as delicate as seashells capable of being shattered by the tiniest tap. The wrong rebuttal might spoil her standing with Shamar. She had nowhere to go among her people except to a king who had probably forgotten her features the moment she left his chamber.

"Ittai came to retrieve my escort. Our kinsman abandoned me in the hills outside of Hebron after I escaped his evil scheme." At the urging of Hamuran and his sword. "I know which cup is mine. I will wash the others."

"Not with that skin you don't. It's defiled." Her uncle sat taller on his stool with his cane hooked over his knee. "And that satchel. Did he carry it for you in the palace?"

An ache in her chest provoked more tears to fall. The few belongings she possessed would have been lost forever if not for a Philistine's concern. *Do not show him any weakness.* "Ittai did not touch my satchel." Or me. "God kept me safe and brought me here to you, Uncle."

"God was it? My father should never have

allowed my sister to marry at an advanced age. Your father's desertion and your mother's ailment brought you to my door."

Her mouth gaped. Not again. Trapped. She was trapped in her uncle's den of deception. If she defended her parents, she would bring forth his ire. Silence surrendered to his lies. Defer. They could discuss her past for years while she had a roof over her head.

Be polite. "Uncle, I…"

Bang. Bang. Bang. Someone rapped at the door.

"Don't stand there." Her uncle lowered his harp. "Answer it."

Praise the Lord for the interruption.

She opened the door to a man holding something in his arms. She blinked at the brightness behind him.

"Are you Shamar's niece," he asked.

Who knew she was here? "Yes."

"A giant of a man told me to bring this to you. It's a gift from the king."

Oh no, it wasn't. Staring at the embroidered robe, dyed green in hue, she knew David had not sent this gift to her. Ittai had sent the robe. And right now, she needed his giant heart to see her through the rest of the day and night. For she only had one more day to spend with her rescuer.

~*~

Thunk. Rimona bolted awake. She stared at her surroundings. This wasn't Beersheba nor the road to

Jerusalem. This was her uncle's former storeroom. Tilted in the corner, a trio of flutes mocked her. She knew not to touch the treasures of her overseer.

"Get up." *Thunk.* "Your banquet is causing a stir in the palace," Shamar muttered. "I need my provisions before they are forgotten."

Rimona's belly gurgled at the mention of food. "Yes, Uncle." She rubbed her eyes and admired the gift of a gown bestowed on her by Ittai. Draped over a square table, it reminded her of the celebration this eve. Vigor surged through her veins. Her uncle could not withhold an invitation from the king, though he could fill her day with chores. Best to feed his stomach and appease his constant ire. The only delight she had seen on Shamar's face since she had arrived in Jerusalem was when he realized he would not need to buy her additional clothes for the banquet. "I will run to the palace straightaway."

Rising, she rolled her mat and set it in the opposing corner from the elaborate flutes. She donned her mother's striped veil and wrapped it tight to her face. Ittai liked the vibrant pattern. She smiled remembering his expression on the plains of Etam. Later, there would be time to make herself presentable for a royal gathering and for her Philistine commander.

Her uncle sat perched at the long table in the music room, bent forward, hands folded. "A feeble body is what I get for allowing you to sleep."

"I will hurry." Halting before the ominous cedar door, she turned. "Where do I go?" A guide had led her through the hallways the previous day.

"Through the courtyard to the main doorway." He waved his hand to rush her. "Left, toward the aroma of bread."

How much sweeter serving her mother had been. Every task received praise and gratitude.

The courtyard bustled with activity. Men and women raced through the stone circle with arms full of belongings. Clipped conversation and mutterings enlivened the morning air. An older man loaded a rolled rug on a donkey. Tapestries decorated the animal's rump. Were all these people palace officials?

The main door swung open. A breeze brushed by her face. The cedar planks nearly knocked her senseless.

"Move," a man shouted, his arms wrapped around a bulky burlap sack.

A high-pitched bellow followed his flight.

What was going on this day? The official acted like a thief. Where were the palace guards? Rimona slipped into the hallway and froze. A shapely, jewel-laden woman blocked her path.

The woman pointed a substantial blade at Rimona's breast. "And what did you come to steal?"

Warmth like a fever overtook Rimona's body. She indicated the stone wall as if the bricks could offer a testimony. "My uncle, Shamar, sent me for his provisions. He said there would be bread."

"Is he leaving?" The woman's enticing charcoal-lined eyes grew round and a bit wild.

"No." Why would the beauty ask such a question? "He's hungry, and he sent me to gather his food. I arrived yesterday—"

"You do not know?" The woman lowered her weapon. "Prince Absalom has proclaimed himself ruler over Israel. The king and his family have fled Jerusalem."

Rimona's thoughts evaporated into a dream, only it was a night terror. "This cannot be." Her words clung to her tongue. "Absalom is in Hebron. I saw him in his chariot."

"He is coming. I do not lie." The beauty grasped Rimona's arm and pulled her down the hall. "I will give you some food. Then you must leave."

Rimona followed after the woman whose gold bracelets clinked with each tug. Her own sandals struggled to find footing as if this world were not real. If David had fled, would Ittai wait for Absalom or advance with David? She knew from the wellspring in her heart that Ittai would defend David with his life. Her ears flamed as an eerie whine clamored in her brain. Her banquet would never come to pass. The host had fled. Any guest who aligned with David was Absalom's enemy. Traitors did not survive for long.

"Here." The finely dressed woman released her grip, put down her blade, and shoved a loaf of bread into Rimona's hand. A waft of cassia perfume filled the space between them. "Take this loaf and a skin of milk."

"Toda raba." Rimona clutched her uncle's provisions. She hesitated. Surely, a woman with this much wealth adorning her body must hold some standing in the palace. "Aren't you leaving the city?"

Stunning, shadowed eyes bore into Rimona. "David is the rightful king of Israel. He is my husband, and I will stay in this palace until he is victorious in battle and returns to claim his throne anew. Several of his wives are staying to stake his claim to the kingdom."

Rimona bobbed her head, indicating the loaf. "You are very kind." If this beauty had born David a child, or was a true wife of the king, she would be trotting on a donkey outside of the city and not guarding provisions. Rimona knew what it was like to be all alone. Left alone by death, not by betrayal. She prayed a few royal concubines would pose no threat to Absalom. "You are brave to remain here in the palace. Your husband must admire your strength."

Frown lines creased the woman's brow. "I will try my best to keep my husband's name alive in the hearts of his people."

"I will pray for you."

"Do not pray for me." A wilted smile tarnished the woman's powdered complexion. "Pray for my husband and perhaps it will cover me." Retrieving her blade, the concubine strode toward another hallway. Her gilded robe swept the floor as she retreated.

Rimona did not know the woman's name. Maybe that was best. Her heart numbed at the thought of what happened to women caught in a rebellion.

She sprinted home faster than when Eglon had chased her into the night. Her throat parched and filled with pain as she reached her uncle's dwelling.

"Uncle, King David has fled from the palace." She

flung the skin on the table and set the loaf before Shamar. "Absalom is on his way to claim Jerusalem and the kingdom." Up and down her chest heaved. Her uncle did not rise or twitch. "We must grab hold of what we can and follow David."

"Why would I do that?" Her uncle tore the end from the loaf. "I know Absalom as well as I know David. Absalom has listened to me play many a time."

"But David is God's anointed king?" she stammered.

"God can anoint another one." Her uncle plopped a piece of bread into his mouth and chewed. Breadcrumbs toppled from his beard. "I will not abandon the treasures in my care. I have parchments to songs of worship. Instruments from all over the world." His stare rebuked her as if she were his student and she had played a foul note. "We are staying and protecting the wealth of kings."

Delight in the day's plans dissipated. She would not dine with the king nor see Ittai one last time. Standing in her uncle's music temple, she understood the trepidation in the concubine's eyes. The resignation to your fate when you are all alone and waiting to meet the armies of the son of a warrior king with solely a cook's blade to wield.

Rimona didn't even have a paring knife.

14

Ittai charged a mule down a rutted path between rows of olive trees. Dew-moistened grass muffled the pound of his mount's hooves and the hooves of the rides for his battle commanders, Hamuran and Banak. He should be sleeping and preparing for a king's banquet, not racing through the valley's foliage shortly after dawn.

"You should have told me sooner." Ittai's reprimand of his best sentry roared above the morning commotion.

"We came and got you immediately when men and women flooded the road." Banak's words rushed forth as he closed the distance on Ittai's lead mule. "We even stopped a wagon to find the reason for such large crowds to be leaving the city."

Ittai grasped a branch aiming to strike his face, ripped it from the tree with one sharp jerk and threw it to the ground.

"Hey." Hamuran shouted as he rode alongside Ittai. "I am not the traitor."

"Keep up or return to your wife." Ittai's jaw clamped tight. His instincts had told him something wasn't right with Absalom's chariot parade. David wasn't concerned when Ittai had mentioned the brief meeting on the plain. The king should never have allowed his son to return to Hebron. But then, how was David to know his son's vow was a ruse for a betrayal?

Ittai crested the rise to the main road, slowed his mule, and surveyed the panic. Banak and Hamuran halted their mounts on each side of him.

A haze of dust clouded the trail. The particles of dirt drifted away from the city. The clop of hooves at a hurried pace, squeaking wagon wheels, and grieving cries jarred the calm of morning. Not one merchant ventured toward Jerusalem. Banak's keen insight proved trustworthy. Loyal citizens were fleeing the city.

Why, God, why? Why was rebellion allowed to flourish against God's anointed king? Why allow this chaos now when exiled men had recently arrived? *Hasn't David served You faithfully by following Your laws and leading the people in worship?* Why was God upheaving a kingdom that served Him?

"The merchant said David and his family are heading into the Kidron Valley. Shall we rally to meet them? Or stay near Jerusalem?" Banak's final proposal prickled Ittai's flesh with its cowardice.

Ittai assailed his sentry with a glare of contempt. "Whose lamb and cheese did you sup on last night?"

"David's." Banak swallowed as if he were tasting a fat hunk of meat.

"Then you have your answer. I did not bring us here because Israel's sun is more bearable than Gath's. I came because David shared his love of God with us. God brought us through the desert without a battle.

But if we must fight, we will fight with David, not against him."

"I agree, commander." Banak bobbed his head. "King David has stocked us well for war."

If only David had the foresight to stave off a revolt. The king had shown confidence during their meeting, not fear of a son's rebellion. Had David given too much authority to Absalom? David, the young, brash raider of Ziklag, had aged and become less bold. The slash of a sword through bone and sinew was a young man's calling. Absalom had to be thirty years younger than David, and the heir had been secretly preparing for combat. The prince who should be defending his father wished to impale his father's beating heart. Perhaps the boundary lines bringing Ittai and his men to Jerusalem were for a defense of God's anointed. David's blood did not flow through Ittai's veins, but a heritage of faith bound them tighter than blood. God had not deserted Ittai, and he did not believe God would desert David. Loyal fighters had arrived in Jerusalem at God's chosen time.

"Commander." Hamuran's voice slashed through Ittai's thoughts. "Shall I ready the men to march into the Kidron? We shall meet David soon enough. He will not travel hastily with wives and children underfoot."

Ittai had taught his second-in-command well. "Yes, have the men prepare for battle. Secure the flank where the women and children reside." He released his officers with the wave of his hand. "I will meet you at the north end of the city."

Hamuran turned his mule toward the grove. He

rested a hand on Ittai's shoulder. "Those loyal to David will have already left the palace. More than likely Rimona and her uncle have fled."

A hint of uncertainty rippled through his confidant's statement. Had Lana told her father about Shamar's antics?

"We must hope Rimona convinced her uncle to flee. Now go." Ittai kicked his mount and advanced toward the city gate. Traveling hard, he ignored an elderly woman straining to carry a large basket on her head while tears streamed down her face.

He could only hope that Rimona's bold tongue had dislodged her uncle from his home. His hope soared on crippled wings.

~*~

Ittai raced through Jerusalem's main gate. He dodged a few small caravans blocking his path while they abandoned the city.

Why hadn't he been notified of David's departure? Ittai's men, while not thousands, were highly skilled in battle. His hundreds of Philistine warriors could hold position against the best legions in Israel. Perhaps David did not know where to find him? Their discussions in the palace lacked a specific location of Ittai's encampment.

On the main street, two boys struggled to load a barrel on a cart bed. They were not much older than Lana.

Fisting his reins tight, Ittai shouted, "Get out of the

city." Children in front of an advancing army would be trampled.

"Are you one of Absalom's men?" one boy called.

He rode past not bothering to answer the insult. Absalom was a beautiful prince listening to grievances at the gate, wooing the hearts of his countrymen, all the while scheming to kill his father. Did Absalom not fear God?

Sweat trickled between Ittai's shoulder blades as he guided his mount up the hill leading to the palace. The sun's rays assaulted the sandstone bricks on David's home. Gone were the guards who paced upon the steps. A few finely robed women perched at the top of the stairs. The women were too lavish in their dress to be thieves. Concubines inhabiting the palace meant David intended to continue his rule. He was laying claim to the throne through their presence. The women hid behind carved columns when they saw Ittai approach.

His heart shriveled at the concubine's lack of defense. Absalom had proven himself a ruthless rebel. That rebel dared to touch Rimona, albeit discreetly, in front of witnesses. What would these women bear when Absalom arrived in his splendor and might? And what would Absalom do to Rimona if she resided a courtyard away from his bedchamber?

"Hah." He urged his mule onward, patting its sweaty coat.

The alley north of the palace stood barren of people. As he rounded into the courtyard a faint melody serenaded the morning. His gut churned at the eerie sound. Was Shamar praising a rebellion of God's anointed king? If this were a battlefield instead of a stone yard, he would impale the traitor.

Darting toward Shamar's dwelling, he leapt from his mount and pounded on the freshly oiled cedar.

"Rimona?" he shouted. He prayed she did not answer and that her uncle had the sense to send her with David. "Shamar!" Music continued to play.

The door whipped open.

"Ittai? What are you doing here?" Rimona's eyes were alert like a mother bird protecting her fledglings. "David has left the city."

"I heard." He glanced over her frame and glimpsed Shamar strumming his harp as if in a trance. Fool. "Why are you still here?" He lowered his voice and let the harp song cover his irritation.

"My uncle will not leave." Rimona clasped her hands. They shook as if she were casting die in a game of chance. "Come and reason with him." She stepped aside and allowed him to enter the room. Her strength and the faint hint of her lily perfume enlivened his heightened senses.

He was upon Shamar in two strides. How small the old man looked perched on his stool.

Psalms halted.

"A visitor should address the head of the household." Shamar turned his direction but continued to caress his harp as if it were priceless. More priceless than a niece. "Why should I scamper from my home like a rat? I know Absalom as well as I know his father. These last years, it has been Absalom who has lounged

137

in the courtyard listening to my songs. I will not abandon the royal treasures entrusted to my care." The elderly musician emphasized his last words. "I serve the household of David. Isn't Absalom a member of the household?"

Ittai restrained the rage drawing his muscles taut. He itched to strike something…someone…anything. "David is alive. He is king over Israel. Where is your allegiance to the ruler who bestowed your position and provided for your needs?"

Rimona drew away from him as if the heat surging through his flesh grew too hot for her skin.

Shamar scowled. "I do not fear Absalom and neither shall my niece. David gave me coin, but Absalom sings my praises. We shall reside in this room and welcome whoever rules Israel." Shamar resumed his song.

Ittai grasped the hilt of his sword. It may not have been appropriate to threaten the elderly musician, but it eased the tension pulsing through his body. "I know what men do when they are drunk on power. Your old bones may be overlooked, but an arrogant king will take whatever he desires, including your niece." A rage he saved for battle flowed through his body.

"Please." Rimona rushed to his side and drew him closer to the door. "I have to trust God will take care of me no matter where I live. I have been praying for our safety and for yours. For everyone's." She forced a smile through trembling lips. "I guess my boundary lines have fallen here."

His heart chilled as if he lingered in a frost. His

warnings were being cast as foolishness. He closed his eyes and drew a hand through his stubble of a beard. She didn't understand men or power or entitlement. Entitlement especially after a war. What would Absalom take from a bold beauty wandering in his view? In this moment, Ittai could not deny his desire for Rimona. If a foreigner desired her, a ruler would ravish her.

"May Absalom remember our meeting on the plain and my hardship." Rimona's gaze stayed upon his face. Her innocence and tenacity touched his soul more than one of Shamar's melodies of praise. Lord, protect her from the recklessness that accompanies victory.

"Rimona, I cannot protect you once I leave Jerusalem." He had to make her understand the peril.

"And I cannot abandon my overseer." Her eyes glistened in a pool of tears. "I will petition God every moment for your return and for David's return to the throne." Rimona sniffled. Her steadfast smile returned. "If only Lana was here to fill my ears with words."

If Ittai had left his mother in Philistia and marched into exile, his heart could not have pained as much as leaving Rimona this very morn.

"I cannot protect you anymore." Ittai's words strained through the fire in his throat. "Understand the dangers."

"Go after your friend, foreigner." Shamar began a new melody. "We do not need a pig from Philistia pestering us this day. I must assemble musicians to welcome our new king."

Ittai begged God to douse his ire. Shamar knew the law of God well. The musician knew his niece could not depart with a man who wasn't her husband lest she be cast out onto the street. And the street was a worse fate than facing Absalom. An urge to cast tradition to the winds seized him. The urge was so great that it was terrifying. But he couldn't carry Rimona off to war without her people's protection. Should he die in battle, Rimona would need her tribesmen to provide for her needs. *God, why do I care? Why did you bring Rimona's loveliness into my tumultuous life?*

He lunged and towered over her uncle.

Shamar's fingers stuttered on the strings.

Bending low, Ittai whispered, "If anyone touches one hair on Rimona's head, I will paint the courtyard with your blood."

"You must go, Ittai." Rimona clung to the door, defeat displayed in her limp shoulders. "Every moment you stay, your life is in danger."

Pressing a fist into his palm, Ittai rotated it as if grinding grain. "When David returns victorious, I will be by his side. I will accompany him to this very chamber and make sure you have provided for your niece. If you haven't..." He indicated the courtyard with a jerk of his head.

"Get out." Shamar's voice cracked, hitting a sour note. "I do not understand your threats in your Hebrew babble."

"Ittai, hurry. You must go. Do not worry about me anymore." She urged him out the door. "God is with us."

He turned and gazed into her glistening eyes. Her unshed tears pierced his leather breastplate. "Do not mention I was here. You have not seen me or my men."

"I do not know where you are going." Her chin rose toward the sunlight. The feisty woman who faced a chariot driver returned, shimmying to stand at her full height. "I do not know where your army is staying. I will be cleaning instruments."

"If you could join Parveda and —"

"I can't. We know that." Her eyes sparked with a gorgeous amber fire. "You must return to me so we can enjoy a king's banquet." Her eyes widened. "I did not thank you for my gift."

"Hide it. Along with your striped veil." She did not need to enhance her attractiveness to tempt Absalom or his renegades. "Wear it at the feast we hold to celebrate David's return."

"I will hold you to that promise, commander."

He backed away beholding her loveliness. Gathering the reins of his mule, he mounted his ride, yet he would not turn and regard Rimona again. For in that moment, a foreigner, a non-Hebrew, a warrior not born from the womb of one of Jacob's wives, fought the urge to trample God's law and whisk a Hebrew woman off to war. A war he would use all his strength and cunning to win.

15

Rimona braced herself against the courtyard wall. Ittai rode out to the alley, his dark hair rising and falling with the stride of his mule. A man and a woman rushed through the courtyard with arms wrapped tight around rugs and baskets. Why not trespass at the palace? The guards had escaped with their king.

She sat on the smooth wall, weary and empty like the husk of a locust dried and discarded from last year's swarm. This feeling had settled on her before when her mother took her last breath and no more praises slipped from her mother's lips. Death had stolen her confidence and what courage remained had followed Ittai out of the city.

In Ittai's presence, she had tendrils of hope for a future. Oh, how grateful she had been for his station on a hill outside of Hebron. He had amazed her with his compassion, for he too had buried a mother. They shared a bond from such a loss. And what foreigner recited the psalms of David to appease a disgruntled uncle? Ittai could have taken his leave and abandoned her to her uncle's folly.

Her spirit begged a grin. Who else in this city had seen a warrior thick with muscle accompany Lana and voice truths about God? In her mind, she would cherish that memory forever.

I lift my eyes to the hills. Where does my help come from?

She prayed Ittai the Gittite lived to see David regain his kingdom. She would pray that prayer often and include her own safety in her petitions.

A fly buzzed by her cheek. She swatted at the pest, shaking her head. Her lone earring of gold and gemstones bumped against her jaw. She fingered the smooth gold and three faceted emeralds. The touch that had calmed her fears for many a year did nothing to buoy her countenance. Her father had vanished at sea. Her mother had succumbed to her ailment. Only their daughter remained. And she remained in a city soon to be overrun with fighters seeking to take a king's life.

She squinted at the sun. "Lord, help me. My earthly protectors are gone. My uncle offers little comfort or concern. A foreigner who was a balm for a brief time has hurried off to war. Watch over Ittai, for this world is a better place with his big heart in it."

Her throat pained. She swallowed past the burn.

A tear snaked to her cheek, its moisture beckoning her back to reality. She flicked the dampness from her face and straightened her head covering.

She had to stay hidden, away from a rebellious prince who may ask questions about the Philistine who had saved her life. Absalom was a bold prince with a loyal army. He would want to know the whereabouts of six-hundred skilled fighters. Ones he may soon face in battle. Praise God she did not know where Ittai or

David were going. At least the battle would not take place in the city before her own eyes.

The clunk of her uncle's cane echoed around the courtyard. She'd best appease her overseer. If what Shamar said was true, her uncle was on friendly terms with Absalom and his household. That relationship may spare her harm.

Rising, she traipsed into her new home, readying false pleasantries.

"What may I oil, uncle?" She pointed to the wall. "Some of those lyres are dusty."

"Dusting on a day like today? You don't reside in Beersheba anymore. Soon, Jerusalem will welcome a new king. We must prepare for a serenade." Her uncle's steps quickened as he headed toward his bedroom. Was he retrieving the bejeweled flutes from her tiny closet?

"Shall I set some stools in the courtyard?" He could tell her what instruments to gather later.

"Courtyard?" Her uncle halted. "I will not hide my songs of praise behind stone. When Absalom is near, we are going to the palace steps."

16

Ittai's mount flailed its head and strained to maneuver through the valley shaded by olive trees. Travelers traipsed over soil the color of crushed walnuts. Orchard paths, rutted and unending, brought forth grunts and cries and muttering from David's followers. Those loyal to the king were on the move, placing distance between their king and a son hungry for his father's throne. A day's time wasn't long to plan a defense against a scheming prince.

Recognizing his band of exiles ahead, Ittai drove his mount toward the middle of the thick groves. His men were easy to spot. They stood taller than most Hebrews, and they had been dressed for a battle since leaving Gath. Diverting into the next row of trees, he came alongside a small wagon packed with provisions. Lana and her brothers sat among bags of wheat and crates of melons.

"Commander," Lana yelled, her neck craning to see past his mule.

Parveda whirled around, her hands firmly on the reins of the team of donkeys pulling her cargo. She inspected his surroundings before glancing at the path in front of her.

"You are alone?"

Parveda's motherly tone made it clear that she expected another traveler to come under her care. Unlike the hill outside of Hebron, this time it was not meant to be. He guided his mule even with Parveda's perch. Disappointment had been waging a war with his pride since he'd left Jerusalem.

"Not every man is under my command."

"Or woman." If Parveda had carried a blade, she could not have pierced his flesh faster.

"And I must find the man who commands us all." He nodded his farewell.

Heart pounding with every hoof fall of his mount, Ittai breathed in the tepid air to ease the sting in his chest. He had to believe, to pray, that Shamar had some standing with Absalom. Ignoring the women's cries rising to branches ripe for harvest, he rode on, slowing his pace only when Hamuran's tall frame came into view.

"Where is David?" he said as he drew beside Hamuran. His question rumbled with enough of a growl to prevent banter.

"Up ahead. Sitting on some clear-cut trees." Hamuran answered as if they had been traveling together for miles, his expression as plain as a blanket. After all their years together, his companion would know Ittai would have briefed him on Rimona's whereabouts if she was lounging on Parveda's wagon. Hamuran surveyed the landscape without asking about Rimona. Ittai refused to remember the tear-filled eyes that beheld him in the courtyard.

"Good," Ittai said. "Parade before him and carry

on." David would see his loyal swords from Philistia. "I will talk to the king."

After traveling a short distance, Ittai came upon a clearing free from the shade of olive branches. Trees edging the open space were half alive. Fire had seared their foliage.

On a wide trunk sat a man, hunched, and barefoot. Scarlet linen embroidered with indigo designs covered the man's head. Ittai sobered as if he had been lashed with leather. David? Israel's king? Where were the loyal attendants caring for the king? Why hadn't anyone brought sandals to the king? Ittai tamped down the need to strike a foe.

Dismounting, Ittai drew closer to the king. Six women and their children huddled together on distant stumps. Some of the women whispered to each other. One sniffled. Older boys stared at the grove of trees as if mesmerized. Younger offspring leaned against their mothers or sat cross-legged on the ground. A few soldiers stood guard of David's family. Where was the king's nephew and loyal commander, Joab? Joab had rarely been seen apart from David in the hills of Ziklag.

Ittai trampled through dew-laden leaves and tufted grass. The odor of livestock burdened the air. Why had the Lord taken David's throne through betrayal? Was this a test of David? Or of Absalom? Ittai's allegiance hadn't changed since his boyhood meeting of the man who had slain a giant from Gath.

David lifted his head as if he sensed Ittai's approach. The king's mouth gaped. His eyes held a glimmer of disbelief as if this was their first meeting.

"Ittai?" David choked out a greeting. "Why have you come?"

"Where else would I be but with you?" Ittai knelt on one knee before his sovereign. A memory flashed in his mind of when a victorious raider readying to claim his rightful throne had knelt before a boy to comfort him at their parting. That famous fighter had become like a father to an insignificant boy.

"You arrived in Jerusalem only yesterday. Should I make you wander in the desert?" David's eyes glistened with moisture. "Where does an old king go? You should return and stay in the city with King Absalom."

Ittai stiffened. He did not like the defeat in David's voice, nor the reference to Absalom as king. "You are the king of Israel. My allegiance is to you and to our God. Absalom never fed my belly with food and my head with wisdom."

David waved his hand, but its limpness did not relay authority. "That was so many years ago. I am not the fearless raider anymore. Take your countrymen and go back. May kindness and faithfulness be with you."

Ittai struck his thigh with his fist. The clap reverberated in the intimate space between him and David. He would not leave the man who had provided for a boy and his mother in their time of need. Ittai would repay David's embrace of a boy with the loyalty of a man.

"As surely as the Lord lives, and as surely as you breathe before me, wherever my lord the king may be, whether it means living or dying, there I will be as your servant." He spoke his assurance forthright to the judge over Israel.

"Oh, Ittai." David grabbed hold of Ittai's hand. Cool was the grasp of the renowned warrior. "I do not know what God has planned for me. My own son plots to take my life. If it were only mine, I could reason with his ambition, but to kill my wives and my children? What madness has overcome my heir?"

Licking his lips, Ittai banished the bitter citrus taste from his mouth. Where were the king's officials and the Lord's priests? Why hadn't God's golden ark, His resting place, followed the king out of the city?

Rocking forward on his knee, Ittai asked, "Where are your priests? Can they not petition God for your safety?"

David's grip grew firmer. "I told Zadok and Abiathar and their sons to take the Ark of God back into Jerusalem when they had finished their offerings. If I find favor with God, He will bring me back into the city and let me worship Him in Jerusalem. Zadok agreed to send word to me about the rebellion when we reach Gilgal."

The king's words sprouted confidence in Ittai. Not only did the priests pray fervently, but the sons of the priests also knew Shamar. They had met Rimona and they had listened to a foreigner recite a psalm. Lord, if You choose, use Jonathan and Ahimaaz to protect Rimona.

"Then my men and I will head north to Gilgal." He squeezed David's hand and gave a brief nod. "I will never turn back and leave you. My men and I will stand by your side." Ittai's voice cracked under the truth of his pledge.

Tears welled in David's eyes. "So many years have passed since I lounged in the hills of Ziklag. God has always provided for me even when He could have cast me aside. I shall remain faithful to my Lord until the end of my days. I could not have asked Him to send me a more loyal friend. I have never forgotten the service of a quiet boy who saw everything." David released Ittai's hand. "Go ahead, you stubborn Philistine. March on with your men."

Ittai's fortitude strengthened with David's praise. "Is that an order my king?" Ittai had never craved a victory as badly as he had at this moment.

"It won't be my last edict." Placing his hands onto Ittai's shoulders, David kissed Ittai's forehead. The royal oils and balms on his skin had faded, but the familiar scent of earth and sunshine remained. "Your rest is over, my son. Now, march onward."

"Always, for you." Ittai rose and straightened his thick leather belt. In all his days, an order had never sounded so sweet.

~*~

Continuing north through the Kidron Valley, Ittai led his mule lest it pull up lame. He and his men marched in line toward the lush mountains in the distance. A man trudged in the opposite direction of the mass of people leaving the city.

Ittai knew that swagger and forward-leaning gait. Why wasn't Joab guarding his uncle? Joab rarely parted from power. Power and prestige came to all who aligned closely with God's anointed king. Joab knew that truth well.

Though, being forthright and vulnerable with David would never have happened if Joab lingered nearby to eavesdrop and taunt. Years ago, when Ittai peeked in David's tent to glimpse the laughter and revelry of God's chosen commander, Joab had seen Ittai at the tent flap and staggered toward the opening, roaring his disgust at a Philistine boy. Escaping as fast as a boy could, Ittai heard David chastising Joab through the ramskin of the tent.

Toda raba, Lord, for my time with David this morn.

"Why are these outcasts crowding the valley?" Joab shouted his insult so that it invaded every Philistine ear. "I don't need exiles burdening the king."

Broadening his posture, Ittai continued forward on his intended path. He would not allow Joab to separate him from his men. "Our king told us to march on." Contempt surged through his veins, but he used the flush of warmth to heighten his senses and foil any sudden knife attack. "We are abundantly supplied by David's hand, and our swords are ready to defend his reign."

"Any men fighting for the house of David are under my command." Joab blocked Ittai's progress. Fists wedged into his sword belt, Joab resembled a raven about to peck and take flight. "My brother and I do not need a Philistine confusing our ranks. The sons of Zeruiah have always fought David's battles."

"And you shall again." Ittai tightened his grip on his mule's lead. He pictured Joab's skull being crushed by his hand.

"Go back to Gath, Gittite." Joab's breath reeked of yesterday's wine. "You have seen the king. He is not the man you remember."

Ittai stared into Joab's sun-scarred face. "Do not tell me what I remember."

"I am in charge of David's army." Spittle flew from Joab's lips. "Everyone listens to me."

Alongside the two leaders, the march north slowed to a shuffle.

Joab thrust a finger in Ittai's face. "You don't have a command here, boy."

The dull thud of sandaled footfalls screeched in Ittai's ears. He would not waste his energy on Joab or cause any more turmoil for David to handle. Ittai did not need rescuing anymore. Soon enough, a battle against Absalom would begin, and all the forces loyal to David would have to fight together to claim a victory.

"Not yet." Ittai used all of his composure to infuse confidence in his boast. "I don't have a command as of yet." He dipped his chin and motioned toward where David had been sitting.

Joab's pupils danced like well-spun marbles. "Carry on for now." He charged toward his uncle's station, grazing Ittai's shoulder with his own.

A thirst for power and a scorching wrath: those

two things Ittai remembered about Joab. The mighty son of Zeruiah had fallen for a Philistine's goading. Ittai stifled a grin, but he knew the time had come to watch for misplaced arrows.

17

Swish. Swish. Swish. Rimona sat cross-legged on the floor of her tiny bedroom brushing invisible dirt from a flute made of ivory. She had not seen one flake of dust on the instrument, but her uncle insisted the flutes must be brushed before they could be wiped with a cloth. Her tedious task hid her from any scouts sent by Absalom. The prince had yet to claim his father's home.

With every twist of her hand, she prayed for the safety of King David and his family. What she wouldn't give to be surrounded by Parveda and her children and their God-fearing commander. She'd best not think of Ittai or she would drip a tear on Shamar's precious ivory. In the presence of her rescuer, she did not fear the next hour. At the moment, she didn't have full confidence that her uncle would protect her over his precious relics.

Oh, how she missed the embrace of her mother and the comforting arms of her neighbor, Leah. Since her mother's death, little comfort had settled on Rimona's soul. Concern for her well-being had come from Philistines instead of her own kin. Eglon would have sold her as a slave to the highest bidder or given her away to settle his own debt. Not a single elder had assured her that they would verify her arrival at the palace.

Harp song filtered through the wall. Truly, the melody of the strings should ease her angst, but knowing the men practiced to praise Absalom's arrival cramped her stomach. Her uncle should be loyal to God's anointed king, not to musical instruments, or a rebellious son. Absalom had feigned a touch of her hand on the plains of Etam. Would he desire to touch more of her now that he ruled Israel and rested in a bed beyond the courtyard? May it never be.

She glanced at the mudded ceiling. *Lord, keep me safe from harm. Help me to find companions who are loyal to You and Your law.*

The song ended.

Silence.

Sandals shuffled on the music room floor.

"Rimona," her uncle bellowed.

What now? Had he found more flutes to polish? She laid the ivory treasure on her bed mat and hastened toward Shamar's main music room. She hoped Shamar found her work beneficial, for her heart couldn't take anymore disparaging remarks about her upbringing or her friends.

Her uncle and his musicians gathered by the row of lyres and drank from cups. Waterskins rested beneath a nearby window.

"Our skins are almost empty." Shamar scowled at her as if she had purposefully drained the skins. Ittai and Lana had barely sipped a mouthful. Shamar's students must have drunk their fill. "I cannot expect musicians to play with parched mouths."

His students had been strumming harps. No flute or shofar had serenaded her this day. She acknowledged the guests with a nod. Her mother had raised her to be hospitable even to the foolish.

"It would be my pleasure to go to the palace and fill the skins." Surely the generous concubine remained on guard in the kitchen.

"Not the palace. There is a well close by where we can fend for our own needs. We must not align with the past." Shamar pointed to the far corner of the room. "Continue down the alley and you will see women hard at work." He emphasized his last word as if he had forgotten the chores he had assigned. Swiveling on his cane, he passed her two thin skins. "We need to be ready for the celebration."

She had other names for what Absalom had done to his father, but a lady had best stow such language in her cheek.

In Beersheba, drawing water was a mundane task. She knew every face in her former town, but in Jerusalem, every face belonged to a stranger. "I'd better go before Absalom and his fighting men fill the city." Did she need to remind her uncle that Absalom came with an army and not a band of harpists?

"Have you heard a trumpet?" Shamar cupped a hand to his ear in jest. One of the musicians chuckled at his antics. "You have time to labor."

Indeed, she did. Shamar hadn't missed a minute. She nodded respectfully with teeth clamped tight, draped a waterskin over each shoulder, and hurried toward the cedar door. Praise be, she was dressed in what Ittai recommended, a plain brown robe and head covering to blend in with the sea of pale bricks and stone.

Men and women charged through the courtyard as if merchants lined the rounded wall with trinkets to sell. They did not have to fear a rebuke from a guard since the king had fled. Would these folk rob what was left behind by those loyal to King David? No one dared to thieve from her uncle or they would be met with his cane. Her uncle's students could protect him from folly, but who would protect her? She darted toward the well as the aroma of roasted lamb enlivened the breeze. Some city dwellers prepared to rejoice instead of mourn.

"Calm down," a woman shouted. The reprimand came from around the corner and from the direction of the well. A scuffle of hooves echoed in the alley. The last time she'd heard such a commotion was when Ittai had ridden away. She swallowed and reminded herself not to dwell on her rugged Philistine, for she had already petitioned God to provide a victory for him and David. A reunion would come in time. *May it come swiftly, Lord.*

Rounding the building, Rimona spotted a cart and a balking donkey pulling on its lead. The concubine from the palace tried to calm the animal. *Tug. Shout. Stomp.* The concubine's gown swept the dirt road while she fought impishly with the beast.

Rimona grinned. She recognized the swath of lightened mane on the beast. God had brought two familiar faces into her path. Her donkey's and the concubine's.

"He is not accustomed to the city." Rimona clicked her tongue and hurried closer, waterskins bouncing against her lower back. "We arrived yesterday after a long journey." She took the reins from the concubine with one hand and stroked her donkey's forehead with the other. The animal calmed and pushed into her hand. His breath smelled of damp hay. "Did you enjoy the royal stables for a night?" she said to her steadfast mount.

"This is your donkey?" The concubine crossed her arms and backed away.

"'Tis a blessing for you, I think." Rimona stifled a grin at the vision of the long-robed beauty battling a determined donkey. "I know how to guide him and prompt him to move." She glanced at the cart bed loaded with jars and flattened skins. "Are you going to the well?"

"Yes." The concubine rubbed her arms and shivered. From beneath the drape of her indigo sleeve, Rimona beheld smooth skin and golden bracelets. "My maid usually draws water from the well, but she is busy preparing food." Her full lips parted briefly, but no more explanation came forth.

The woman's presence on the narrow-bricked path was like a ruby glistening in a pile of limestone.

"Show me to the well, and I can draw our water." Rimona rotated her shoulder to display Shamar's empty skins. She coaxed her donkey farther down the road that was bordered by buildings and almost glimpsed the hills of Beersheba in the animal's wild eyes. Swallowing past the thickness in her throat, she said, "My mother had trouble walking, so I made many trips to our well."

"You will be seen with me," the concubine whispered. "There are people in this city who are loyal to Absalom."

"Aren't we staying in Jerusalem? Let them believe we rejoice with the rebellion."

"Why didn't you leave?" The concubine's question hovered a wisp above a whisper. "I saw the rider in the courtyard."

Was she gawking at Ittai? A possessiveness surged through Rimona's veins. How odd a feeling to desire a man's presence and devotion. A man she hardly knew. *Stop it.* She had to get to the well and return to the music room swiftly. Even a royal concubine perceived the danger to officials who remained in the City of David.

"I didn't have a choice in the matter." Rimona concentrated on the cistern wall ahead and briefly glanced at the tempting eyes of the concubine. "Shamar would not leave his treasures, and he is the only kin I have left."

The elegant woman staring into Rimona's face appeared much younger than when they were in the palace. The shadowed hallway and the threat of a knife had clouded Rimona's remembrance of their meeting. "I know what it is to be alone. I do not have any children of my own, and my husband has fled into the valley."

"My prayer is that your husband will return to you soon." Rimona met the woman's forlorn gaze and nodded as if her petition had already been answered by God.

Carrying on, Rimona settled the donkey a few yards from the well. Two women finished their labors. Another girl lingered in the shade of an overhang from a generous roof. She slept with her arms wrapped around a wide-mouthed jar. The slumbering girl did not flinch at the approach of Rimona and—?

"What is your name?" Rimona asked. She and the concubine shared an uncertain future, yet Rimona did not know how to address her companion.

"It is best if you do not know my name. My presence in the palace declares that David has not relinquished his rule." The dark beauty squinted past the well to the wall surrounding Jerusalem. A wide city gate was a short trot away. "Absalom may not be kind to my acquaintances."

Surely, knowing the woman's name couldn't cause any harm. "I've met Absalom," Rimona said, hoping to calm some of the concubine's anxiousness.

"Meeting a man and understanding him are not the same." The beauty grabbed a skin from the cart. "Those women have finished. Lead your donkey closer to the well. I can manage empty jars and skins."

Rimona made sure the sleeping girl made no claim to the well before drawing water and filling the containers. The concubine carried them to and fro all the while her golden bracelets reflected starbursts on the sand, dirt, and brick.

"Knowing your name would help with conversation." Rimona braced her hands on the damp wooden bucket. Would the woman acquiesce and reveal her name?

Sweat pooled above the concubine's lip as she lounged briefly on the wall. "This water comes from the Gihon Spring. It runs beneath the city. Call me Gihon if you must."

Why was the woman being coy? "But that is not your name."

"It is now." Gihon swiped her hands removing the grit from the stones. A sweet scent, faint, and alluring, wafted Rimona's direction. "I would not have filled so many vessels so fast without your help." A contented grin washed over Gihon's features. "Toda raba." Gihon hesitated. She patted the donkey as if thanking him too.

"My name is Rimona." When the last waterskin was loaded into the cart, Rimona untied her donkey.

Gihon's brow furrowed. "You are Shamar's niece. That is all I need to know."

Men's voices diverted Rimona's attention. Dust drifted above the city wall. Movement near the gate sent a cool shiver over her sun-warmed skin. Men marched side by side through the distant gate. Her donkey bucked its head at the commotion. Had Absalom arrived? She gawked at men carrying poles not swords or shields. The golden wings of cherubim glistened head high among the pole bearers.

Air rushed from Rimona's lungs like wheat kernels pouring from a merchant's sack. The Ark of

God had returned to Jerusalem. Levites carried the presence of God toward the tabernacle. She recognized Jonathan and Ahimaaz, the priests' sons, who waited by the gate, surveying the line of servants. Her uncle had introduced her to the young men, and she had answered their questions about her travels. How often does a priest see a Philistine commander escort a Hebrew woman into the palace court or recite psalms of praise?

She bit her lip. Salt sizzled on her tongue. The ark should be with King David and Ittai. Why was it being brought back to the city?

"Hold these a moment." Handing a stunned Gihon the donkey's reins, Rimona hefted a water jar onto her shoulder and ambled toward the procession. The priests' sons were not strangers, but she strolled in their direction cautiously, leaving enough distance to show them respect.

"Have you seen King David?" she asked Jonathan who had spoken freely after Ittai's worship of God. She tipped the water jar ever so slightly to feign an offer of a drink to the lanky worship official.

The chief priest's son scanned the area near the gate. "You are too kind," Jonathan answered.

"Please." Her beg stuck in her parched throat. "Is he well?"

Jonathan leaned toward her, his fist covering his mouth as if to cough.

Would he chastise her for mentioning David?

She flinched and back-stepped from the sons.

Jonathan cleared his throat. "He is. Gone." More

sputtering. "Gilgal."

Rimona met Jonathan's gaze and nodded. Before she could ask about Ittai, the sons traveled on with the procession. She whirled and darted toward Gihon who stood like an ornate tower next to a wide-bellied donkey.

"We best return to the courtyard," Gihon said. The strengthening sun failed to cast a glow to her pallor.

Setting the water jar onto the cart, Rimona reclaimed the reins to her donkey and tugged him away from the well. The soft leather in her hands couldn't comfort her dread. If God's servants, the priests of His dwelling place, were afraid to speak of David in the city that bore his name, what would befall a concubine in his palace and a woman whom Absalom had already caressed?

She recalled Ittai's plea.

Hide.

18

On foot, Ittai continued to climb the low mountain covered with olive trees. Many of his men traveled without mounts, so Ittai decided to spare his mule the extra weight of a rider. His Philistine forces journeyed behind him in a wide fortified mass hidden by sprawling branches over twice the height of their leader. Boys eager to learn about battles led resting mules so the beasts did not wander.

"You are a man of few words this day, Hamuran."

They converged on a mature olive tree and Hamuran veered around to the other side of the trunk. "I prefer fighting on plains than among branches." Ittai's second-in-command battered a low-hanging sprig and rejoined him.

"These trees will hide our forces."

"And how many will that be?" Hamuran's eyebrows rose not in a challenge but with a steady gaze of curiosity.

"Six hundred more than yesterday." Ittai's trusted friend did not know David as Ittai knew him. Philistines heard the songs and stories of David's valor and victories. Were they dismayed at a gallant fighter weeping on a stump before women? Hamuran had never wavered in his trust of Ittai's plans. His loyalty was a blessing from God. "It appears our arrival was timely."

"We met and conversed with our enemy. Our provisions were stocked by a king." Hamuran dodged a rock in his path. "And we rescued a Hebrew woman who calmed fears outside of Etam."

Ittai stared at Hamuran. His friend did not grin or chide. His stern features were contemplative not challenging.

"Yes, we did." Ittai quickened his pace. He did not care to dwell on Rimona's situation near the palace. He wasn't near the city to protect her if trouble arose. The thought of innocents being attacked caused a wildness in Ittai that he needed to conserve for a battle. "I pray for God to give us victory and to protect the innocent in Jerusalem."

Hamuran halted briefly. "At times I feel I am in a dream of God's. The outcome has happened, yet I must keep moving forward and do my part in order to understand God's purpose."

"This is not a dream. Waking tomorrow is not a promise I can make. Blood will be spilled in victory and in defeat." Ittai bound his emotions deep beneath his breastplate and trudged onward. He had hoped in gaining exile that he would find a new home, not a new war.

"I know you do not sleep, for I do not hear your snores." Hamuran hurried to catch his commander and clamped a hand on Ittai's shoulder. His friend's trust rejuvenated Ittai's spirit. To have the allegiance of one who was not a brother was a blessing to an orphan.

Ittai needed that strength and assurance for his soul was full of the faces of fallen men who had fought valiantly and lost.

"I would follow you into any battle." Hamuran's words were meant solely for Ittai's ears.

"Follow God into battle, not me."

"But you follow God."

"You are making my head hurt." Ittai squeezed his temple and shrugged to remove Hamuran's hand from his shoulder. Ittai's role in this war was uncertain. David had established commanders at his side. Ittai's men needed to gather their strength and boldness from God, not a single man.

From between the trees, a boy scampered toward Ittai. The youth waved a thin, leafy branch enlivening the air with a sweet scent.

"Are you the Gittite?" The boy panted from his sprint. "The king has asked for you. He is over that rise." The messenger pointed to the west.

"Who is with him?" If the king was alone with his family, then Ittai would summon some of his men to attend to him.

"Joab and his brother, Abishai." The messenger flailed his arm. "Come, come."

Ittai retrieved his mule's reins from a young helper and mounted his mule.

"Banak," he shouted.

His revered scout rushed forward.

"Lead the men in ranks."

Defined muscles snaked along Hamuran's forearms as he prepared his mule for a sprint. "Sounds like the king has awakened."

"I pray he has." Ittai edged his mule forward. "Make haste."

Hamuran leapt atop his mount. "Don't want to face Joab alone?"

"A bit of advice." Ittai acknowledged Banak and Hamuran with a stare full of caution and wisdom. "Don't ever face Joab alone."

"Watch out," Ittai roared as he weaved between tree and traveler. Men, women, and children, heads covered, cheeks streaked red with tears, fled from his path. His mule snapped at passersby. Hamuran also called out warnings to those who had fled their homes and were following their king. Too many of these people were officials and city dwellers. What skills did they possess to assist in battle? Battles were fought by men with prowess and strength. Women and children camped at the rear of the forces, bringing food and drink when needed. Ittai had seen what happened to women whose men lost in war. Ittai needed all his wits to command his men in this chaos.

David had been a fierce warrior in Ziklag. Though, in the past day, Ittai had not witnessed the same fire for victory in David. Was it his age? Over thirty years is a long time to be fighting enemies. Was the shock of his son's betrayal befuddling David's cunning? Or did the advisors and commanders around David grow complacent and ignore the revolution simmering in their midst? Even if David was somehow diminished in body and spirit, Ittai would see his mentor through this conquest. And when Ittai claimed victory over the haughty Absalom, he would batter the city gate and find Rimona. In his mind, he envisioned the dark-eyed delight of Rimona when he arrived to set her free from her musical prison. He would seek her again, God willing, even if that freedom were for only one night at a banquet.

Lord, give me Your strength and wisdom. May I uplift Your servant, David, in counsel and might.

Near the top of the summit, Ittai slowed his charge. Hamuran's mule trotted near his flank. Up ahead, David sat on a donkey. The king lifted his hands toward the clear sky. His face glistened with sweat while tufts of gray hair sprang from his head covering. Finally, someone had seen to their king's needs and provided a mount.

Joab and Abishai positioned themselves on each side of David. As Ittai approached, Joab squinted as if he had gone blind. Joab was playing coy, for the man could recognize Ittai a slope away.

Ittai halted and waited for David to acknowledge his arrival. A slight breeze blew Ittai's long hair against his cheek. He swiped the distraction from his face and centered his attention on the raider whose long-ago provisions had kept Ittai and his mother from starvation.

"Ittai." David motioned him closer. "I have lost a trusted advisor. My faithful counselor Ahithophel has conspired with my son. How much more sorrow can I bear?" David tugged at his robe. His features wrinkled like his garment. The king, haggard as he was, showed more fortitude than earlier in the day.

"You have many loyal supporters, my lord." With word and presence, Ittai would reinforce whatever courage David had left after his son's and confidant's betrayals. "Let Ahithophel answer to God for his deceit. The man accepted your trust and position. For him to scurry to Hebron makes him a liar before our God."

"God must turn Ahithophel's wisdom into babble." David closed his eyes and tilted his chin toward the treetops. "Lord, confuse Ahithophel's counsel." The king's voice strained to be heard. His gaze fell upon Joab. "The blood that runs through Ahithophel's veins is the same blood that runs through my son Solomon's veins. Why would a man turn a blind eye to his kin?"

Joab fidgeted on his mount, creaking the leather protecting his chest. "He is an old man living with the ghosts of dead soldiers. You are the rightful king of Israel. Ahithophel thinks too much of his standing. He will regret his allegiance." Joab's glare in Ittai's direction could have set the grove ablaze. He kicked his donkey and continued up the mount. "We must keep moving."

Abishai rode after his brother.

"I agree." Ittai straightened. When had his thoughts or deeds ever aligned with Joab? Until now. The thought set like a stone in his gut. "Son of Jesse."

David turned his attention to Ittai.

"Who taught me this truth? I set my eyes to the hills. Where does my help come from?" Ittai's question rang with the assurance of its answer.

David thrust a fist heavenward again, but this time he opened his palm as if to catch raindrops. "My help comes from the Maker of heaven and earth." His praise settled over the trodden soil. "It is good to be reminded of my songs once again"

"Yes, it is." Ittai leaned over his mule's mane. "Forget Ahithophel. His sharp tongue will be dulled by the One True God. Though, we need to be on the move. We must remember the women and children." Lowering his voice, he added, "And Joab's impatience."

The king grinned, a knowing grin, one conjuring a fighter from decades ago. "I am glad God brought me a man from years gone by. You are reminding me of truths I need to hold onto." He jerked his head in Joab's direction. "We must ride."

Finally, Ittai had glimpsed the warrior who waded from one victory to another as easily as wading through the foam of broken waves.

David turned before traveling onward. "I see you brought someone to watch your back." The king indicated Hamuran.

Hamuran bowed his head. Shade from a twenty-foot branch shadowed half his features. "I am here to warn him of every flinch, for there are more conspirators in your palace than rats on goat's milk."

David's jaw gaped. He arched a brow and beheld Ittai. "And I thought the woman you brought was bold. Your confidant is forceful as well." David kicked his donkey and trotted after his nephews.

Forceful? Rimona? A spark of remembrance

brightened Ittai's countenance. He prayed Shamar kept her tucked away among his harps.

~*~

At the top of the wide mound, where the shade and cover of olive branches was no more, a man leapt and screamed. His wail likened to a small note on the expansive summit. Even from a distance, the man's torn robe revealed pale skin usually hidden by cloth.

King David broke from the ranks of his nephews and trotted his donkey toward the distraught traveler. His donkey's hooves kicked clods of dirt into the afternoon air.

"God has answered David's prayer," Ittai said to Hamuran. "I remember that man and his beard from the city gate. Hushai is an advisor to the king."

Hamuran's nose wrinkled as he assessed the commotion up ahead. "The other advisor was a traitor. Perhaps this one is too."

"This one is going back." Ittai kicked his mount to join the reunion.

"To Jerusalem?" Hamuran followed close behind.

Ittai slowed his arrival, allowing Hamuran to catch him. "We need eyes and ears in the city if we are going to win a war. We will meet the priests' sons at the fjords, but if no one relays Absalom's plans from the palace, we will be met with a shrug."

Turning and surveying the people climbing the steep grove of trees, Ittai scratched his beard. The air closer to the heavens should have filled his nostrils with fragrance and wonder, but dust clogged his senses and caused grit to claim his tongue. He spit on the trampled soil. "Absalom has men who are prepared to fight. David's fighting men are spread out over the kingdom. Some in the desert and some across the river. I've never gone into battle with stunned, worn-out city dwellers who are afraid to die."

"Nor have I. We need a trusted confidant in Jerusalem to delay Absalom's advance." Hamuran stretched his back and scanned the ranks of Philistines trudging with the supplies. "Will Joab agree with us about sending the advisor back to the city?"

"I don't care if Joab agrees. I only need David to agree, and I know the king will listen to me. And you." Ittai met Hamuran's confident gaze. The look that passed between them would frighten any mother blessed with the care of two such boys. Ittai grinned. "The king knows we don't do flattery well."

19

Rimona awoke to an unsettling quiet, more troubling than her uncle's clomping cane. She dressed quickly in her plain brown robe and rushed into the music room. Where was Shamar? Had he risen early? Or had he left her alone during the night? She did not care to live in a city where the ruler was in dispute. Who would protect the widows and the orphans? Would those loyal to King David be hauled into the public square and attacked? Oh, how she missed her home with neighbors who cared about her safety. Living in Jerusalem made her anxious for her future.

On the long table, her polishing rags remained from the previous night's work. The faint scent of olive oil hung in the air. The row of lyres along the wall gleamed rich and ready to be plucked.

A tapping sounded at the door.

She grabbed the edge of the table. Her uncle wouldn't knock. Who visited this early in the day? Soldiers? Scouts? Would they break down the door and take any wealth? Or women? Her heartbeat thrummed in her ears. Absalom couldn't have arrived in the city. A shofar would have sounded to announce his arrival. Knowing Absalom as she did, he would not enter Jerusalem in the shadows of morning. The beautiful prince would prefer sunlight glistening on his chariot and sparkling upon his gold-banded hair.

Banging came. Louder than before. "Shamar?" a man's voice questioned instead of demanded.

Clearing her throat, Rimona took a deep breath to rival the sound of her uncle's growl. "He's not here."

Steps hurried away.

"Thanks be to the Lord." She rested her forearms on the table and continued to pray. "Please protect King David, and Ittai, and all the people traveling with them. Watch over me, Lord. I am an unwanted orphan in this city."

When her prayer ended, the door whipped open. Shamar hobbled inside. A young man trailed after him like an heir after an inheritance.

Her uncle jabbed his cane at a wooden box set where Jonathan and Ahimaaz had strummed their harps. "You will find the instruments in that crate. Take them to the palace steps."

The young man bowed and carried his load out the door and into the courtyard.

"Why didn't you let him in?" Shamar chastised her with a scowl. "We have plenty of work to do. Absalom may arrive at any moment."

"I did not know we were expecting anyone." She did not share her uncle's enthusiasm for Absalom's arrival. The prince gave her an odd feeling when they met as if he searched her being to see what value he could steal or use for his benefit. King David had been on the throne all of her life. She would remain loyal to the man God placed on the throne. Loyalty did not appear to be one of her uncle's attributes.

Shamar shuffled to a stool and rested. "What instrument do you play?" Her uncle asked as if everyone possessed a musical skill. She had labored over her mother and assisted her neighbors with sewing and cooking. Harp songs in Beersheba were rare except for a wedding or festival

"Well, I—"

"I need a single word," Shamar snapped. "Harp. Lyre. Flute. Cymbal."

She pinched the table's edge and allowed her fingers to assault the dead wood.

"None. I sing a little. My voice calmed my mother's pain."

"The woman was dying." Her uncle puckered his lips and shook his head in a chastising sway. Did he enjoy the sensation of his head shake? She did not, for his every move heaped more disdain on her presence. Where was his compassion for the ill? His sister suffered without a single offer of comfort from his mouth or from his messenger.

"I spent my life learning instruments, studying music, and practicing to receive the notice of kings." Shamar raised his voice to impress the empty room. "Every note you hear played in the tabernacle to worship God, was taught to a musician by me. And now when I need peace in my life, my tribal elders send me a woman to support. A woman who has no skills."

Her ears did their best to filter the slander of her family, for she needed her uncle's oversight in this tumultuous city. Though she would never forget how selfish he had been to abandon his family over a disagreement about marriage. She hid her hands that had become claws ready to scratch the smugness from his face. From deep inside her dignity, she withdrew pleasantries instead of scorn. "I'm sure I can do something to help you. I am willing to sweep the courtyard and the front of your home." Lingering inside when at all possible. "You must eat to keep your strength. I can churn cream for our bread."

Shamar rose from his seat and hobbled her direction. Was buttered bread on his mind? He struck the table with his hand. Steadily. Rhythmically. The thud of his skin on the wood reverberated between her shoulder blades and slid to her tailbone.

"Can you keep a beat?" he asked.

She nodded in cadence with every wrinkle-handed slap of the table.

"Good. You will accompany the musicians with the tambourine."

"Here? In the music room?" Her mouth tasted of soiled rags. Drawing attention to herself was not her plan.

"Why would anyone join us here? I'm having a platform built outside of the palace. Absalom must be welcomed with the harp and lyre." He raised his arm, shook an imaginary tambourine, and wiggled his waist. Even his cane swiveled during the awkward dance. "You will celebrate Absalom's entry with us."

She forced a smile to show enthusiasm at his suggestion. Tart saliva pulled at the back of her throat as she mimicked a dutiful niece playing a joyous tambourine. Would he cast her on the street if she refused his request and insulted his standing in the court? Danger would abound in the alleys and markets after dark, especially when legions of men arrived. The people in Jerusalem were strangers. Who would risk harboring a woman who had been seen with a Philistine entering David's palace? Worse, would they think her soiled or a prostitute? Believe that her uncle refused her because of her wicked ways? She licked her lips and continued her pretend tambourine playing.

"Yes, we will welcome the new king." Her voice sounded as if she still slumbered.

Why couldn't she remain tucked away in her bedroom? If, indeed, she produced a lively beat with her tambourine held high, every curve of her body would be under Absalom's scrutiny. This day, when she met the traitor king, she would not have the comfort or protection of sitting on a donkey surrounded by Philistine warriors. Dread squeezed her heart. The same dread when Eglon threatened to slice her tongue. The same aching dread when she watched Ittai ride away. No massive rescuer waited in the nearby hills. Yet, she did have one rescuer ready to offer assistance. An image of Ittai and Lana reciting David's words filled her mind and attempted to calm her soul. *Where does your help come from? From the Lord, the Maker of heaven and earth.*

She prayed the Lord would be on the streets of Jerusalem helping her shake a tambourine in rhythm with Shamar's musicians and with the motions of a modest stone statue.

20

Ping. Another rock ricocheted off Ittai's bronze-plated helmet. King David did not flinch. The king's forces and followers were making good progress toward Gilgal near the river. Ittai prayed the word they would receive was that Absalom was celebrating in Jerusalem before advancing on his father. Only time, and a messenger, would tell of Absalom's plot.

"Leave, you man of blood. Leave this place." A Hebrew by the name of Shimei raced along a ridge. A shower of dirt rained on the king's procession. "Get out, you scoundrel. You'll come to ruin."

David rested prominently on his newly gifted donkey. He did not contest any of Shimei's insults. None of the officials on his right, nor on his left, shouted a defense at the slinger of stones.

Rocks struck the neck of Abishai's mount, spooking the animal. The donkey bucked its head and brayed, side-stepping into Joab's ride. Joab chastised his brother.

Abishai calmed his mount and turned toward David. "Why do you allow that dead dog to curse you? Permit me to go over and cut off his head."

"I will set his face on a pole for all to see," Joab added.

Silence. David rode on, his posture as stiff and straight as a roof bearing plank.

Ittai admired David's restraint. The humiliation sung from the hillside caused Ittai to clench his teeth and envision Abishai's wish of beheading the vile man. He had never witnessed a king of Gath being treated with such contempt.

"Not again," Hamuran muttered as a shower of pebbles and dirt covered his shoulders.

"Curse you, man of blood," Shimei continued his rant. "God is rewarding your son with your kingdom." Raucous laughter echoed over the path above David and his supporters.

Joab leaned toward his uncle. "Lord, allow your own bloodline to shed Shimei's lifeblood. He is a disgrace to Israel."

David grinned as if the slinger were singing praises. "He's from the tribe of Benjamin. The man is angry over my predecessor's demise. The Benjamites mourn King Saul's death to this very hour. Shimei is delighted that I am on the run again." David reached and grabbed Ittai's arm. "I was on the run from King Saul when I met this Philistine."

The warmth and firmness of David's touch invigorated Ittai's tired body. Every man, woman, and child in David's company battled exhaustion from their hurried pace.

"Boundary lines fell for us in pleasant places in Ziklag." Ittai clasped David's hand. The praise of his mentor was a welcomed cassia-scented balm among the stench of unwashed bodies and sweaty livestock.

"You were a boy in Ziklag," Joab said. "I don't remember you going on any raids." *Thunk*. A good-sized rock struck Joab's shoulder narrowly missing the king. "Shimei, I'll truly have your head," Joab roared.

Ittai did not wish to see the king pelted, but inwardly, he praised any strike on Joab. Biting his cheek, Ittai held back a grin at Joab's discontent.

"You are all men of blood." Shimei leapt with joy at his successful throw. "The towns of Israel will spit you out, David. God has given your kingdom to Absalom."

Joab trotted his donkey a few paces ahead of the officials and guards spread out along the path protecting David. "My lord, silence can come swiftly."

David dismissed Joab with a wave of his hand. "Shimei is correct. My own son is trying to take my life. Shimei brings rocks, but my son brings swords." David lifted his face to survey the Hebrew sprinting on the ridge, staying even with the procession. "What if the Lord has led him to curse me? What if the Lord has placed the profanity on Shimei's lips? It may be that the Lord will take pity on me when He sees my distress and repay me with good."

"The Lord has repaid all of us with good." Ittai coughed from inhaling the dust on the dry trail. "The Lord has delayed an assault on our flank. I say we have already benefitted from God's goodness."

Hamuran brushed debris from his lap. "Do you believe Absalom has reached the city?"

Joab and Abishai exchanged an expression of mockery.

"That is where the palace lies." Joab pointed at Shimei and motioned a slit throat.

Ittai prayed for a delay, but he had seen Absalom's pride and conceit on display outside of Etam. The son desired the kingdom, and its throne remained in Jerusalem. Where Rimona remained. He prayed for Absalom to meet them on a battlefield of grass and not of city stone. Conquering an army house by house flooded streets with innocent blood.

"I know my son." David's voice shattered in his throat as he cast a glance at Hamuran and Ittai. "There was a time I believed I knew him well. But he has not forgiven me for a lack of justice in my household. Absalom will not rest until my body is buried under a pile of stones much bigger than Shimei's rocks." Tears glistened in the king's eyes. He deflected an incoming barrage. A glimmer of his younger self flashed in Ittai's memory. "Surely, Shimei desires my body to be crushed by stones."

"That prairie dog is a bitter man." Ittai knew that a commander conversing about his own death demoralized fighting men faster than a plague. He needed to pray and then remind David of God's faithfulness.

God, You brought me to Jerusalem on the eve of Absalom's revolt. May I be a swallow of wine and a lick of honey to David's confidence in himself and in You.

Ittai blocked another of Shimei's stones with a small shield. The sun-warmed bronze beneath his fingers jolted his senses.

"My lord," Ittai said firmly. "If God is causing a

man to hit you with stones, then God is here with you, with all of us who call upon His name. I have no doubt that Hushai will arrive in Jerusalem, and the One True God will show your advisor favor. Hushai will befuddle Absalom's plans to assail you."

"I hope you are right, Gittite." Joab sounded skeptical.

Ittai prepared for ample criticism from David's nephew.

"You foreigners underestimate Ahithophel's standing and wisdom. He is upheld as one of the wisest seers in all of Israel."

"That may be true, son of Zeruiah." Ittai stretched his muscles, broadening his form. He did not have to defer to Joab anymore now that both men rode at David's side. "Though, I never underestimate God's standing."

A scattering of dirt landed on a group of officials. They splayed their arms and flapped their hands like disgruntled geese.

David laughed at the commotion. "Who knew loyalty would come to this?" When his chuckle quieted, he grew stoic. "I have no doubt that Hushai will confuse my son with his eloquence. My friend will send word of Absalom's plans. The priests and those serving in the tabernacle are loyal to God and to me. They know that every fool remaining in Jerusalem has become a spy. I trust them to bring me word regarding my son."

Would the messengers also have knowledge of a musician's niece stowed away near the palace? He should have been more forceful with Rimona. He should have beseeched the king to protect her. If only he knew David saw him as a mighty commander and friend worthy to travel at his side. Such standing could protect any woman, even a woman as alone in the world as Rimona.

David needed his entire army to fight as one if victory was to be certain. And Ittai was certain of one thing, David had to reign victorious, or exile for Ittai and his men would evaporate faster than a raindrop on a desert stone.

Rotating to survey the mass of people in his wake, Ittai prayed Absalom's battle plans would arrive swiftly. For deep in his gut, he knew they needed to be ready to defend their position soon, or the innocents trudging behind a beleaguered king would be slaughtered.

21

Rimona stood on her uncle's platform, hidden by harpists, with the sun torturing her head covering. Her wooden station gave her a view of the main street leading to the palace and a reprieve from the crowd of people waiting to welcome "King" Absalom. Even the thought of his title clenched her teeth. How could an Israelite act with such disregard for God? Absalom heaped disdain on his father, not honor. Gossip from the crowd revealed Absalom's thirst for blood. The prince sought the murder of the man who had given him life. How could a son plot his father's demise? May such lawlessness never come to pass. To this day, she still remembered his forbidden touch on the plain outside of Etam. She shifted behind a plump musician to avoid being seen by the rebel prince.

"Use your thumb." Shamar grasped her arm and shook it, clanging the tiny bronze cymbals on her tambourine. "You are too slow and too loud with your palm."

Why was her uncle astute to her playing now? She had pounded her instrument all day, only stopping to offer drinks to the harpists and flutists. Her hand tingled from striking the smooth leather for hours.

"I will try to soften the rhythm." She stepped

toward the edge of his musical podium leaving her uncle room to provoke his other players.

A loud, low hum rose into a full trumpet call. The mutterings of the crowd turned into a roar. From the direction of Jerusalem's main gate, the ominous howl of the shofar continued.

He's here.

Rimona's body chilled. She shivered and turned to survey the entrance to the city while the horn's *oooh-aaah* carried the announcement of Absalom's arrival all the way to the stone steps of the palace. She had climbed the same steps with Ittai and Lana when peace reigned in David's household. Soon, turmoil and war would be brought to David's royal residence.

Movement in a front window of the palace caught her attention. Was Gihon watching the steps for soldiers? What defense could ten concubines muster against a formidable army?

Clapping rang out at her side.

"Hold it higher." Shamar glowered at her and mimicked a frenzied tambourine. "Let the cymbals welcome Absalom to the palace." Patting his hip, Shamar said, "Move to the beat of your thumb."

Her uncle's screams, the blasts of the shofar, people's shrieks of anticipation, and the thud-dud of her own instrument sent a piercing ache through her skull. Even the calming spice scent of myrrh that her uncle had insisted she rub into the frame of her tambourine, made her stomach and senses ill.

"Long live King Absalom," the crowd shouted. Those gathered along the street cleared the center of the road.

A brownish-black horse, its mane dancing in the wind, pulled a familiar ornate chariot closer to the palace.

Her palms dampened at the sight of the beautiful prince, his hair wild and curling to his waist. Scarlet and indigo sashes decorated his chest while the sun glistened on the same gold bands wrapped around his ears. She wiped her hand and continued a faint thumb and palm rhythm on her tambourine. Absalom traveled alone again. No wife or woman accompanied him in the slow-moving cart.

"Louder. Faster." Her uncle's hand kept time to the song. "Our king must hear our music of praise this day."

She didn't want to praise Absalom. David had been anointed king over the tribes of Israel, and people she had grown to care for were marching at David's side. If only she could shimmy her tambourine and be transported to Parveda's cart.

Officials and soldiers cleared a path to the palace steps for Absalom and his glorious chariot. The rebel waved at cheering men, women, and children welcoming him as their ruler. Absalom stood aloft on his perch soaking in his stolen praise. Words of adoration did not seep from her mouth. Her lips pressed thin as a thread as she timidly shook her bronze cymbals.

"King Absalom," her uncle shouted. He rocked on his cane practically bursting forth in a dance.

She prayed the noise of the people and the harp

strings would drown her uncle's summons.

The chariot swung wide sending the crowd scampering away from Absalom's skittish horse and unforgiving cartwheels. The froth-mouthed beast stopped in front of Shamar's musical stage.

Stilling her tambourine, she surveyed the drop from the podium. The distance was too high for her to avoid a scene or the surety of a broken bone. Head lowered, she aligned her body so a harpist on a high stool blocked Absalom's sight.

Her uncle bowed while his musicians continued playing. "Welcome home, my lord."

"Ah, Shamar, you delight me with your music." Absalom's robust voice commended her uncle's service. "Finish your songs and bring a few musicians into the palace chamber."

"Of course." Her uncle *thunked* his cane on the planked floorboards and straightened his stooped-shoulder form. "Anything for you, my king."

Leave straightaway. Rimona's mouth became as dry as a cast away onion skin. Hide me, Lord.

The chariot creaked as it began to move.

Keep going!

Clopping hooves silenced.

Dare she peek? The musician blocking her presence concentrated on his instrument. She eased a hair width to the side and met the dark, sharp-as-a-hawk gaze of Absalom. The pound of her pulse deafened any note from serenading her ears. She had failed Ittai. An ache like a stab to her breast overcame her being. Casting her gaze beyond the prince toward the palace steps, she palmed her tambourine as if proceeding toward an open tomb.

"My counselor, Shamar." Absalom's praise echoed over the chanting of cheers.

Her uncle trembled and stretched a hand toward the traitor. "Yes, my lord."

Chaos around her vanished as if she and Absalom were the only two travelers on the streets of Jerusalem.

"I am fond of the tambourine. Make sure I hear its song inside the palace." The king's throaty chuckle hollowed her belly. "Rimona of Beersheba, you are more becoming in stripes. I look forward to hearing about the remainder of your journey." Absalom slapped his reins and continued on to claim his throne.

She nodded as only one caught in unjust rule could do. Her jaw pulled tight from the souring of her saliva. Absalom remembered their encounter. His memory wouldn't bear well for her future.

Shamar's stare questioned her mention, but instantly, the scariest of light dawned in his eyes, and he appeared as merciless as Eglon who had desired to sell her as a slave.

Hope drained from the marrow of her bones, for God's anointed king and God's rule of law had abandoned the city. Wickedness had arrived. Now, she would have to avoid and defeat it in shadowed chambers latched by Absalom's hand.

Lord, where are Your boundary lines taking me?

~*~

"You deceived me." Shamar shoved her onto a high-backed chair in the chamber in which she, Ittai, and Lana had greeted King David. The shapes of grapes and pomegranates carved into the chair dug into her flesh through her robe. "You are in favor with the king, and you kept it from me? What other secrets do you keep?"

Rimona poked the frame of her tambourine at her uncle. The beast needed taming. "I spoke of my meeting with Prince Absalom when I arrived in Jerusalem. King David knew all about it."

"Do not mention his name. Absalom is our king, and you will serve him and do as he pleases." Spit flew from her uncle's lips and settled in his beard. "Sit in this corner and do not overpower my harpists with your clanging." Shamar stomped toward his gifted students leaving a pungent body odor in his wake.

Had her uncle set her apart to catch Absalom's eye? Was she an offering in order to gain prominence? May it never be. She shook a soft rhythm and straightened her playing posture. Shamar had set her near the wall from which David had entered and greeted his guests only three short days prior. So much had occurred since her arrival in the city. Her loyalty remained with David and with her steadfast rescuer. Oh, how she prayed for God to save her friends from ruin.

The far door opened. Rimona glimpsed the small oasis Lana had cherished. An older man and two guards entered. Covered with a fine dust of dirt, the visitor marched through the vast room with an eager, slightly leaning gait.

"I will see King Absalom," the elder demanded. "I served the father and now I will serve the son." The pledge echoed amidst the stone walls.

Rimona squinted at the aged man. Was it Hushai? He had conversed with Ittai and her at the city gate and had brought them to see David. Conspirators lurked in every alley and on every street corner in Jerusalem.

Hushai rushed by without an acknowledgement. "Long live King Absalom," he bellowed.

A guard opened the cedar door into the royal rooms. The door closed, but not all the way. What a fool she had been to believe Hushai was a loyal counselor to David. Her uncle cleared his throat. She shook her tambourine anew and concentrated on the song, not on the intrigue in the palace.

"Is this the loyalty you show to my father?" Absalom's muffled charge came from the hallway. She cast a glance at Shamar lost in his instruction. Her uncle was deaf to the conversation beyond the wide door.

"Shall I not serve the one chosen by the Lord and all the men of Israel," Hushai replied. "I will remain with him."

Rimona stood, feigned pleasure in her accompaniment, and shifted closer to the doorway.

"Do not inquire of Hushai," came a harsh retort. "Have I not told you to set out at once with twelve thousand of your men? Attack your father when he is weak. Strike first, kill the former king, and your rule will be secure." She did not recognize this voice, but it came out forthright. She feared the earnestness of the advice would sway Absalom.

Lord, doesn't David have one friend left in the city, save You? And me?

"Ahithophel's counsel is useless." Perhaps David had three friends in Jerusalem. Toda raba, Hushai. "You know your father is a fighter. He hid from King Saul in caves. He and his men will lie in wait in the hills. He may be old, but no one is as cunning as David on the run."

Soft muttering ensued.

"Trust me," Hushai ranted. "David will attack first, and all your men will flee. Wait in the city and gather your forces from the surrounding tribes, so your army will be as numerous as sand on the seashore. Your large army will crush David and his men."

Her muscles grew taut with every plot of David's demise though she was aware of something the Hebrews were not, and that was the battle prowess of Ittai, Hamuran, and Banak.

"You wish me to linger in Jerusalem?" Absalom said. "To wait on the elders of the tribes to send more men? What will I do while my father gathers strength?" Anger seethed through the slightly opened planked door. She was thankful that she was not a counselor to the king.

"Make yourself a stench in your father's nose as we have planned." Ahithophel uttered more foolishness.

With men speaking over one another, she could

not hear clearly. Ahithophel had mentioned David's concubines. Voices praised Hushai. Ahithophel cursed. Something was happening tonight. Her brain ached from deciphering wicked schemes. The clink-clank of her clattering cymbals added to the pain. Was Gihon safe? She had not seen any of David's wives when she arrived at the palace.

Men's voices trailed off. Thanks be to God that Absalom had advisors to entertain.

Returning to her chair, she slumped in her seat and swept stray strands of hair underneath her plain head covering. She grazed her golden earring with the three emeralds, fingering the faceted gems. Memories of her mother and father flooded her mind. She had a loving family once. If only she could be running the hills of Beersheba, carefree, and secure. Her cherished jewels added little comfort this day amidst the conflict of kings.

"God, help me be strong and courageous," she prayed softly. "Give me your wisdom among so many devious schemes."

The cedar door swung open. A trample of feet interrupted the music. Absalom entered the grand hall, but he did not approach her uncle who was an official and a personal music instructor. The traitor king strolled to her perch nearest the wall.

Did he suspect she'd heard his plans? Did he believe her to be a spy? Her heart tap-tap-tapped faster than the tiny cymbals on her tambourine.

Absalom's gaze swept over every curve in her form and settled on her hips. She swallowed past the burn in her throat. Her tongue and teeth tasted of vomit. Placing her tambourine in her lap to block the king's sultry perusing of her body, she bowed her head, acknowledging the self-appointed leader.

"King Absalom." She gripped her wrist to still the tremble of the tambourine.

"You did not wait for me in the valley." He smiled, displaying his white teeth. She believed there was more to his statement than questioning her location in a grove of trees. He wanted information about Philistine soldiers. Absalom would never coax a betrayal of Ittai from her lips.

"I came inside the city, my lord." She motioned to her uncle. "My home is with Shamar, your musician, now."

"And the Philistines?" Absalom eased closer. Nothing larger than a sliver of a breeze would fit between their bodies. The newly appointed king smelled of ripened berries and fresh blood. "Did the foreigners accompany my father?"

A lion lurked before her. She blinked, fluttering her eyelashes, feigning ignorance. "I did not see the men leave." The truth. She only saw Ittai leave.

"You are a brave woman, Rimona. Not many women could survive a trip from Beersheba surrounded by foreigners. Your uncle is a determined and highly skilled man. The blood in your veins is strong." Absalom dismissed his guards to the other side of the hall. Back turned toward her uncle, he continued his address. "I am a ruler with no heir. The sons born to me have died. My wife's womb is troubled." Absalom rocked on his sandals as if comforting himself.

Why was he speaking of offspring? To her? Truly there were better more prestigious women to invite into his bed. Those with wealth and alliances.

How did one comfort a king? "I'm so sorry—"

"This is your instrument." Discreetly, yet boldly, and in the presence of her overseer, he swept his fingertips on the top of her hand. A hand hidden by the drum of her tambourine. His touch sent a shudder throughout her whole being. Even her shoulders quivered from the brash stroke. She grew ill from his indiscretion. Absalom's flawless features drank in her reaction.

"It is. My tambourine." Her voice barely registered.

In Ittai's presence, her insides became a bubbling spring. Absalom brought out disgust served in a barren wilderness.

Absalom grinned like an emboldened lover. "You and I will create a son strong enough to rule Israel." He whispered his lust through lips that reminded her of a suckling goat.

Where was his wife now? This shouldn't be happening. Not here. Not anywhere in the City of David. A flock of birds flapped and squawked in her stomach making all her senses take flight.

"I shall have an heir to carry on when I am gone." Glee filled Absalom's sculpted face. "I will send for you promptly tomorrow night after this day's revelries are finished." He winked and began to parade from the hall. "Shamar," he called, "you will be receiving gifts this very day." The king vanished through the cedar door in haste. His guards followed after him.

Her uncle bowed as the procession retreated. "Toda raba, my lord."

Slumping in her chair, she dropped her tambourine. Round and round the drum rolled until it hit the stone wall and *tinked* a tune all on its own.

With God as her witness, she would never share a bed with Absalom. The man was a deceiver with murder on his mind. Her love and loyalty rested on two men who worshiped the One True God and tried to follow His ways.

Tonight, after dark, she had to brave treacherous hills and rock one more time. She had to find her Philistine rescuer and her true king, David, and try to rescue them. While also rescuing herself.

22

Ittai dismounted north of Gilgal near the bank of the Jordan River. He slung his elbows backward and stretched his bones. Heat rose from the shore of the river like the side-wind of snakes. He prayed Hushai's reputation and standing in Jerusalem would sway Absalom and stall the prince's advance.

"Why are we stopping?" Joab trotted his mule ahead of his uncle and turned back as if bringing a charge. "We must cross the Jordan at once. Absalom and his men will be sniffing our mules' tails before night fall."

Debate from a Philistine's lips would stoke Joab's fury. A fury that flamed at the slightest spark. Ittai deferred a rebuttal to the king of the land.

The king wiped his brow with the back of his hand and surveyed the riverbed from atop his mount "Hushai will send word of Absalom's intentions."

"Intentions?" Joab scoffed. "Your son has assumed rule of your kingdom and will hunt us down like a wild boar. We need to cross and find a stronghold to amass more men." Joab's tone was more insult than insight, yet David sat motionless, his features devoid of wrinkle.

"We don't know when my son arrived in

Jerusalem or how quickly he summoned counselors. Where was your wisdom when we plotted with Hushai on the mount? Why place an old man's life in peril if you did not believe his information would help us?" David impaled his nephew with a stare that would have panicked any other advisor. "Perhaps my son will have mercy on me. He may now be celebrating in the palace and not stalking his father."

"You are blind, Uncle," Abishai, Joab's brother said. "Absalom has no loyalty to his own blood."

"Can you not hold your tongue? You sons of Zeruiah would rather slit my son's throat than barter for peace." Veins ridged on David's neck. His forlorn body quaked. "Was your agreement to wait at these fjords a lie?"

"It's hot." Ittai patted the damp fur of his mule's neck and perused the small band of warriors gathered around David. The scent of warm and wet animals filled his senses. "What harm will it do to give Hushai more time to inform us of Absalom's plans? Our forces hold more women and children than a Passover feast. Let us rest our people and water our livestock. I could use some refreshment myself."

"So, we should think about our stomachs and not our severed heads?" Joab mocked Ittai with laughter that transported him to the hills of Ziklag. "No wonder the rulers of Gath exiled you."

Hamuran rocked forward on his mount as he always did before lunging into battle.

"Feed the men at our flank." Ittai raised his order-giving voice. He could take on Joab alone. "If we fight from the north and from the south, our men will need to be strengthened." He nodded toward the king who had the authority to bless or denounce all strategy.

"We need time for our loyal followers to find us." David dismounted and handed his reins to a servant.

"Time?" Joab did not flex a muscle to care for his men. "We don't have much time."

"God numbers our days and sets each one in motion." Ittai surveyed the ripples of the Jordan. Joab may remember Ittai as an ignorant, pagan boy, but now a formidable commander stood before the king's nephew. "I came the day before last to Jerusalem. I came with six-hundred battle ready men. "You," he said, meeting King's David's stare, "gave me provisions for my army."

Ittai turned toward Joab who paced a rut in the ground. "Your uncle and his family were able to leave Jerusalem unharmed. We even have a spy entering the city to tell us of Absalom's plans." Ittai strutted around his mule and positioned himself between Joab and David. He cast a glance at Abishai whose face was as snarled as his brother's. "I believe God can give us time if we ask for it. You cannot sway my thinking that my arrival wasn't commissioned by God." Fighting the tightening of his throat, Ittai said, "Who taught me this song? I lift my eyes to the hills." He grinned with cracked lips. "Where does my help come from? My help comes from the Lord, the Creator. Hasn't He made the heavens and the earth. And this road upon which we travel?"

Abishai clapped a beat. "Are you going to dance

for us, too?"

"Silence," David shouted. "How long must I wait to hear you call upon the name of the Lord, you sons of Zeruiah? God sets rulers on their thrones. If God wills, we will claim victory even if we tarry for a few hours." David folded his arms as if the tarrying had begun. "We will wait. It will give my kin time to wash the blaspheme from their mouths."

Joab dipped a knee. "Have we not been loyal to you, my king." Joab accentuated his allegiance to his uncle. "If it is your command to stay here, then we will abide by your decision." He indicated his brother with a nod.

"You will obey my orders as always." David bestowed a regal assessment upon the small band of leaders. His gaze settled on Ittai. "All three of you."

Joab reared backward as if struck. "What are you saying?"

Hands braced on his hips, David looked as if he were about to address the people of Jerusalem. "When my entire army is amassed, you sons of Zeruiah will each command a third of my men. Ittai will command the remaining forces." David pronounced Ittai's status for every good ear to hear.

Hamuran let out a whisper of a whoop, loud enough to spook his mount.

But it was the granite-hard glare of Joab that gave Ittai pause. Could he trust the sons of Zeruiah to fight at his side, or would David's bloodthirsty kin scheme a Philistine commander's demise.

Ittai glanced at the heavens and praised God for

David's loyalty. Ittai and Hamuran would need all the help they could get.

~*~

Waterskin in hand, Ittai traipsed to where Hamuran lounged against a boulder not far from the front lines of their men. His companion stopped chewing long enough to give his commander a nod.

"Appeasing Joab's ire, are we?" Hamuran motioned for Ittai to hand him the skin.

"There is no appeasing Joab." Ittai gave his companion the waterskin and sat on a nearby rock. "However, I can appease the animal that carries my weight. The king will find he is missing an apple."

Hamuran scooted a basket closer to Ittai's perch. "Lana wanted me to mention how she baked the bread all by herself. She seasoned the mutton as well."

"Don't speak so loud, or you will receive a betrothal request." Ittai removed a sizeable piece of bread from the basket. "How will I feed myself when that girl is married?"

Cocking his head, Hamuran's forehead crumpled with a perplexed expression.

"What?" Ittai said through a mouth full of mush. "I washed my hands in the shade."

"You wouldn't have to rely on Parveda and Lana's cooking if you found a wife."

Ittai let the taste of roasted grain flavor his tongue. Wives were a distraction. In war, he needed all of his wit and wisdom to keep his men and their families safe. For years, he had escaped death in the fiercest of battles. His companion continued to assess him. Was Hamuran waiting on him to mention Rimona? His friend knew better than to tease him about women.

"You are the one who tells me I stink after days in the sun and that I snore like a coughing donkey at night."

Hamuran grinned wide with an almond skin stuck on his tooth. "If you had a woman, you wouldn't be sleeping. As much. You'd sleep sounder." Hamuran winked, still wearing his silly grin. "Well, some nights."

Ittai shifted on his stone seat. "If you continue with this babble, I'll make you ride with the blood brothers. Let's see how Joab endures your chiding."

Hamuran sobered and took a drink of water. He leaned closer to Ittai, his back turned to the nearby men. "Have you heard the gossip from the city about Joab? He arranged Absalom's return to Jerusalem after Absalom murdered the king's firstborn son."

Ittai clamped down on a piece of dried mutton and chewed the peppered meat into a pulp.

"Absalom's deceit must be a burr in Joab's gut. I am a nuisance to the sons of Zeruiah, but to be betrayed by your own cousin, your own blood." Ittai swallowed the spicy mutton. "Absalom is more despised than a Philistine exile seizing some of their command."

"Joab cannot seek revenge when the king mourns for his son to this very hour." Hamuran slapped his hands together and rubbed them near the hem of his tunic.

Ittai laughed. His girth jiggled at Hamuran's statement. His men gawked in his direction. Ittai knew Joab. He knew of pinches and punches to a boy's arm. He knew of provisions lacking from what David had promised. He knew of the rumblings of a hollow belly. He knew of insults regarding his mother. Slurs Ittai would never repeat to another being. He knew the heart rooted in darkness. He knew. A young, fatherless boy would never forget his past. But a Philistine commander, now a Hebrew commander, would use this knowledge and wisdom given by God to protect a king whom he loved. No one, not even Joab, could sever a bond forged years ago between a boy and a man anointed for greatness by God.

"Joab always seeks revenge." Ittai stood and addressed Hamuran whose giddy smile had vanished. "But I am not the most hated man in Israel."

Hamuran patted the hilt of his sword. "I am ready to fend off Joab's blade anytime, anywhere."

The breeze from the riverbank bathed Ittai in cooler air thick with the scent of succulent grasses. He balanced with one sandal on the granite rock and surveyed the carefree river. "Listening to the people, we now know Absalom's blood will stain Joab's blade before mine."

"King David will protect you." Hamuran grabbed some grapes from the basket. "From Joab and his brother."

"Only God can protect anyone from Joab. He has too many shadows in his heart." Ittai reached and plucked a few grapes from his friend's cluster. "My hope remains with Hushai. He must sing Absalom's praises. Delight the new king, so the old man's deceit shrouds Absalom's cunning like a bounty of royal wine."

If Hushai could give King David more time to assemble forces, then Ittai and the sons of Zeruiah had a chance at victory. If Absalom advanced in the next few hours, then the Jordan would run red with blood.

23

Evening shrouded Jerusalem in hues of gray. Torches with a fury of orange flames lit the roof of David's palace. The fire's brilliance captivated the crowd amassing in the streets around the king's dwelling place. People filled the courtyard, their murmurs making her uncle's songs a nuisance in the background.

"Stop fidgeting," Shamar warned her. "Or I will force you to stand on the stone wall for all to see. You have been off beat all evening."

Rimona's uncle turned to his small band of flutists. Gone were the harps that serenaded Absalom's arrival in Jerusalem. Shamar waved his hands furiously as if trying to lift the high-pitched notes all the way to the king's ears. She sat on the wall a few feet from her uncle and shook her tambourine without a care to the rhythm.

Where was Absalom? Would he be addressing the city from the rooftop? Perhaps in the darkness, he would not glimpse her in the courtyard. A summons would be her undoing. She needed time to gather provisions and escape the city with her dignity while Shamar slept. Surely, she could find the true king's forces near Gilgal. Someone would know where King

David was camped.

Smoke from the tiny blazes illuminating the palace rooftop irritated her nostrils. It did no better to breathe through her mouth. Men, shoulder to shoulder, blocked her view of the palace walls and stole her air. Women congregated in the alley where she had traveled to draw water. What was Gihon doing this night? Was she locked away in her own home?

As if speaking Gihon's name summoned the woman to the edge of the roof, there the beauty stood in a sleeveless tunic with Absalom at her side. Stones mortared to the height of Gihon's thighs kept her from falling. Absalom wouldn't push her from the palace, would he? Rimona's chest ached as she leapt to her feet. Her veins chilled at the peril her friend faced.

Gihon did not turn her head to the east nor to the west. Chin tilted toward the emerging stars, she stared at the darkening sky as if she had become the mortar between the stones.

"People of Jerusalem," Absalom shouted. "My father left ten wives here in my palace."

The crowd shouted insults at Gihon. Some cheered Absalom's name.

Tears formed in Rimona's eyes, pulsing to be set free. She didn't belong here in this rebellion.

Absalom grabbed hold of Gihon's arm. Not a trinket glistened under the torchlight. He shook her frame as if to draw her attention, but Gihon did not behold the traitor. "I am king of Israel. The rock beneath my feet is my dwelling. What remains of my father's is now mine." Absalom yanked Gihon closer and grasped her face. His mouth devoured her lips.

Dropping her tambourine, Rimona gagged.

Raising his mane ever so slightly, Absalom yelled, "I will take everything that is mine this night."

Men, women, and children jeered at Gihon as she received the unwanted lust of a rebel.

Rimona scurried over the courtyard wall and backed toward the music room, feeling the filth from Absalom's actions invading her skin. She would not, she could not, be part of this crime against God, against Gihon, and against David. Through a pool of tears, she glimpsed the rooftop. Guards dragged her friend toward a tent staked on the top of David's palace. Another beauty was ushered to the edge of the roof all to Absalom's delight.

Rimona ran toward the alley, dodging bodies, toward the well, and toward the city gate. She would not lie with Absalom and bear him a son. Doing so would bring her to ruin.

Lord, how could You allow this to happen? Everything in Jerusalem and beyond belongs to You. Why allow this chaos?

Her sandals pounded the road outside of the city until her heart lodged in her throat. Gasping for air, she darted toward a rock hemmed by the shadows of thick bramble bushes. She rounded the foliage and knelt by the rock, hidden from passersby. The gurgle of water sounded nearby. Praise God, she could drink her fill.

A sob threatened to roar from her lips. *Lord, I have no protection.* I need another rescuer. Her eyes grew hot as an image of Ittai filled her watery vision. She should have fled with him that morn.

What was she going to do now? Curl up right here and wait until sunlight? How far was Gilgal on foot? Were there any beasts lurking to lap water? A slight throb pulsed in her ankle where she had been injured fleeing Eglon. Burying her face in her arms, she prayed, "Keep me safe, Lord. You are my refuge." She sniffled. "What else does the song say? I will praise the Lord, for even at night You instruct me." Glancing through a pattern of bramble branches, she draped herself over a large rock and let the warmth emanating from the stone calm her nerves. "Lord, I need that instruction now."

A small body rushed by Rimona's hiding place toward the gurgle of the water. Was it a child? Rimona crouched behind the boulder. Who would send a servant this late to draw water?

Rimona followed the line of bushes, hunching so as not to be seen. When the foliage ended, she stopped and scrutinized two broad shouldered forms by a pool. The men spoke to a girl under the starlight.

"You are sure he will not reason with King David," a tall man said in a deep voice.

"He has taken the king's wives in the sight of the city." The girl panted her reply.

Wait. Rimona recognized the thin, pointed features of the man. His speech was familiar as well. Jonathan waited by the pool. The priests' sons were here with her. She surveyed the stars glowing in the sky and whispered, "Toda raba, Lord."

The girl fled as quickly as she appeared. Her sandal slaps echoed in the night air.

As soon as the messenger was gone, Rimona emerged from her hiding place, bowing, and greeting her friends.

Jonathan stumbled over a rock and clung tightly to Ahimaaz.

"Rimona?" Jonathan's voice warbled. "What are you doing here?"

Ahimaaz tugged on his friend's robe. "We must leave. Too many people are about tonight."

"Don't leave me." She drew closer, but not too close. "I've run away from my uncle. From the shame Absalom prepares to heap upon my head. Don't lea—"

"Who hides in the bushes!" a command came from the road.

Jonathan motioned for Rimona to take cover. He strode toward the stalker, his long strides reaching the path before anyone could round the line of bushes.

"It is I, Jonathan, son of Abiathar, the priest. I have come to dip some water for worship. Zadok's son is with me at the pool."

The throb of Rimona's heartbeat drowned any deciphering of Jonathan's banter.

When Jonathan returned, he flailed for her to follow him to a grove of trees. A pack of donkeys were tied in the brush.

The scent of donkey dander and chewed grass was a welcome perfume to Rimona's nose.

"We must hurry. Choose a donkey." Jonathan practically leapt onto his mount. "From the rise in that stranger's voice, I do not think he believed I came so late to draw water."

"Where are we going," Rimona rasped as her donkey trotted after Jonathan.

"To Gilgal by way of Bahurim."

Those were the best instructions she'd heard all day.

~*~

Late into the evening until almost morn, they rode. A white froth hung from her donkey's mouth. The animal's breaths grew rushed. They would have to rest the animals soon before they collapsed from exhaustion. Rest would never come to her body until she was reunited with God's anointed king.

"We are almost to Bahurim. I can see the shadows of the ridge," Jonathan said.

Ahimaaz halted his donkey and jumped from his ride. He raced toward a rocky plateau overlooking the road they had recently traveled through the valley. His curls bounced as he traversed rock to rock like a skilled huntsman.

"What are you doing?" Jonathan's sharp questioning was at odds with his mild manners.

Stopping near the ledge of the plateau, Ahimaaz squinted at the terrain. "I am not overlooking a prompting from the Lord. I have sensed we are not alone this night." He jabbed a finger at the dissipating darkness. "There's movement in the valley. We have been followed."

"They could be shepherds." She would offer any hope, for a woman captured in the wilderness may not make it back to the city. "Lord, protect us," she prayed.

Jonathan dismounted. He rushed toward her. "Give me your mount."

Panic seized her soul. "You are speaking foolishness." Was he? How far could they run on foot? Her hands trembled as she gripped tighter on her reins.

"Trust me." Jonathan's voice softened. "If we are found with sweaty mounts, they will know we rode all night from Jerusalem. We must find a home with loyal followers of David. They will hide us. We'll set off on the other side of the ridge and head toward Gilgal."

Ittai would be camped near the city of Gilgal. Her limbs obeyed Jonathan's order. She slid from her ride and traipsed after Jonathan. Ahimaaz sprinted past, the high slope of the plateau giving him speed.

Their donkeys were unbridled and slapped on the rump, sending them toward the Jordan River.

She and the sons of the priests scaled over rock, slid in a stream of pebbles, and maneuvered through brush until they came upon a dwelling nestled off the road. *Lord, I am trusting You that our lives do not end with a rap on this door.*

Bracing his arm on the threshold, Jonathan knocked on the door as breaths *whooshed* from his chest. The lanky musician motioned for Ahimaaz and her to wait near a tree not far from the side of the house.

The door creaked open.

"Please, I beg of you. I am Jonathan, son of Abiathar, a priest of our Lord. I need refuge, for my blood will be spilled this night if I am not hidden from Absalom's men." Jonathan stooped, his gaze set firm on the homeowner. "Another priest is with me and an orphan from the city."

A man rushed outside followed by a woman clutching his tunic.

"Hurry," the man said. "We have cut grain from the field. Climb into our well and we will cover you with our harvest."

Rimona raced after Ahimaaz, veering toward a walled well in a clearing by the home. She recited praises to God for His provision.

"The orphan is a woman," Jonathan said, grabbing a tarp from atop the well.

"She can come with me." The woman pointed toward the door of the house. "Hide in the room with my daughters. No one will notice one more girl."

Rimona glanced back to see Jonathan and Ahimaaz being lowered into the well. She ran after the wife and entered her home. What a blessing to travel over a smooth floor of hard-packed soil. No more jagged stones and rutted pathways to batter her feet.

The woman ushered Rimona into a room. Three girls slept on a large straw-filled bed. Two of the girls sat up as Rimona whipped off her head covering and loosened her sandals. She slipped under the woven blanket between her hosts' daughters. One of the girls looked old enough to marry soon. Another was about Lana's age. The third was only a few years old. The babe slumbered peacefully.

Soothing warmth comforted Rimona's body as she settled between the two youngest daughters. A waft of soap perfumed the air as the youngest girl cocooned into Rimona's chest. Oh, to sleep like a babe amidst this turmoil.

"You are loyal to King David," the middle girl whispered.

Rimona tried to turn her head without disturbing the little one. "Yes. I journeyed with two priests from Jerusalem."

"We should pray," the sister who resembled Lana's age said. "Hear O' Israel," she began softly. "The Lord our God, the Lord is one. Love the Lord your God."

"With all your heart and with all your soul," Rimona continued.

The older sister jumped in. "And with all your strength."

Hoof beats filled the courtyard outside of the home. Men shouted for the homeowner.

Every muscle and bone in Rimona's body throbbed. Eyes closed, her lips sputtered a prayer for protection, chanting it over and over. Her whole body stiffened when the door slammed.

A touch like a feather swept across Rimona's cheek. She opened her eyes and met the brown-eyed gaze of the babe. Tiny fingers continued their caress of Rimona's face. The soft touch calmed Rimona's fear. *Toda raba, Adonai. Watch over Your faithful servants.*

Shouts.

Mumbled conversation.

Hoof beats.

Silence.

Could it be Absalom's men had left?

Rimona kissed the baby girl's forehead. What a treasure these people possessed to have such a family. Her heart twinged at the thought that she would never know the delight of having a child.

A short time passed before the mother came into the bedroom.

"Hurry now. You must be on your way." The woman waved one hand and held Rimona's sandals in the other.

"May the Lord bless you all," Rimona said as she secured her head covering and hurried from the room. She didn't look back. What lay ahead for her own being, she did not know. She doubted her uncle would ever oversee her future again. Jonathan had cast her as an orphan, and she had never been more alone than this very night.

She joined Jonathan and Ahimaaz near the well.

"Take my donkeys and provisions," the homeowner urged. "Anything in service to David."

Jonathan shook his head.

Her spirit plummeted at the thought of running to Gilgal.

"I will pay you for them." Jonathan rummaged through a pouch tucked into his belt. "We released three donkeys not far from here and sent them toward the river." He handed the man a few coins.

"That is too much." The man tried to refuse.

Jonathan tugged on the man's arm and forced payment into his hand. "You have saved our lives this night. Receive God's blessing."

The man nodded.

She mounted her fresh-legged donkey, grateful for the beast, a satchel of bread, and a waterskin. Along the rocky ridge toward Gilgal, she followed Jonathan's lead and listened for any wayward scout that may be riding on the main road.

Nearing the outskirts of Gilgal, the sun threatened to dry her lips to chaff. Large oaks shaded the soil allowing a respite from the heat. Her donkey snapped at leafy branches testing the path's boundaries.

Her mount balked.

Men emerged from behind tree trunks. Several men had swords drawn and seemed ready to strike. Jonathan halted his beast and raised his hands in surrender.

"We mean you no harm," Jonathan shrieked.

She shivered as foot stomps advanced toward her from the rear. Her bone marrow became like butter.

Turning, she stifled a scream.

"Banak?" Her cry had become a greeting.

Praise the Lord!

24

Ittai remained rooted to the bank of the Jordan. David lounged in the shade of an oak with his nephews close by. Hamuran inspected the line of men stretching along the roadway. The rhythmic serenade of the river did nothing to calm Ittai's rage. The flowing water with its uniform notes reminded him of Shamar. The musician had chosen parchment and inked refrains over the safety of his niece.

Men raced toward the oak. They shouted for the king.

Banak and Hamuran escorted two men toward David.

Ittai strode to greet his commanders. He recognized Jonathan and Ahimaaz from Shamar's music room. The visitors were not strumming harps.

David rose from his station on the cut stump. He rushed toward the small band of men with Joab and Abishai ever present in his shadow.

"My loyal servants." David opened his arms and embraced each messenger. "I rejoice at seeing your faces. What news do you bring from Jerusalem? Was Hushai able to persuade my son?" David stepped backward allowing Jonathan and Ahimaaz to bow and show reverence to the king.

"My, lord," Jonathan began. "We have ridden all night to bring you this news." Jonathan hesitated, catching his breath. "You must set out immediately and cross the river. Hushai's advice has given you time to seek a place of refuge, but your advisor is not certain his counsel will hold."

Ahimaaz clasped his hands and shook them as if he jostled a die within his palms. "You must hurry. We were followed to Bahurim by men loyal to Absalom. We cannot be sure they won't spoil Hushai's plan to delay your son."

Not a grin, nor a frown, nor any emotion enlivened David's face. "Then my son has not set out to kill me and my men?"

The priests' sons beheld each other with eyes wide in silent communication.

Ittai lumbered closer to the messengers. "What was the advice given by Absalom's advisors?" Hushai may have persuaded Absalom to wait in Jerusalem for a while, but Ahithophel surely had planned the rebellion with Absalom. The esteemed traitor could overturn Hushai's counsel at any moment.

"Well." Jonathan rocked forward, closing the distance between him and his king. "Ahithophel counseled that your son should amass an army and massacre you and your men."

David's eyes narrowed. "But Absalom has not left Jerusalem? My son remains in the city."

"For how long?" Joab sidled up next to his uncle. "Did you not hear these men? Absalom sits on your throne, and he will not give it up. It is a matter of time before he attacks your forces and your family. We cannot survive an assault here on the open road."

Wisdom from a jackal's mouth. Joab had the birthright to challenge David.

"My son has been deceived by false counsel. Can I not hold out hope that he will see the error of his ways and humble himself?" David's gaze searched the men present for affirmation. No agreement came forth.

"My lord, the God of Abraham, Isaac, and Jacob offers forgiveness, but there is more." Jonathan held out his arm indicating David's stump. "You may want to sit."

Joab thumped his forehead with his hand. "We are at war. Speak your peace quickly before our blood stains this dirt."

Ittai found himself agreeing with Joab more often than he desired.

"A woman came to us while we waited outside of the city," Jonathan said.

"Your woman." Ahimaaz pointed toward Ittai. "The one you rescued. Shamar's kin."

The lap of the river roared in Ittai's ears. *My woman.* Hamuran and Banak observed him with interest. "Rimona? Shamar's niece? What was she doing outside of the city?" Alone, he suspected. His hand tightened into a fist at a vision of Shamar. "Where is she?" If they abandoned her, he would...

"She's with the women," Banak answered. "We intercepted these men and Rimona." Banak puffed his chest. "No one gets by my scouts."

Jonathan bent his neck ever so slightly toward

David. A hair of a movement Ittai caught and heeded. If an unwed woman fled a city, one who had recently fled for her life, Absalom was never humbling himself before his father, or before God.

Palms pressed together like a petition before the Most High, Jonathan nodded to David. "The woman told us that before she left the city, she witnessed"— Jonathan cleared his throat— "she saw your son defiling your wives on the rooftop of your palace. For all eyes to see." Gaze downcast, Jonathan mumbled a prayer.

David screamed in anguish. The rightful king of Israel slumped against Ittai. "No. It cannot be," the king sobbed. "How can I be dead to my son?"

Ittai had little experience comforting men. He patted David's back "You are not dead."

"Not yet." Joab kicked a rut in the ground. "We must cross the river at once. Will we go to Mahanaim? Other rebels found it easy to defend." He spat at the trunk of the oak. Wavy lines of shade cut his features like a jagged blade.

David separated himself from Ittai. He scrubbed his eyes free of tears. Scarlet eyelids marred his complexion. "I will be welcomed in Mahanaim." David's lips quivered. "I have secured their borders with Ammon and Moab. They will honor the peace I have brought them."

Joab motioned for his brother to draw near. "We will ready the ranks. I do not trust Absalom to listen to anything but his own lies."

The king cleared his throat and fought to conceal

his emotions. "Will you accompany us across the river?" The king nodded to his spiritual messengers. "I am in your debt for the word regarding my son."

"Our presence at the tabernacle will be missed if we stay away too long," Jonathan said. "We are often in Bethel. No one will suspect a journey this far north."

Ahimaaz bowed. "It would be my honor to accompany you, but Jonathan must return to the city and to his family. We would not want any harm to come to our fathers if our deeds were discovered."

A fresh pool of tears built in David's eyes. "I am forever in your debt. May God bless your travels, Jonathan, and protect your families. I pray he will see fit to protect mine."

"May it be so." Jonathan echoed the sentiment.

Banak led the messengers to the supply carts.

Hamuran took a few steps toward the road. "I should prepare the men to march." He waited, casting a glance at David.

"Yes, we will follow Joab and his men across the river." Ittai would not leave the king without a commander.

"Follow?" Hamuran quirked his brow. His confidant knew enough about Joab that acquiescing the least bit of power could lead to one's death.

"I don't believe the men of Mahanaim would welcome an army of Philistines even with their king at the helm." Ittai laughed hoping David would find the rivalry humorous. The shell of a king shuffled toward his wooden seat.

"Any words for Rimona?" Hamuran asked.

Words? Greeting? Confession? Consternation? What did an exile say to a woman who refused his offer of escape only to find her in his midst after Absalom's sordid display.

"She should have come with me at the beginning."

Hamuran grinned. "I will mention the king delayed you and that he needs your services. I won't cast blame. I know better." Hamuran's gaze lingered on David slouched under the great oak.

"Thank you." Maybe time would place some encouraging words on his tongue. "I will make sure we cross the river safely, and then I will speak with Rimona."

Nodding, Hamuran took his leave.

What did an exiled orphan say to a devastated king and father? Ittai's own father was a fog of a memory. A feeling without facts.

Ittai trudged over and crouched by the king. "God saw fit to bring us messengers from Jerusalem. We should set out before their words are meaningless." Ittai's gut clenched. Commanders did not linger after a warning.

A raven cawed above their heads. The bird's obnoxious tune tested Ittai's restraint.

"It's my fault," David muttered. The king didn't behold Ittai. He stared like a mystic expecting a vision. The river rolled along without a care to rebellion or a war or a slaughter. "My son learned this from me. Absalom is seeking justice for my past sins. So is Ahithophel."

"You fought for God. For Israel. Even in Ziklag,

you hid from King Saul instead of trying to kill him for the kingdom." Ittai would defend David with his life. He knew the heart of this man. A man that had compassion on a starving boy and gave him food and clothing. David made the orphan believe it was rightfully earned due to work and friendship and loyalty. Oh, Absalom. What have you done to your father?

"No." David shook his gray locks. The king sat limp and unwashed like a beggar. "I took a woman. I should have been off to war with my fighting men, but I stayed at the palace. I saw the most beautiful woman bathing on her rooftop. She couldn't see me, though I feasted my eyes. I knew it was wrong to summon her, but I wanted her. I was the king. My lust knew no bounds." David's chest quaked. "You think me a good man. When the woman was with child, I killed a good man so my sin would stay hidden and so I could have his wife. Only God held me to blame. He took the child. The babe of my sin." The raven cawed as if heaping scorn on the king. "God knows our hearts and our ways. God always knows."

"None of this matters to me." Hadn't he seen kings take women for pleasure? "You do not need to punish yourself." He inched closer to David. His knee ground into the soft soil. The scent of wet earth tried to calm his confusion. "God knows your heart. He has heard your words of repentance. God is watching over us now, even sending us messengers." And Rimona. A sense of peace settled on his soul.

Lines creased David's lips. "The woman who

became my wife and bore me other sons is Bathsheba, Ahithophel's granddaughter. He must harbor a chasm of hate for me for the shame I caused his family, and for the death of a mighty warrior. I hate myself, yet I have made every offering and repented for every minute of my sin before God."

Lord, help me comfort and counsel my friend. "This doesn't excuse Absalom's rebellion."

A tear escaped from David's eye and trailed over his cheek, perching on his lip. "My firstborn son took one of my daughters into his bed and defiled her. Tamar was Absalom's sister. I was furious with my heir. I should have accused him before the priests and sought justice for my beautiful daughter. How could I when my sin was the same. I wept. I raged. I did nothing of consequence. My heart wept over this abuse and sin, but I did nothing to reprimand my son. Absalom was enraged at my lack of action and brought justice himself. He killed my firstborn in a ruse, and I lost another son to the grave. Why should Absalom be stopped from killing me? I have failed my family."

"Your sons have failed you." Ittai choked back tears. What he wouldn't have given for a father like David. "Your sons knew the laws of God, of God's justice. They failed to let God be God."

"Oh, Ittai. Why couldn't I be that raider of Ziklag that you remember so well? One who rights wrongs and is feared by men because God rests at his side?"

Hamuran was right. Ittai was not good with words. How did one comfort a warrior king who fought champions and claimed victory? He would tell the truth and share the knowledge in his heart.

"You are the raider of Ziklag, and you will always be that man to me." Ittai's throat grew as thick as the reeds along the bank. "You lead a nation in worship of the One True God. Your words and deeds brought that God into my life. Look at the forgiveness you extended to Absalom after his sin. A sin against you and against God." Ittai stood and brushed the mud from his knee. The raven darted to the other side of the Jordan. "God has brought us this far even with Absalom and Ahithophel aligned against us. If God desired your death, it would have happened in Jerusalem, and you wouldn't be sitting under an oak with a smelly exile like me. Your son is the man who must answer to God for his actions. I must answer to God as well. And I will not explain to God how I let a traitor kill a man after God's own heart."

David rose and laid a hand on Ittai's bronze-studded breastplate. "Don't flatter me. I am not the raider of Ziklag at the moment."

"No, you're not. Aren't we going to Mahanaim?" Ittai grinned through unstable lips. "You are the gray haired, disheveled raider of Mahanaim, who needs a dunk in the river." He met David's gaze and gripped his mentor's hand. "I cannot think of a man that I am more honored to fight for. I don't know the mind of God. But I have witnessed your faithfulness to Him, and I have seen His faithfulness to you." Ittai stepped away from the king, remaining close enough to still clasp his hand. "I will walk with you as you join your family and your officials. And I will considerate it an honor."

The king tugged Ittai closer and kissed Ittai's chin. "What kind of commander are you? You walk with an old man and let Joab take the lead."

"I would stroll with you all the way to Mahanaim. And I know you would never leave a sword-wielding Joab at your back."

David laughed once, deep and hearty. "See, I did teach you well."

25

Ittai hadn't come to offer a greeting or a reprimand. Rimona had lost hope of seeing her commander after the lush riverbed had become a sea of rock, dust, and endless brown hills. Parveda had advised her of Ittai's new position. Overseeing a third of an army scattered over foreign terrain did have its challenges. Why should an esteemed commander care about an orphaned woman, especially one who had recently refused his offer of protection? Perhaps not seeing Ittai was best. A gift from the Lord. For if he fell at the hands of Absalom, she would miss him all the more.

Lord, You are the protector of the orphan, the widow, and the weak. Help me to rely solely on You.

Solitude was becoming Rimona's faithful friend. But how could she embrace a life with a scandalous rebel pawing at her flesh? Images of Absalom's bed sickened her. Absalom may not be too sympathetic to her uncle when she couldn't be located. No doubt, her standing with Shamar unraveled with her escape from the city. At best, her uncle would consider her a harlot.

"Would you like to ride?" Parveda's patterned veil puckered with the breeze revealing her long dark hair. "I do not see any fortress in the distance."

Rimona had lost herself in her thoughts amidst the drone of hoof stomps, footfalls, and the occasional squeak of a worn cartwheel. "In a while. I don't want to disturb baby Simeon." Parveda's youngest son lay draped over Rimona's shoulder. The boy should be able to slumber without a care to battles. "My feet have trod more of Israel in the last few days than in my twenty-four years. I'll let you know when I cannot take another step."

Parveda grinned as if they were sharing a meal in safety instead of fleeing a tyrant. "Walking is good for you. It frees the mind to ponder."

Ponder what? The upcoming war with Absalom? The death of her friends? Being carried off as plunder in defeat? She halted briefly and let Lana gain ground. The dutiful girl led a trio of mounts packed with supplies. A slight throb resounded through Rimona's feet.

South of the caravan of families, a cloud of dust rose from the sparse plain. The cloud grew fatter. More than a single rider approached. Had Absalom discarded Hushai's advice and set out after his father?

"Riders are coming." Her warning disturbed Simeon. The boy lifted his head only to fall back asleep snuggling tighter into her neck and chest.

Parveda slowed the mule pulling her cart. She stood and stared at the impending cloud. "I knew I would see his face today."

"Hamuran's?" Did husbands spend time with their wives on a march?

"Your rescuer is arriving." Parveda giggled like a

girl. "He is later than I expected."

Wasn't Ittai leading David's men? Truly, he didn't ride to seek her? Was he angry at her refusal to accompany him out of Jerusalem? Why reprimand a woman when lives were at stake. She licked her lips as her mind whirled with excuses for Ittai's presence. She cast a glance at Parveda and Lana. Both of her friends smiled too wide for her liking. Ittai could have many reasons for his journey. Didn't the women cart the supplies for his fighting men?

Ittai rode in front of a group of soldiers covered in leather, bronze, and a hefty amount of dust. Philistines were large people and the sight of these warriors advancing as one caused a slight panic to seize her muscles. If she were Simeon's size, she would be toddling under a cart. She shivered as if she had recently waded through the Jordan.

Ittai trotted his mount toward her, acknowledging a few greetings as he maneuvered through carts and wagons.

Her belly became a whirlpool of exuberance and regret.

"Rimona of Beersheba." Ittai's dark brown eyes bore into her like a beetle into grains of sand. "Or should I say, Rimona the Bold."

She nodded, careful not to bump Simeon as Ittai halted his mule. "You will have to do a better job of hiding, Commander, for I found you again."

"I'm glad you did." His jaw flared ever so slightly. "Jonathan told me of Absalom's debauchery in the city."

Warmth, not from the sun, tingled upon her cheeks. He hadn't blamed her outright for refusing his offer of protection. If she had left with him, her eyes would have been spared the vile acts on the rooftop.

"Why do you bother us?" Parveda beheld Ittai with a chastising grin. "Shouldn't you be with my husband?"

Ittai cocked his head. His plumed-helmet gleaned under the midday sunlight. "Your husband is learning what it is like to serve with the king's nephews. I'm making sure the king's son doesn't try to split our forces in two."

Was that a wink? What did Ittai have to say that couldn't be said in front of others?

Parveda shaded her eyes. "Your men look thirsty. Lana and I will offer some refreshment." She quirked a mischievous brow. "Lana, tie the animals to the back of the cart and take your brother from Rimona."

Lana complained about the chores. When the girl removed her sleeping brother from Rimona's breast, the bath of cool air pimpled Rimona's skin. She rubbed her shoulder using her arm as a shield. Ittai's presence would intimidate the most powerful of men, yet she would not leave, not until she made him understand why she stayed in the courtyard.

Ittai's lips pressed thin and curled at the ends as if their time together had been previously planned.

Why was she staring at Ittai's lips? She cleared her throat and absorbed his raptured attention.

"I was a fool not to flee with you, Ittai." She swept a hand alongside her face and tucked strands of hair inside her head covering. A lock of hair caught on her earring. She kept her gaze upon Ittai while she tried to disengage the golden hook. "You have watched over me since Hebron—"

"I knew you would not come with me." His confession stumbled over hers. "For my own peace, I had to try to convince you." He tugged gently on her earring. "You told me about these gems after our meeting with Absalom."

She nodded as her eyes tingled, coaxing tears to stand ready. How had Ittai remembered about her emeralds? His compassion was like a hug from her former neighbor Leah.

"I know why you stayed." Tenderness softened Ittai's gruff voice. "It's why my mother stayed in a land that was not kind to her. Your father is gone. Your mother is gone. And all you have is your uncle." The stroke of his thumb over the gems tugged on her lobe. "I was the foolish one asking you to leave the protection you had under your uncle's roof." He withdrew his hand.

"No, Ittai. You were not foolish. You were wise." She righted her head covering. "My uncle didn't protect me. He treated me like a servant. I couldn't stay and do his bidding in the palace."

"Or be a king's concubine?"

She stiffened. "Never! I could never be with such a man." She flapped a hand at the mounts he and his men had ridden "Wild mules couldn't drag me into Absalom's bed. I knew the prince was vile when we met him on the plain."

"That is the Rimona I remember." Ittai leaned closer. "You're a strong woman who stands against men in chariots and men with harps." He sputtered a laugh as if they were at the king's banquet, wearing fine clothes, and without a care in the kingdom. How could he be jovial with a war looming? Her temples pulsed as her body went from relief, to worry, to elation, to…what? What was to become of this man who had rescued her from Eglon and offered an escape from Shamar. Truly, he could see the pool of tears creating waves in her vision.

"Ittai, I'm worried. About you and Hamuran. About King David." She sniffled, trying to hide her weakness. "All these women and children heading toward a war."

"I know, Rimona." For once he said solely her name in a voice that was as gentle as a mother's hug. "I know what it is to be a small boy with no skills and a belly that grumbles every day. Mornings brought the fear of starvation until I met David and he led me to the One True God. Your God." He reached for her, stilled his hand, and then hooked a thumb in his thick leather belt. "I have to trust in God. Our Maker knows how this battle will end." The handsomest of smiles appeared on his face. "What did you hear me sing in your uncle's home?"

"I believe you spoke it." Tears dampened her cheeks. She swiped them away and took in all that was Ittai. "It truly was more of a recital." She chuckled at the memory that she would always cherish, a memory of a warrior and a young girl praising God before two amazed harpists and one dismayed uncle. "Our help comes from the Maker of heaven and earth."

He back-stepped from her and ended their brief reunion. "Stay with Parveda. She has been through many battles. Her wisdom and instincts cannot be taught. You will be safe under her care."

Fearing another geyser of tears, she nodded. "I will. Hamuran has the most hospitable family." An idea popped into her brain. "I should be as hospitable. Would you like a drink?" In the distance, Parveda offered a waterskin to one of Ittai's men.

His dark eyes beheld her as if she was the craftiest of foes. "I'm as refreshed as I will ever be." He scratched his beard, but she was certain she glimpsed a smile. "Remember my instruction." He grew serious. "Once the battles begin, all my memories of a fearful boy and a widowed mother disappear. I become a battle-hardened warrior chasing victory. And I won't stop fighting until David regains his throne."

"I wouldn't expect you to." She had never been prouder of Ittai. Not in Hebron, not in Jerusalem, and not in a courtyard. An exiled Philistine fought for her people and for her king.

"Shalom, Rimona the Bold." Turning, Ittai sprinted toward his men.

"Shalom, Ittai the Gittite."

She stood staring at men she had only met days ago as they rode off to protect a Hebrew king and his people. She stroked her earring and prayed for Ittai's safe return. How did Parveda do it? How did she kiss her husband and send him off to fight for his life? A child's cry broke her contemplation. Lana struggled to contain her brothers among the provisions.

Ambling between pack mules, Rimona made it to Parveda's cart.

"The men say there are trees not far ahead. I will welcome the shade." Parveda handed her a cup. "You must drink, or you will be trampled by wooden wheels." Her friend caressed Rimona's shoulder. "Enjoy life and live in the present. You must be strong and courageous in the Lord."

Rimona sipped the tepid water. "That is what Ittai said."

"Do not make me confess a man is right." Parveda cackled and took the cup.

In a flicker of a thought, Rimona pondered if it would have been better not to see Ittai again. The sight of her brave commander brought hope for a future. Was this what her mother felt when she married? Was this the love about which maidens sang? No matter where her boundary lines fell, she would praise God for the chance to befriend Ittai the Gittite. And if he died in battle, his sweet smile and the feel of her rescuer standing as a pillar on a hilltop outside of Hebron, would haunt her all of her days.

Be strong and courageous.

26

Ittai and his scouting party rested in the shade of old growth pines. The fortress of Mahanaim was a short ride in the distance. The high stone wall of the city would protect David and his followers from a barrage of arrows, rocks, or any projectile Absalom put to flame. Like a trampled ant hill, Mahanaim was alive and swelling with activity. Caravans of David's supporters descended on its gates. Praise God honorable and God-fearing men resided on this side of the river.

Picking at the bark of a nearby tree, shards of wood flaked from the trunk and poked a callous on Ittai's hand. Not a single stab of pain radiated through his finger. When had rough skin become a blessing? Tilting his head to assess the treetop, he bemoaned the high branches. No archer could perch in the pines without a boost to reach the lowest branch. Ittai had fought on seashores, plains, and mountain slopes. Forests claimed more lives than any other terrain. He prayed Absalom would not lurk behind tree trunks.

"A rider is coming," one of his men called from a nearby hill.

Racing to the edge of the forest, Ittai identified their visitor. He knew the pattern of the leather breastplate and the haughty raise of the arm. Joab approached.

A simmer of a memory shot a ping of fright through Ittai's frame. He was not a small boy scurrying from Joab's rage. David had made Ittai an equal to his nephew in standing and command. Ittai would prove his prowess to David and to the sons of Zeruiah.

"It's the king's nephew." Ittai shouted to his scouts. "Prepare to head to the city."

Was David in trouble? Perhaps the officials in Mahanaim did not welcome an army at their gates. Ittai mounted his mule and rode to meet Joab.

Joab slowed the charge of his mount. With one hand, he waved a sack in the air. "Shalom, Gittite. I have a gift for you." Joab launched the bag at Ittai causing Ittai's mount to balk at the assault.

Ittai grabbed the tied burlap sack. "What is in here? Did you bring me a swarm of asps?"

"You insult me. I could have thrown your cheese in the tree and made you climb for it. It smells almost as bad as you do."

Ittai clenched his teeth and swallowed a retort. He studied Joab with interest and suspicion. "Cheese?" Never in all his days had a commander brought him cheese.

"It's from a cow." Joab grinned, thinning the scars on his face. "My uncle has wealthy friends in these parts. They have brought bedding and food, good food, for our men to enjoy."

Handing the sack to a nearby scout to disperse, Ittai kicked his mule and drew nearer to his fellow commander. "You rode all the way out to these pines to deliver a meal? Alone?" Ittai laughed. "Did you find Absalom hiding at the city gate and you are the lone survivor?"

"Mahanaim is too far from Jerusalem for my cousin to amass a following with his lies. But he will come." Joab stared at the trees as if expecting a foe to be hiding in the branches. "Absalom has been plotting this rebellion since he regained his father's favor."

"From the murder of his brother."

"Half-brother." Joab's tone sobered. "You know a lot about my family. Too bad there is not much to know about yours." Joab quirked a brow and stared with the smug expression of a conspirator.

"Why are you here?" Ittai raked his tongue against his teeth and spit on the needle-strewn ground. Even the hint of pine sap in the air could not calm the resentment rising in his gut.

Joab slumped on his mount as if he were ready to converse with a confidant. Even in his casual stance, he looked about to hatch a scheme. "The king is asking about your whereabouts. I have been at his side for years, yet he worries about a foreigner."

"He shouldn't worry. I marched past Hebron and Etam unchallenged." Ittai shouldn't take pleasure in insulting Joab's tribesmen, but he did. "I'm not about to ride into an ambush."

"Shut your mouth. I don't have time for your boasts." This was the Joab of old. His former tormentor scowled. "I need you at the city gate."

Truly, he had heard the son of Zeruiah wrong.

"You, need me?" A chuckle gurgled from his throat. "Since when have you ever needed my help?" Ittai sobered. Was this a test of God? Or had something happened to Rimona? A whirlwind of fright tried to seize his thoughts. He wouldn't let his mind wallow in dark places. Parveda would watch over Rimona in the city. He met Joab's stare. The stare that noticed every muscle twitch, or jaw tick, or drip of sweat. "Do tell."

"He wants to march out with us." Joab shook his head. Ittai knew that slight shake meant frustration was sparking and if it was left to fester, a fiery rage would strike. Joab only spared one person his rage. David was the blessed one. "The king understands war. If he rides into battle, it won't matter where you, or I, or my brother fight. Absalom will pursue his father on the plains or in the thicket."

Rubbing a hand over his stubbly beard, Ittai disguised his grin. David wasn't listening to his trusted nephew. "You want me to align with you and tell the king to stay in the city?"

"You've grown brighter, Gittite. Come along and put an end to his nonsense. He'll listen to you." Joab turned his mount toward Mahanaim. "What are you waiting for?" Joab clicked his tongue. The click clack had better be for the mule. "Absalom and his men to arrive?"

Ittai shouted for his scouts to follow in line. He would return with Joab to prevent David from leaving the sanctuary of Mahanaim. The king's death is what Absalom and his army sought. If David fell by the sword, his loyal army would scatter, and Absalom would bathe the soil in blood.

The short journey to the city provided Ittai a chance to glean information about his foes. He trotted his mule alongside Joab. "Who commands Absalom's army? I know you've chastised every mighty man from here to Philistia."

"You've grown smarter, boy." Joab gave Ittai a side-eyed glare.

"But I'm not as patient." Ittai maintained his self-assured stature.

"My mother's sister's son. Another nephew of David's." Joab stated the offender's relation as if he were choosing a hunk of cheese from the gift sack. "It's an affliction of power, Gittite."

"Or of poor kinsmen. Of which I am proud I have none." Ittai tamped his gloating. *Lord, these boundary lines are becoming crazier by the day.*

Joab kicked his mount. "Lies from a thieving orphan."

~*~

As Ittai and his scouts approached David's new-found fortress, Hebrew travelers averted their paths. Ittai could blame their avoidance on his stench from baking in the heat, but he knew the fighting men saw him as an enemy, a pagan, and worse, an unclean Philistine. If they only knew some of their bands would fight beneath his command.

King David lounged at the main gate to the city, perched on a chair whose dark wood, oiled to perfection, begged the notice of every passerby. Officials stood at the king's side, noblemen Ittai did not recognize. These men had not traveled from Jerusalem. Their robes and flesh were free from stain and their features had not wrinkled from the terror of fleeing a tyrant in the night.

"Ittai." David clapped his hands in a joyous rhythm. He flailed his arms waving Ittai toward his mahogany throne.

The exuberant welcome should have been a soothing aloe to Ittai's spirit, but the mannerisms and beat of the slaps reminded Ittai of Shamar's betrayal of his niece and his beloved allegiance to inked parchment.

An aroma of roasted lamb filled Ittai's senses and banished his infuriating memory. God saw fit to bring Rimona into his care once again, and knowing how Parveda organized the families of his men, the savory aroma was surely the work of Parveda's hand and most likely Rimona's and Lana's as well.

"My lord." Ittai halted his mule a short distance from the king, sparing him a breeze of body odor. "You are as rested as I have seen you on this journey." Ittai scanned the city gate. Joab had disappeared. Ittai doubted he had received such a glowing welcome.

David indicated the men of wealth at his side. "My loyal friends have brought us gifts beyond measure. If I had ordered supplies, they would not have been as abundant as what my friends have brought to us. I have been blessed by their generosity. Barzillai has opened his storehouses."

The nobleman named Barzillai bowed his head, nearly losing his turban. A patterned sash hung from his aged shoulders. "The desert makes men tired and thirsty. This is the least we can do to show our allegiance."

Ittai's stomach rumbled. He pressed a hand to stop the noise and unleashed a louder roar.

David laughed. His wealthy followers joined him.

Sweat beaded above Ittai's lip. He breathed deep to try to stop the rumblings from his gut, but most of all, he tried to stop the anxiety cramping his stomach. David's laughter wasn't abuse. David wasn't Joab. The king needed a respite from his grief. Ittai grinned. He could give David this small victory and join in the revelry.

Nodding to the king's guests, Ittai said, "I rejoice with the scent of your gifts roasting on the fire."

"Come and eat. You are the last of my commanders to enter the city." David stood. The King of Israel was standing and urging him to enjoy a meal. Ittai absorbed the welcome from David and wished a son of Zeruiah witnessed the hospitality.

"I received some cheese from Joab, yet he is supping on the whole cow." Ittai bobbed a show of gratitude to David's benefactors and dismounted. "My men and I are in your debt."

"Protect our king." A younger nobleman indicated David. "He must retake the throne and return to Jerusalem."

"I will lead my men to victory, Shobi." David reclined in the chair. "They are loyal like none other."

How was a foreign-born warrior supposed to denounce a king's wishes? Ittai shifted so his broad form shadowed the king and guarded his words from the noblemen's ears. "I rarely, if ever, agree with Joab's advice, but he has given you wise counsel on where you should fight this battle."

"You want to pen me in this city?" David's tone sharpened. Ittai remembered it well. The nobles backed away from their king, but Ittai held his footing. David's orders and curses were nothing new. Ittai could recite them since childhood.

"Yes," Ittai said. David liked direct answers. "If we have to flee, Absalom will not care if half of us fall. His eyes will be searching for you. You are worth ten thousand of us." Ittai halted and admired the vast wall protecting Mahanaim. "Behind these stones, you live to fight another day. And I, nor the sons of Zeruiah, will have our thoughts divided on the battlefield."

David fisted his hands and banged them against the smooth arm rests. Ittai allowed him time to seethe and ponder. Warriors sought battle. Idleness made fighting men go mad.

With one last thud of his fists, David scrutinized Ittai. Tears glistened in the sovereign's eyes. "Will you be gentle with Absalom? God offers forgiveness, Ittai. I have seen it and felt it and fallen on my face before it." David grabbed Ittai's neck and brought him nose to nose. "Promise me, you will show favor to my son."

Mind reeling with images of chaos, blood, and deadly blows, Ittai nodded. "I will do my best. May God bring Absalom to me and not to the sons of

Zeruiah."

David's eyes clamped shut. "If only I had three of you, Ittai. I am forever in God's debt." David straightened, sitting as a mighty ruler. He waved his hand. "Off with you, Gittite. You need a bath and a meal."

"I am always happy to do the king's bidding." Ittai acknowledged David's benefactors and headed outside of the main gate to assess his men.

Huddled in conversation with two others, Ahimaaz, the priest's son and messenger, sipped from a cup and ate grapes from a basket slung over one of his companion's arms.

"Ahimaaz," Ittai called. "Come with me." His order had the harpist scrambling to get rid of his drink. Ahimaaz hurried toward Ittai.

"I need to organize these visitors into ranks and assess their prowess. You can pray with them." Ittai strode amongst men sitting on packed soil and with weary mounts. Ahimaaz trotted to keep pace with him.

"Would you like me to pray with them while they fill their bellies?"

Lord, I need patience. "I want you to pray that their bellies aren't disemboweled on the battlefield. War is coming."

"Commander," a voice rang out.

What now? He turned. Ahimaaz scurried away with a quick "Shalom."

Hamuran raised a basket above his head as if it were a trophy spirited away from the main gate into the outskirts.

"My wife and Rimona are sorting provisions for the men. I say your basket is bigger than most." Hamuran winked, handed Ittai the basket, and let out a low whistle. "More men come by the hour. Let us hope they know how to wield a sword."

"There won't be time to learn." Absalom had heeded Hushai's counsel and hadn't pursued his father in earnest, but Absalom was impatient for victory, and Ittai had no doubt the renegade son was on the prowl for blood. Did the son know of his father's prayer?

When evil men advance against me to devour my flesh, when my enemies and my foes attack me, they will stumble and fall.

Hamuran plucked a piece of honeycomb from Ittai's basket. "I hope we get one night of rest." His friend's words held more defeat than anticipation.

"So do I." For he knew one evil man was on the advance. And Ittai had vowed to protect David with his life no matter how many foes attacked.

27

The tearing of cloth made Rimona's teeth ache. Sitting on the edge of Parveda's cart, in an alley in Mahanaim, she poked a sharp knife into mighty fine sheets. The blade glided through the bedding with ease. Rimona shuddered envisioning how knives would slice through flesh soon enough. The roasted meat that scented the air earlier had given rise to smoking fires. Ash and sparks danced toward the darkening sky from a nearby fire pit. Although, many stomachs were satisfied with the delicacies of David, her insides threatened to spill the roasted grain and salted mutton she had supped on earlier.

She would work into the wee hours of the night ripping cloth for bandages for one may be needed to save Ittai, Hamuran, or other warriors injured in battle.

"Do not hold the cloth too high." Parveda leaned against the other side of the cart and worked a knife against the hem. "I do not want to insult the officials who believed we would sleep under this bedding. The cloth is better served to wrap the wounded."

Rimona would do all she could to assist Parveda and the injured. "Will you be setting up some beds by the city gate?"

Parveda cast a glance at Lana and her sons playing

with carved animals in the corner of the alley. "No. I will be going outside of the city. Stationed at the back of the lines."

"Why would you do that?" Rimona's arms tingled as she envisioned facing Absalom in his chariot, the wheels slicing her to pieces. "You have children." Rimona lowered her voice so as not to disturb Lana and her brothers. "Let me go. If I were to die, there is no one to grieve me."

"Stop that talk," Parveda rasped. "I would grieve you. So would my family. I can think of another who would mourn your loss." She widened her eyes and dipped her chin. "Have you bandaged an arm with a hand missing?"

Rimona's mouth gaped, but no words came forth.

"Could you put honey on a burn?"

"I could…"

"You shouldn't," Parveda scolded. "Honey will hold the heat in the skin and the man will scream until your ears melt. Water. Water is what you use on burned flesh." Parveda drew back and stilled. She waggled her finger. "Barrels and jars. We will need to gather more than what I brought."

Barrels, jars, and death. Had Rimona ever had a stranger conversation? Why was she even here in a faraway city talking about war? If Eglon had delivered her to her uncle, she wouldn't have met Ittai the Gittite outside of Hebron. Or Absalom on the plains of Etam. She could have hidden away in the music room and mourned her mother. Now, she feared she would grieve several more deaths. Her throat grew tight.

"How do you do it, over and over? How do you grieve and go on to the next battle?"

"If you are alive, grief will find you." Parveda grasped Rimona's hand with her strong, nimble fingers. "If you do not grieve, then you have never loved or experienced the joys of life. God gives us blessings, and He takes them away. In His own time, not ours." Parveda's eyes glistened in the moonlight. "Are you fond of Ittai?"

Rimona brushed one sandal with the other. She set her knife on the cart bed and stared at her and Parveda's intertwined hands. "I don't know that I have ever loved a man other than my father and grandfather." Her cheeks flamed hotter than the glowing embers in the fire pit. "I want to cry when I think I may not see Ittai again. I think about him all the time. Even tonight as I cut bandages and before when I packed the basket. I do not know what I will do if I never see him again." Her nostrils tingled as she remembered her rescuer. She would not cry in front of the children and cause them concern.

Parveda squeezed Rimona's hand. "God has placed Ittai in your life for a time and only God knows how long that will be. We will pray it is years beyond this battle."

"You seem so confident in my God." Rimona smiled at her overseer. "Um, our God." She shook her head covering. Who would have predicted that she would be sitting in Mahanaim talking to a Philistine mother about the God of Abraham, Isaac, and Jacob? Oh, how her boundary lines had changed.

"You are confident in our God or you would never have left Jerusalem and the protection of your uncle." Parveda let go of Rimona's hand. The cool of the evening settled upon Rimona's skin. "I trust you understand why I must do everything in my power to assist my husband and his men." She grinned, thinning her full lips. "It's like packing a basket for a special commander."

"Toda raba," Rimona whispered to her friend.

Parveda nodded toward her children. Her babe, Simeon, sprawled in Lana's lap. The girl held a carved camel and wiggled her hand to make it move and entertain her other brother.

"I had another child." Parveda spoke, but she did not gaze at Rimona. Her voice was weak as if tired from journeying far into the past. "A few years after Lana, I birthed a boy. He was beautiful. Long like his father with the sweetest eyes. He never cried." Parveda cast a glance at Rimona, her eyes misty. "My beautiful boy would not feed at my breast. Since he did not scream, I let him rest. I fell asleep myself and when I checked on him, his body was stiff and cool. Those sweet eyes were still open, but I knew he would never truly see me again. My baby had died." Parveda hunched forward and rocked, her arms cradling her waist. "I buried my sweet boy under an acacia tree near a creek bed in Gath. I mourned leaving my family when Hamuran was exiled, but I didn't know how I would handle the grief of leaving my boy. I would never be able to kneel by the creek and whisper to my son."

Tears streamed from Rimona's eyes. She swept them away and pretended to rub dust from her eyes. How could Parveda not wail?

Rimona reached over and embraced her friend.

"Time, Rimona. Time will assist with grief." Parveda slipped from Rimona's arms and gathered her youngest son, setting him on her hip. "God gave me more children to love. When I look at them, I know I must be strong."

"Be strong and courageous," Rimona echoed.

"Those words come from a Hebrew battle commander." Parveda rested her cheek on top of Simeon's onyx-colored hair.

"Yes, they do. Joshua exhorted my people to be strong and very courageous and to take the land that God had promised them."

"And that is what you will need to be my sweet, Rimona." Parveda motioned toward the knife on the cart bed. "We need more bandages."

"So, you will bring me along to help you?" Rimona had cared for an ailing mother but never for those impaled or bloodied in battle.

"I will. For the walls of this fortress are not as powerful as our God."

~*~

Rimona stretched along the solid stone wall of the alcove trying to sleep. Her fingers throbbed from holding the knife for hours and pulling apart stubborn weaves. Lana, snoring softly, lay beside her. The young girl gave off a soothing warmth and a faint scent of hyssop, but nothing calmed the chill seeping into Rimona's bones.

Scenarios, some blissful and some terrifying, played over in her head, one right after the other. She didn't have the experience of loving a warrior. Her own father fished and traveled, never drawing a sword.

Lana rolled on her other side and gazed at Rimona, her lids barely open.

"Aren't you tired?" Lana's question faltered as she breathed deeply.

The girl possessed her mother's confidence and trust. *Lord, may her confidence rub off on me.* Rimona unhooked her emerald earring. Even the gold and gems were cool to the touch.

"Lana," she whispered. "I have a gift for you."

"Hmm." Lana's eyes fluttered and then opened wide.

Rising on her elbow, Rimona dangled the earring for Lana to see. "I want you to put this in your pouch."

"To keep while you are with my mother?" Lana's nose crinkled as she grasped the jewels.

"Forever. It is yours now." Rimona forced the words through her stinging throat. "It will remind you of when you, Ittai, and I met a king."

Lana shook her tangled locks as she fumbled with the pouch on her belt. "What about your family?"

Rimona stroked the girl's hair. "I have a new one now."

And she would do everything within her power to

keep her new family alive.

28

Torchlight, a fiery orange, banished the gray of dawn. Runners approached from the direction of the Jordan. Ittai tightened his sword belt and tested the ease of his blade's unsheathing. His palm itched against the bronze hilt. He traipsed closer to the main gate of the city from his camp along the outer eastern wall.

Ooo-aaah. A shofar blast. The echoing hum from atop Mahanaim's wall called soldiers to war. Absalom was coming with an army in his wake.

Hamuran appeared at his side without the snap of a twig as a warning. His second-in-command reminded Ittai of the messenger's torches. Hamuran, tall and lean, wore a golden plume on his helmet. Arrows rarely grazed the feathers, but Ittai knew where his companion fought with a vapor of a glance.

"I wish Hushai had stammered his counsel for a week." Hamuran rubbed the back of his neck beneath the bronze band. "Our men could use another day of rest."

"They've had worse." Ittai set his hands on his waist, above his sword. The leather hem of his breastplate grazed the top of his hands. "Joab and Abishai are coming. I wonder what the men of blood have been plotting."

"Do you trust them to have our backs?" Hamuran cast a wary glance.

"I trust my back to fare better than Absalom's." Ittai scrubbed a hand over his chin. No whiskers bristled upon his fingers. Too much hair and one could lose their helmet and give an enemy a hand hold for a beheading.

Hooves clopped against the main road into the city. Joab and Abishai halted their mounts a few feet from Ittai. The stink of body odor, while not overpowering, soured the dawn air. Ittai breathed in the anticipation of war.

"Gittite." Joab nodded his direction. No acknowledgement of Hamuran slipped from Joab's lips. "My brother will head south toward Rabbah. I will defend the plain and cover you in the forest."

Silence.

Hamuran's plume twitched like a hungry hen pecking at flies.

Curse Joab for giving him the forest. Though, he and his men had scouted the pines and Ittai knew its foils. *Thank You, Lord.*

"No one remains to guard the city? You are confident the officials won't deliver David to Absalom if his forces assail the wall?"

The sons of Zeruiah exchanged a laugh.

Woe to you, Hebrews. A commander who did not consider all possibilities in warfare, usually died because of his oversight.

Abishai patted the rump of his mount in a smooth

rhythm. No helmet protected his skull. "Absalom would be a fool to send a force from the west. The Ammonites have treaties with my uncle. They will kill anyone setting foot on their lands as long as David is alive."

"So, your men will have an easy day?" One step. Two. Ittai strode closer to Abishai's mount. "If we need reinforcements, you will come to our aid?"

"If you need assistance." Abishai's last word held a hint of ridicule. "I will dispatch my men."

Joab leaned forward on his mule, creaking his leather. Abishai stilled his odd stroking of the mule.

"Make sure you have a shofar," Joab said as if war plans were a bother. "Two short blasts if you are losing too many men, Gittite. One long blast and the war is over. Absalom will have fallen."

Ittai grasped the mane of Joab's mule. The man's eyes bulged like ripened plums contorting his face. "You mean when we capture Absalom," Ittai said. "David wants his son taken alive."

Joab jerked his mule backward. "I heard my uncle. Am I deaf?" Veins bulged on Joab's neck. He cast a glance at his brother. "Absalom is family. We will take care of our cousin."

Ittai unfurled his hand and let a few strands of coarse hair drop from his palm. He stepped backward and allowed the sons of Zeruiah to leave and gather their ranks. Ittai knew not to trust Joab. He had seen the same smirk on the hillsides of Ziklag. If Absalom didn't come face-to-face with Ittai, he would be slain. Vow or no vow.

"Nice plume, Gittite." Joab shouted from his mount. "The color matches your blood."

Hamuran shuffled to his side. "And men say we are the barbarians."

~*~

Ittai and his commanders of thousands rode past David. The king stood in front of his mahogany throne a few yards from the main gate. Raising his hands, David blessed and praised the leaders of his army. Joab and Abishai rode on ahead, their fighting men marching south. At Joab's side, rode Ahimaaz. The tabernacle servant rounded on his ride, his gaze darting to David and then to Ittai. Ittai couldn't save the priest's son from Joab's talons. The sons of Zeruiah were accustomed to fighting alongside the Ark of God. Assuming Ahimaaz might become chief priest one day, they took him instead.

"Protect my son," the king shouted to his commanders. "Be gentle with Absalom." The king's order was forthright and held the optimism of a father.

Ittai sat straighter on his mule. A slight ache pulsed in his temples. Never had he heard empathy ring out for the leader of an opposing army. He prayed that amidst the thick of war, Absalom could be recognized and apprehended. He also prayed for Absalom to strike Ittai's forces, for he knew the sons of Zeruiah would stop at nothing to seize Absalom and blame his death on a wayward sword.

Behind David's waving arms, through the main

gate, women filled carts and wagons with supplies. Faithful wives prepared the cart beds to receive the injured. Ittai would not scan the gathering for Rimona. His focus must be on the survival of his warriors. Enough older men remained in the city to see to her safety. Loyal followers of David continued to gather on the road leading into Mahanaim supplying a steady stream of protection. God would have to watch over Rimona and the wives of his soldiers. He would seek her afterward if God saw fit to give him an afterward.

As Ittai and his men approached the forest, a strange sensation rippled across his forearms. He should praise the cover provided to his ranks by the mature trees, but needles and dead branches littered the forest floor. Ittai would find a way to battle so that his men did not become kindling for a fire.

"This is what Joab assigned to us?" Hamuran shaded his eyes to survey their battlefield. "I knew he resented you, but to burn you alive?"

Ittai's jaw stung as sour bile pooled in his mouth. "The sons of Zeruiah oppress those who threaten their wicked schemes. I know them too well to place all my men among these trees. Lead half our ranks to the plateaus." Ittai pointed north where chiseled rock formations could hide a grand army.

"How will I know when to reinforce your men?" Hamuran rolled his shoulders as if his armor had shrunk. "If this forest blazes, I won't be able to see you or Absalom through the smoke."

"Do not worry about Absalom. Our goal is to secure David's rule. If God places Absalom in our path, we will seek his capture. If God chooses to send him elsewhere"—Ittai frowned and met Hamuran's intense scrutiny—"it is war."

"Like no other. We usually fight against the Israelites, not with them."

"Order the ranks into small bands. Make sure each group has Philistine swords and at least one archer. Banak and I will hold the forest. You hold the outskirts."

Hamuran flinched. "I'm usually at your side."

"I need you to do what you do best." He didn't want to cast doubt on Hamuran's abilities, but his companion had a family to live for, and now Ittai cared for someone who needed the support of that family. He needed Hamuran to secure the highlands and return to Mahanaim a victor. "You can keep us alive. Your stealth can't be matched in the hills."

"And it can in a forest?" Hamuran pierced him with a stare as sharp as a javelin.

"No. But I'm the commander. I'll meet the brunt of Absalom's forces, and you'll make sure no Hebrew reinforcements advance from the river." Ittai clapped a hand on Hamuran's leather-clad shoulder. "I trust your oversight of the battlefields. Mine and Joab's." He quirked a knowing brow at Hamuran. "If you have to rescue me, you may have the seat of honor at the king's celebratory banquet."

"You're never wrong." Hamuran grinned. "Yet I'm always right." His companion kicked his mount and raised his sword in the air. "Formations." Hamuran's command reverberated over the landscape.

Ittai's heart pounded a secret war cry. *Lord, may all our boundary lines lead to You and to victory.*

~*~

Stationing his men behind the fattest tree trunks, and a few in high branches to shoot arrows, Ittai crept farther into his shaded battlefield. The sun couldn't scorch his men from above, but shadows danced on the uneven ground teasing and testing every war response he possessed. His muscles protested from the tricks. Opening and closing his fist for the fiftieth time, he was ready to wield his sword in David's stead.

Rustling, like the scamper of a rodent, drew his attention to a pair of pines growing as one evergreen. Ittai signaled to Banak and his men stationed nearby.

Ittai removed a perfectly rounded rock from his pouch and flung the stone in the direction of the noise, striking the soil. A body jerked from behind the pine. One of Ittai's archers reacted. The enemy fell forward, fully exposed, and with an arrow protruding from his side.

Cries bellowed from behind the fused trunk. A soldier retreated, shouting in Hebrew. Ittai eased from his position. A shriek split the thick sap-scented air, and then silence ruled again. Absalom's spies had fallen. The men were too loud to be accomplished warriors. Without another challenge, Ittai moved his men near the edge of the forest.

Ittai swept his gaze over the threat on the plains. A bead of sweat traveled down his neck and beneath his chest armor. Thousands of Hebrews blocked the view of the flatlands. Line after line of fighting men waited for the spies to return and inform on David's army. Absalom's spies would never arrive with wisdom. Praise the Lord.

"Orders?" Banak's words barely registered. His commander's ruddy cheeks glowed with perspiration.

"Fall back," Ittai said to Banak and his fellow commanders. He swept his tongue over his teeth hoping his instructions rang out with force and not the muffle of a cloth-filled mouth. "Get more men in trees. Make sure they have ropes."

"To hang—

"To sling down. An army on the move cannot be easily impaled with arrows. Or sword." Tiny tics pulsed upon Ittai's lower lip. "Banak and I will take a few bands of men and strike before their officer's eyes grow accustomed to the shade." Two commanders lurched to carry the message before Ittai dismissed them. "Listen for a long trumpet blast. We must hold this forest with our blood and bone."

"Banak shuffled his feet. "Shall we summon Hamuran's forces?"

"They would be slaughtered before they reached the forest. We have to draw Absalom's men into the darkness." Ittai punched Banak's bronze-and-leather chest armor. "Whether we live or die this day, God will be with us."

After a curt nod, Banak secured his helmet. "May we be strong in the Lord."

And then came what Ittai did best: war.

~*~

Oooh ahh. The long howl seeped into every pore on Ittai's bloodstained body. Longer and louder the blast sounded again, and again, and again. No one would have an excuse to spill more blood.

Hebrews retreated toward the plain, their stomping cushioned by limbs and lifeblood of the fallen.

Ittai wanted to scream. He and his men had held the forest. The Hebrew forces had devoured the trees pushing Ittai's men southward toward Joab's ranks, but the defense of David had not given way to the barrage of Absalom's men. Hubris and greed afflicted death on good men this day. Acrid smoke filled Ittai's lungs causing a cough. How many of his men had perished in the flames of the forest, barely able to roll away from the intense heat of the fire? Sparking swords over parched nature created a third enemy, one not led by Absalom or David, but by the breeze and retreating bodies all aflame.

"Ahhhh." Ittai emptied his putrid lungs. If any warrior dare follow his shriek, he would slay them twice over.

Banak and two men rushed toward his heart's cry. "That horn is not far off."

Ittai sobered. Abishai fought too far south to be sounding a horn at the edge of the forest. Joab hailed victory with the shofar, but if true, Absalom was caught or killed. And if caught, the traitor wouldn't be alive for long.

A cool stream of foreboding streaked through Ittai's veins. "Follow me. We must honor David's decree and take his son to the city."

Ittai bolted around trees and through the haze of smoke. His men panted to keep up, spitting the ash from their mouths. Ittai swallowed the pungent film resting on his tongue and almost vomited.

Lord, keep me from Joab's snares. Whatever commander or loyal fighter is alive, cast your mercy upon them. And Rimona. Futile. It was futile. He couldn't spare her from the horror of war. Would she see him differently when he returned covered with other men's blood? David. He fought for a king set on a throne by God. He would tell himself that truth for the rest of his days.

Footsteps approached, loud and sure of foot. Ittai halted his advance and waited. As the stomping grew near, Ittai lunged and seized a man by his throat. His rage almost snapped the man's neck.

"It-tai," the man rasped.

Ittai jerked and released his lethal hold. "Ahimaaz," he roared. "I could have killed you."

Ahimaaz bent at the waist and stroked his neck. "Joab," he wheezed. "Joab has Absalom. I am going to tell the king."

"He's alive?" Ittai asked, befuddled.

The priest's son stepped away from Ittai and his men. He shook his head. "You are too late. I'm taking the news to the king." Ahimaaz sprinted toward the plain in the direction of Mahanaim.

"Coward." Who raced to break a father's heart? Ittai turned toward Banak and his two officers. "Be on alert. We greet an asp with fangs at the ready."

A chorus of laughter rippled toward the treetops. The raucous cheering twisted Ittai's gut. *Why, Lord? Why did Absalom meet Joab's forces instead of mine?*

Ittai stormed ahead and charged into a small clearing void of brush or bramble brush. A lone oak had banished any growth from taking root. Blinking, Ittai fought the sliver of sunlight for clarity of sight. His men cursed. Ittai rotated his sword in hand, turn after turn after turn. "Lord, help us."

A body swayed from a low-hanging branch in the oak. Long, curly hair tethered the body to the tree. Three javelins protruded from the chest of the man. If it was a man. Ittai knew in his heart that the body bathed in scarlet was Absalom. Muscle and bone had been bludgeoned. No longer could Absalom be Jerusalem's favored prince. Joab's armor bearers gloated near the body. Their swords gleaned red and slick with Absalom's blood.

"You're going to take this to the king?" Ittai pointed his sword at Joab. A threat? Possibly? Condemnation, definitely. "How could you disobey the king?" Ittai's sword traveled the line of Joab's armor bearers. "You have struck down the king's son for your own vengeance."

"For the king's vengeance, Gittite." Joab's snarled and spit like a sickened panther. "My uncle is blind to threats on his throne. I have murdered for him before, and I will murder again," Joab screamed his promise, his blade shaking in his fist. "You dare insult my orders with only three men at your back."

Out of the corner of Ittai's eye, someone lunged. From behind a tree, a Hebrew soldier leapt. Banak rounded, sword ready, but high. The enemy plunged his knife into Banak's armpit. Banak slumped backward against the trunk of the tree.

Fire. White and searing like the heat of the fire that charred his men. That fire blazed inside of Ittai. Storming forth, he speared the Hebrew and withdrew his blade. The enemy collapsed, struck down. With righteous fury, he stalked Joab. Another of Ittai's commanders tended Banak. Ittai's scar-faced nemesis gloated.

"Now, you assail me with two men, boy. How you held the forest I will never know."

Ittai would kill them all with his bare hands. He glared at Joab's contorted expression. Was that fear on the face of his foe?

Commotion overtook the clearing. Voices and marching feet invaded the small space. Ittai rounded halfway. A warrior in a golden-plumed helmet led hundreds of men, Ittai's men, forward. Hamuran's forces surrounded Joab and his revelers.

Hamuran came alongside Ittai, a satisfied grin puffing his usually gaunt cheeks. "My commander held the forest by stealth and reinforcements, Joab. From the cliffs, I could see every advance. And now our commander has hundreds of fresh forces to do his bidding."

"With Philistine fools."

"Ah careful, old man" Hamuran warned. "I may act and repent later."

Ittai beheld Hamuran with admiration. "How did you get here so fast? The trumpet only blasted a short time ago?"

Hamuran's forehead furrowed, shifting the bronze band of his helmet lower on his face. "You jest. I heard the howl an hour ago. That is why I'm here in the forest. Ask any of my men, and they will tell you."

Where does my help come from? The Maker of heaven and earth. The Creator of forest and rock.

The weight of Absalom's tortured body creaked the oak branch adding its disdain for Absalom's killer. Ittai glowered at Joab.

"What are you going to do with the body?" Ittai asked. "You've mangled the boy beyond measure. No father should gaze upon his son like this." Ittai stepped forward, casting a shadow upon Joab and his lesser frame. He perched within striking distance, but Joab wouldn't dare knife Ittai in front of his men, and Ittai stood ready for the tiniest of flinches. "Even you, son of Zeruiah, won't be able to talk your way out of this offense. Your severed head will hang from the gates of Mahanaim."

"We'll bury him here. Dead is dead" Joab retreated toward his men. "Right, Gittite? We both gave David a victory. Mine is simply sweeter."

Ittai's pulse throbbed in his dirt covered neck. He had never hated a man more than Joab. Forgive me, Lord.

"See to Absalom." Ittai delighted in his voice's boom. "I have a loyal commander to attend to since you left an enemy alive, Joab."

Joab traipsed under the oak tree without an acknowledgement of Ittai or his army.

"Remember this, Lord," Ittai whispered.

Banak groaned from his station by the tree. "Remember me."

Ittai hugged his second-in-command and gave him a friendly push in Banak's direction. "My exceptional commander and a few of his men will carry you to the women and stewards. That coward's blade missed your heart. We should offer a prayer of thanksgiving."

Banak grimaced as Ittai and Hamuran lifted him from the ground. "Can you say the prayer after we get home?"

"Surely," Hamuran said, "And we can offer a prayer at the banquet that I will be attending." He winked at Ittai and swallowed his gloat.

Home. Ittai didn't think of Mahanaim as home. But for once in his grown life, he had someone he delighted in seeing, and reminiscing with and imagining in his future. And this time, in this exile's heart, it wasn't King David.

29

Late afternoon, Rimona drained a waterskin into a bucket. The walls of Mahanaim shaded the soil at its borders sheltering injured fighters from the blistering heat of the sun. Bleeding men who had not been struck down on the battlefield arrived slumped over donkeys or dragged upon soiled cloaks by weary runners. Women hurried in all directions gathering supplies and offering water to the wounded. Every fleeting moment, Rimona checked the hurting for Ittai or Hamuran. In the distance, on the battlefield, ribbons of smoke continued to twirl and join wisps of cloud. She could not fight sword to sword, but she would aid those who fought for a righteous king.

"Hurry, Rimona." Parveda's wave became agitated. "The men with burns need fresh water to ease their suffering."

Rimona grasped the handle of the bucket and rushed toward a cart holding two men. Her fingers trembled, sloshing water on her robe. A man shivered and shook on the near side of the cart. Fire had singed his flesh. Rimona's stomach hovered at the brink of spilling with all the stench of smoke and raw skin.

She had taken care of her mother, bathing and washing her body, but nothing in Rimona's life had prepared her for this misery. Thankfully, older men from the city and newly arrived fighting men, bandaged the maimed and broken. Women attended, but they did not touch the exposed flesh of the fallen.

"Here we go." Rimona set the bucket to the side of the quaking man. "Cool water will help with the pain." She prayed it would, for she was not a liar. The man mumbled, but he did not soak his arm.

Rimona nodded at an attendant as he submerged the burn patient's arm in the bucket. She turned from the stench of raw meat and toward her friend who piled strips of cloth in the corner of the cart. "How do you do this war after war, Parveda? Holding your breath from the smell of blood and praying your husband is not lost?"

Parveda's lips puckered. "I pray often for the injured men who make it off of the battlefield and for those warriors who die where they are slain. What else can I do?"

"Praise God we have not seen our men in these wagons." Rimona went to cover her mouth and thought better of the touch. When had she started considering Ittai as her man? Enough to voice it out loud. "I mean, Hamuran is your husband, and Ittai, is well…" She stammered finding a word to describe her rescuer. Warmth spread over her cheekbones.

Parveda brushed strands of hair from her eyes. "Ittai is your man. I don't know of any other commander who leaves his men when war is at hand to search for a woman. Certainly not one he met only days before. Love can be like that at times. Swift of heart." A hint of a smile graced Parveda's dirt smudged face. "You and Ittai are so similar."

How could a rugged commander from Gath and a young Hebrew woman be similar? Running into Ittai's form outside of Hebron, was like running into a mountain. Rimona shook her head. "I don't believe we are the same." She grasped an empty waterskin to fill at the well and followed Parveda while her friend replenished the stacks of bandages on each cart.

"You are both devoted to the people you love." Parveda glanced at the looming wall of Mahanaim. "I have seen it with Ittai. He is loyal to God and to his fighting men. He would give his life to spare any one of his men in battle. And you, Rimona,"—Parveda shielded her dark brown eyes from the sun—"you let life slip by while you cared for a sick mother. I say it's about time each of you found someone."

"Perhaps." Rimona forced an agreeable smile. The tips of her ears flamed with all this talk of Ittai. Even now, she worried about her bold commander and feared for his life. On occasion, she did dream about being held in his strong arms. But he was a Philistine. Could she marry outside of the tribes of her people and break God's law? Would her uncle allow it? Would she be an orphan and an outcast?

Rimona picked up an empty food basket and turned to head back to the city for replenishments. "I don't know what to think or feel right now. We are in the middle of a war."

"There will always be war." Parveda came alongside her, the bandage satchel folded and flattened. "That is something else you and Ittai share. A strong will to fight for what is right."

God, show me what boundary lines You have drawn for me.

The clop of hooves and a rumble of excited voices drew her attention toward three men riding donkeys toward the cart beds filled with the wounded. In the center of the riders, a man sat tall on his mount. A gold band sparkled across his forehead. His robe, and the garments of the men at his side, brought the burlap brown plains to life with scarlet and mustard and indigo designs.

Rimona swallowed. The taste of ash lingered in her throat. King David approached.

The king lifted his arm overhead. "Praise to my faithful stewards and fighting men. You bring honor to our kingdom."

Men shouted their adoration for the king. A few injured cried out in thanksgiving for the king's arrival.

Parveda tugged on Rimona's sleeve. "We are in their path."

Rimona side-stepped to make way for the king. She blinked at the man whose legend and songs were celebrated all of her life.

King David halted his donkey. His officials followed his lead.

David's thick-lashed eyes beheld her as if she were his child, and for once, few wrinkles grooved his chiseled features. "I have met you. You accompanied Ittai to my palace."

"My lord." She bobbed her head and gripped tight

to her metal bucket handle. The king grinned filling her belly with riptides. "Yes, we met in Jerusalem. I am R-Rimona, of Beersheba." Her affirmation rumbled on parched lips. "Ittai rescued me from a troubled kinsman. His men saved me again when I fled from Jerusalem." How much should she say to the king? She grabbed hold of Parveda. "This is the wife of Ittai's trusted commander."

The king acknowledged Parveda. "I have met your husband. He is a good man. He is as loyal to Ittai as Ittai is to me."

"Thank you, my king." Parveda bowed her head. For once, Rimona thought she felt Parveda tremble. "We are very fond of our men."

Rimona's mouth gaped. Why did Parveda speak such to the king? Would David believe she was Ittai's woman? The warmth at the tip of her ears engulfed her whole body.

King David grinned as if he had savored a fine meal. "I am very fond of your men as well. I pray they return safely. If only my kingdom were filled with such loyalty and faith, we wouldn't be here in exile." The king grew serious. He tilted his head. "Rimona." His beloved gaze rested upon her anew.

Rimona could have been blown to the Jordan by a single breath. "Yes, my king."

"You are doing precious work here." The king glimpsed the injured warriors. "My great-grandmother hailed from Moab. She left her family and her gods to care for a Hebrew mother-in-law. From what I am told, it was her tender spirit and her strong faith that captured the attention of my kinsman. Who would have thought the lineage of the king of Israel would flow through Moab." King David chuckled, as did his officials. He stroked his bearded chin. "I might have mentioned her to Ittai when he was a boy. You should ask him about her. Her name was Ruth. It seems I need a kingdom full of Ruths."

"I will ask Ittai if he remembers." Rimona tried to smile, but her lips quivered. As a child, she had heard stories of David's lineage. Reminiscing would be for naught if Ittai didn't return from the battlefield. Rimona rubbed her arms, embracing herself like her mother had done throughout her life. A peace swept over her as if God stood at her side, comforting her, and affirming that she would never be alone. "Thank you, my lord, for remembering me."

Parveda gently elbowed her waist.

"For remembering us."

"May the Lord bless you and keep you." The king stared at the expanse of people treating the wounded and those moving the men into the city. "May the Lord bless you and keep you all." His voice soared above the moans and muttered praises of the ill.

Once the king and his officials had traveled past, Parveda's elbow became sharper in Rimona's side. "Ruth. What a wonderful name for a daughter."

~*~

After David returned to the gateway of the city, a long horn blast sent a shudder from Rimona's shoulders down to her toes. Could it be? Could the battle have been won? No forces advanced against the city, so Ittai must have held the forest and Joab the plain. She met Parveda's misty-eyed stare as cheering erupted from Mahanaim and from a few of the injured in the closest carts. Relief swept through her bones as the shofar continued to announce King David's victory.

Not much later, a chorus of shouts drew her attention to the main gate. A man raced on the road from the direction of the forest. A haze of dust followed the messenger. Fighting men cheered his approach. Suddenly, another runner appeared. The elated calls of triumph eclipsed the moans of the suffering.

"Do you recognize those men," Parveda asked, breaking off a piece of honeycomb for an ailing warrior.

"I believe one is Ahimaaz. I saw him run from spies outside of Bahurim. They must be bringing news of victory."

"Or of Absalom's fate. If he is dead, the fighting will end straightaway."

"He was to be captured." Rimona turned and beheld her friend, capping the waterskin in her hand.

Parveda quirked a brow, casting doubt on Rimona's belief. "When you are fighting to stay alive, it can be difficult to show mercy to the man ordering his army to kill you. Even if the commander of the advancing army is the king's son."

"Absalom, Oh my son, Absalom." Cries erupted from the direction of the main gate. "Absalom, my son." Grief-stricken wails scaled the walls and permeated the air.

Rimona recognized the voice that had spoken wistfully of his lineage earlier. If only Absalom had the faith and humility of his ancestor Ruth, good God-fearing men would still be alive.

"Absalom! My Absalom." The king continued his lament.

Why Lord? Why do we have to live through this craziness? Rimona had lost a parent, but she had never lost a child, even a rebel child. Her eyes tingled with tears remembering the joy her family brought to her heart and the sorrow in Parveda's eyes when she recalled the death of her babe.

Rimona slung the waterskin over her shoulder and prepared to make another trip to the well. Absalom may have been slain, but she did not want any more fighters to die. She would tend the wounded until she came face to face with her commander.

Before she had traveled a short distance with her skins and a pack mule, riders charged toward the main gate. Men laden with shields and swords rode their mounts in earnest. Joab led the procession with his sword held high. Where was Ittai? Had she spoken hopeless nonsense to Parveda? Why had Joab returned and not her commander? Could Ittai be one of the men who had perished in the forest?

Lord, You must bring Ittai back to me. I don't need to be his woman, but I want to live in a world where there is a man named Ittai the Gittite.

30

Ittai charged his mule toward the city gate. His gut twisted in frustration at Joab, at Absalom, and at war. How dare Joab sneak away with a few trusted men leaving others to crush Absalom's bones beneath a pile of rocks. Confidants had relayed the truth that Joab had impaled Absalom while the prince hung helpless from an oak branch. One fatal blow would have killed the traitor, but three javelins? Joab's taste for revenge was never slated, not even by murder. Twice and thrice his vengeance reigned over Absalom's corpse.

Allowing runners to take word to David about his son was standard in war, but David was like no other king. The man loved his son. Betrayal did not hamper the king's devotion to Absalom. No womb had born Ittai a child, but he loved Lana like his own daughter. If she had wandered from her faith and sought to kill him, would he delight in her death? He knew deep down in his soul that he would try to find an ounce of mercy and remember a sweet girl who loved him for most of her life. Memories knew no master. Cherished memories remained ingrained in one's mind along with tormenting visions. Ittai knew that no man could control their appearance.

Squeezing the reins, Ittai ignored the burn

radiating from his knuckles. His hands were still stained from the slaughter of Absalom's army. He would wash later. After he waded through Joab's wrath and the desperation of a dear friend and king.

As Ittai neared the main entrance to Mahanaim, he refused to scan the women aiding the wounded. He needed his wits to combat Joab. A glimpse of Rimona would scatter his thoughts to the future and not to the present turmoil.

Fighting men slouched near the gate. Grouped together around campfires farther from the wall, their posture mirrored defeat, not victory. The scent of smoke and sun-drenched leather assaulted his nostrils.

An official perched by the gate met Ittai's gaze. A look of recognition dawned on his face. The noble raised a hand and motioned toward Ittai.

Slowing his mount, Ittai halted a short distance from the official. With the blood of war clinging to his skin, Ittai knew he was unclean in Israel for several days.

"You are the Gittite commander?" The official's words stumbled over each other as he pointed to a nearby house. "The king resides in the gatekeeper's home."

Ittai nodded and raced his mule toward the dwelling. People scurried from his path. He leapt from the animal and stormed into the house. He would apologize for his manners later.

A barrage of insults filled a room off to his right.

"You have made it clear that I mean nothing to you. Your commanders are cursed for their deeds and your rebellious son is praised." Ittai recognized Joab's disrespect in an instant. "Go out and encourage your men or no one will be left with you by nightfall."

Taking a deep breath, Ittai opened and closed his fists, allowing his palms to remain open. *Lord, calm my rage. Allow me to advise the king with wisdom and understanding.*

"Go!" Joab shouted, hunched over his seated and sobbing uncle. "If you don't welcome your men, it will be worse for you than any other calamity from your youth."

Ittai sauntered into the room, his gaze intent on Joab. He planted his feet alongside David's chair and crossed his arms over his armored chest. Nothing short of an earthquake would dislodge his presence. "You may go to the gateway and recognize the fighting men. The king and I will join you in time."

King David beheld Ittai with a face as mottled as a weaning babe. "Oh Ittai, my son is dead. My precious son."

"This is nonsense. Get him to the gate," Joab ordered as he stormed from the house.

Kneeling before the king, Ittai made sure to leave a small distance so as not to make the king unclean. He had never seen his friend completely undone. The strings of David's fortitude had unraveled and lay strewn on the dusty dirt floor. *God, please help me renew David's strength.* "I know you are hurting, my lord. I know your heart is heavy. I wish there was some way to trade my life for your son's."

"No, never." David sobered and brushed the tears

from his face. "I'm a fool to mourn my son. I know the truth. I can't seem to make my heart agree." David sniffled and held Ittai's gaze with eyes as watery as the Jordan. "Why couldn't you have been my son, Ittai. Your father would be proud to see your courage and skill. I'm not your father, but I am proud to see your faith and goodness. What would I do without my Gittite?"

Ittai's chest grew heavy as if the wall surrounding Mahanaim had fallen and trapped him beneath its grandeur. He inched closer, his knee grinding into the packed soil floor.

"I know it's difficult, my lord, but your men have fought through fire and blade for your survival and for the survival of your wives and children. If you could praise their deeds, I will stand by your side and aid you in any way I can."

A tear glistened on David's cheek. "You are right. I must honor the living and the fallen. God has seen fit to rescue me once again. Me and my family." The king stared at the ceiling, his features still and stalwart as if he had traveled to a different place. One not so troublesome. "The Lord is my rock, my fortress and my deliverer. My God is my rock in whom I take refuge." David's lip trembled as he attempted to smile. "You will come with me, Ittai. To the gate."

"Always." Ittai cleared the thickness from his throat. "I will be by your side."

"You know, Commander,"—David turned and tilted his head, his damp hair falling to his shoulder— "I will need another trusted advisor when we return to

Jerusalem. I hear one of my counselors has taken his own life since Absalom did not follow his wisdom. Jerusalem is a nice place to settle."

"I would be honored to serve you anywhere you lay your head." Ittai rose and motioned toward the door. "Shall we greet your loyal fighters at the gate and proclaim God's protection."

David nodded. "Wash your face Gittite. You're not a little boy anymore chasing piglets for dinner. You will frighten half the people in this city."

"And the other half?" Ittai grinned and relished the banter with the raider he had admired all of his life.

"They will swoon over those brooding eyes and pronounced chin. I could always tell when Joab raised your ire. Your eyes bulged fatter than melons." Finally, the tiniest hint of the man he knew in the hills outside of Ziklag flashed into being. Ittai fought a burst of emotion so big it would swamp the city.

David shuffled toward the sunlit doorway.

Ittai followed, remaining close, but not too close to his sovereign king.

"Mmm, Gittite," David mused, lost in a refuge of thought again, "do you remember my ancestor? A Moabitess named Ruth? She was loyal and full of faith like you."

Ittai vaguely remembered the name.

"Come along." David quickened his steps. "I will remind you while we sit by the gate."

And Ittai had no doubt he would. For the confident raider had returned.

~*~

When the sun began to set and the sky became the color of ripe embers, Ittai lumbered into the city to gather a cleansing jar. His skin had become itchy and ridged like frayed rope.

A girl dipped a ladle into a tall vessel and filled a pitcher with water.

Was it? Could it be? "Lana?"

The girl turned. Her mouth gaped and then smiled with a happiness that gripped Ittai's soul.

"Commander." She continued her silly and gut-wrenching grinning. "My father was here a while ago. He says you are camping outside of the city."

"We are. For a few days. The Israelites have laws about cleanliness after war."

Lana pouted. "A few days isn't too bad." Her eyes brightened. "Have you seen Rimona?"

Why would she ask such a thing? Was something wrong with Rimona? Had she been injured somehow? His heart scampered around his chest like a surprised desert rabbit. "She's all right, isn't she? She was with your mother." The thudding in his ears could easily overpower Lana's gentle voice.

"I think she's sad." Lana offered him a drink from her pitcher.

He declined. "Sad? About the war?"

"I don't know. She gave me this before the battle started." Lana rummaged one-handed to open a small pouch attached to her belt. Her eyes grew wide with delight as she dangled Rimona's gold and emerald earring. "Rimona said it was to remind me when all three of us visited the palace."

Ittai took the earring from Lana being careful not to touch her skin.

"I haven't showed it to my mother." Lana tapped her sandal as though she might be chastised for accepting the jewelry. "Do you think she'll let me keep it?"

Scrubbing a hand over his chin, Ittai wished he could see the bold woman who brought these gems to life. He clutched the earring in his palm. The facets of the emeralds fit comfortably against his flesh. "What if I keep this earring for a short time? I'm sure I can arrange something with your mother."

"Thank you, Commander." She bounced on her toes. "I'd better get back before my brothers start crying for another drink." She stilled. "You aren't coming." Her pout returned.

"Soon. In a few days."

Lana smiled and hurried off with her water.

Ittai opened his palm and stared at the earring. How far away that day seemed. The day he reunited with David and requested exile in a foreign land. A land he fought for with his life. As he turned toward the city gate, one of David's wealthy benefactors approached. Barzillai's turban sat straight on his silver hair, but his sash caught in his belt.

The elderly man raised his hand in greeting. "Blessed be you, Commander. You helped bring victory to my friend. If only I could have sustained his kingdom with my fighting skills."

Ittai bobbed his head in a show of respect. His plumed helmet shifted on his head. "Receive my thanks for all the supplies you provided for my men. You gave comfort not only to the king but to many a weary traveler."

"I know what it is to be weary. I have seen several years." Barzillai clasped his shriveled hands. Jeweled rings sparkled on several fingers. "May God give you rest this night from your battles. Shalom, my friend."

The gems in Ittai's palm grew heavy as if he carried a bronze sword.

Before David's benefactor hobbled away, Ittai said, "My friend. You know this land better than I. Perhaps you can help this warrior win one more victory."

31

Rimona balanced a mortar on her lap and ground wheat for bread. Parveda and other women patted the dough thin and placed it on a baking stone. Children helped distribute the bread to the fighting men lounging inside and outside of the city. Those who had killed in battle were unclean for seven days. By law, the warriors isolated themselves so as not to accidentally touch someone who hadn't witnessed the chaos of war or touched the dead.

Even the aroma of roasted wheat and olive oil couldn't alleviate Rimona's worry. She knew to pray to God and ask for the desires of her heart, but it had been three days since the battles ended, and she had not spoken to Ittai. How she longed to praise his victory and David's victory while beholding his rugged features. Who would have thought that a Philistine exile would have captured her heart and continued to cradle it in his strong hands? Her rescuer hadn't returned to share his tales of triumph with her.

It is well with my being, Lord. You watch over the orphan and the weak. Truly, I don't need Ittai to watch over me. You have done the oversight beyond measure. First, in the hills outside of Hebron, in Jerusalem, and now in the city of Mahanaim.

With Absalom dead, she could return to Jerusalem and live near a king who knew her by name. She doubted Shamar would accept her back under his roof. She shuddered at surrendering to her uncle. The music room rivaled a prison.

A squeal from one of Parveda's sons pierced the alley where the cooking fire smoldered. One of the boy's round stones had ricocheted off the wall and fallen into a small jar. His jubilant dance forced a smile upon Rimona's lips.

"Here, here," Rimona sang as the young one's hips shimmied.

Fat and wet, a tear slid down her cheek and plopped into her crushed kernels.

Sighing, Parveda grabbed her mortar. "We have oil to mix with the flour. It is time you had something to eat outside of these stone walls."

"I can't leave all the work to you." Rimona reached to reclaim her grinding bowl.

"Uh, uh, uh." Parveda pulled away just as Lana approached carrying two baskets.

"Are you ready to go?" Lana's gleeful question had Rimona going over the morning chores in her mind. Where had the girl been since waking?

"Walk with my daughter." Parveda flapped her hand, shooing Rimona away like one of her children. "Eat some bread, and you will feel better. The poor grain in your mortar is tinier than dust."

Rimona stood, grasped two mats, and followed Lana down the alley and out the main gate of the city. Would she glimpse Ittai among his men? Small camps of warriors spread out over the landscape like locusts swarming a barley field. Where would Ittai's men settle? The farthest camps were almost unrecognizable.

Warmth from the sun rested on Rimona's shoulders as she and Lana traipsed the wide, well-traveled road. The weave of the mats prickled the underside of Rimona's arm.

"I can carry one of the baskets." The girl had been hugging the baskets tight to her chest. Perhaps Lana savored the aroma of the bread. Rimona intended to tuck a mat beneath the basket handle.

Lana skipped off the road toward a sprawling acacia tree. The branches, broad and full, were shaped like an upside-down rowboat. Plenty of shade covered the bare ground above the roots.

"We're here." Lana pointed to a flat piece of ground. "You can unfurl the mats."

"Have you been this far out of the city before?" Rimona laid the mats in the shade. "This tree is truly an oasis from the sun."

Lana set a basket on each of the mats. She clutched Rimona's hand and led her to a single mat facing the road. "I'm hungry. Let's eat." The girl tugged Rimona to sit beside her.

"Don't you want your own place to sup?" Rimona didn't mind the girl's company, but why had she carried two prickly mats if they were to share?

"This mat is for me."

Rimona heard Ittai's deep, familiar voice before his mountain of a form revealed itself from behind the trunk of the acacia tree. Her bones became weightless as her rescuer stood before her grinning the smile of a commander who had set a cunning trap.

"Ittai." His name came out as a squeak. "You're here. You won." She was babbling because her heart was bouncing all over her chest and doing its own jubilant dance.

"Rimona." The rumble of her name on his lips nearly had her sprinting back to the city in fear. Fear of where this may lead and fear of the grief she would feel if this was his farewell. "Indeed, we won. We claimed victory for King David, but I don't believe I'm long for leading men into battle. The king is looking for new advisors. I believe I've earned his trust." He beheld her with eyes the color of tonka bean and amber. "I have fought in many wars. The victories gave me status and wealth, yet I have no one to comfort me when I return. No one but God that is."

"So, you feel alone." She twisted her hands not meaning to interrupt, but she wanted to talk and learn and dream. "We're both orphans," she babbled. This is not how she envisioned their reunion to be. She licked lips that had become like scorched reeds. And, oh, if he didn't follow her tongue with his calculating stare. "I know loneliness as well."

"We should eat our meal." Lana tugged on Rimona's sleeve. Rimona had almost forgotten Lana lounged at her side.

"Shall we." Ittai sat in front of her allowing enough distance to keep her clean and to show her respect. The anticipation in his gaze was better than a caress.

Lana uncovered the food in their basket. "You choose first."

"Hmm." The girl's words weren't registering in Rimona's brain. Ittai was here, under a tree, alive and hungry. Hungry to spend time with her.

"Rimona," Lana said, her tone becoming more forceful.

Lana's wide eyes beseeched Rimona to eat. Yes, she should choose something.

Tap. Tap. Tap.

Rimona glanced into the basket and noticed a square box made of cedar. The box was strategically placed on top of the flatbread. The cedar's sweet, soothing scent tempered the bread's aroma.

"What is this?" She held the lightweight box in her hand.

"Open it," Lana said, her head covering tugged close to her chin.

"I agree with Lana's wisdom." Ittai leaned closer. His eyes were aflame with a tease. "It's my secret."

He knew what was in the box.

Her fingers trembled as she opened the cedarwood. She gasped. Sparkling on top of the plain-colored wood was her earring. The one she had given to Lana. The one she held dear as a reminder of her family. The one that comforted her when her mother slipped away. Her three emeralds weren't alone. Alongside her earring was a mate as perfectly beautiful as her cherished earring. Her cheeks blazed as tingles of emotion throbbed behind her eyes. "Oh, Ittai. You...how did...why?" A wavy tide of tears obscured

Ittai's handsomeness. "But I gave Lana my earring." She glanced at Lana who was holding her head covering wide for all to see her ears. Two replicas of Rimona's earrings, smaller, but equally as beautiful, hung from the girl's lobes.

"I wouldn't steal from my commander's daughter." Ittai winked at Lana, smiled, and then tempered his exuberance. "I've missed you, Rimona. I prayed to God to give David victory and to spare my life so I could spend time with you. To sit on a blanket and talk about childhoods and children. To have a future together." His eyes were twinkling again and causing a flutter she couldn't contain.

He reached for her, grazing the dirt at the edge of her mat with his fingertips.

"Ittai, you cannot touch me for four more days. And then…"

His brooding eyebrows quirked. "I touched you on a hill outside of Hebron?"

"You were saving my life."

"And now it is time for you to save mine." His intensity deepened causing her spirit to soar toward faded stars. "I believe God's boundary lines have brought us together. More than once. I'd like to start a family of my own and…"

"With me?" *Truly? Praise be. Right now?*

Ittai's boisterous laugh was a harp song to her soul. "Only with you, Rimona. Only with you."

32

Fifteen Months Later
Jerusalem, the City of David

"Rimona, the cart is ready." Ittai's lighthearted summons echoed through the window of their home. A home not far from the palace that had belonged to a nobleman who had aligned with Absalom. The homeowner had vanished before the rightful king regained his throne. Living close to the palace had its benefits. Ittai visited David often, and when he and Rimona weren't in the city, they managed land near the valley with Ittai's men and their families. Parveda and Lana were a constant treasure in her life. Parveda was an accomplished midwife and the first one to glimpse Ittai's heir.

Rimona swaddled her baby boy and hurried out the door.

"We could walk down the street," Rimona offered. "The fresh air would be good for Nathaniel."

"The boy gets enough air. He is growing so fast. You won't be able to hold him soon." Ittai's chest swelled broader than the length of the cart. Donkeys and all.

"Did you pack the basket of food?" Rimona

sniffed the breeze. The faint aroma of garlic scented the cart bed.

"There may be a few stuffed olives missing." Ittai grinned and helped her into the cart before sitting beside his family. "My wife is beautiful and a revered cook."

"Revered only by you."

Her husband glanced down the street and discreetly placed a kiss on her temple. The seat in the cart made her closer to Ittai's height. Tilting her chin, she didn't allow him to retreat without a kiss on the lips.

She and Ittai traveled past the palace and turned west to visit a large two-story house. Guards were stationed outside the door day and night. The men nodded to Ittai. Her husband's fighting prowess had gained him notoriety throughout the kingdom.

The door flew open.

Gihon danced on tiptoe to glimpse Nathaniel. "You are late. Did the giant eat all of my food?"

"The baby was fussing." Rimona handed Ittai his son while she slipped from the cart.

"Give him to me. He calms when I sing." Gihon cradled Nathaniel in her arms. "This child needs more family. I cannot leave this house because of that rebel's heinous sin, but your uncle has no reason to shut himself in his music room. You and Nathaniel should be more important to him than instruments and singing."

"I can think of one reason Shamar hides in his music room." Ittai's dark brows rose high on his forehead.

"Do not hurry back, Gittite." Gihon fluttered her hand. "I have stored a bushel of words for your wife."

Rimona retrieved the basket of delicacies and followed Gihon into her home, one she shared with the nine other concubines who had been left to secure the palace when David fled. Because of Absalom's defilement and death, they lived as widows. Rimona had banished the images of that night from her mind. All she would remember about that day was God's protection of ten women, two sons of priests, and a musician's niece. In His time, God had brought her a loving husband, new friends, and a healthy child.

Gihon entered her home and lounged on an oakwood bench covered with cloth pillows. She sputtered her lips and smiled at her youngest visitor. Nathaniel giggled at the beauty's affection.

Rimona laughed as her eyes fought back tears.

Toda raba, Adonai. The boundary lines You drew for two orphans, one from Beersheba and one from Gath, have fallen in delightfully pleasant places.

A Devotional Moment

My command is this: Love each other as I have loved you. Greater love has no one than this: to lay down one's life for one's friends. ~ John 15:12-13

The world likes to draw lines between people: them and us. "Them" are people of a different race, economic status, job description, religion, gender, geographic location...you name it, and the world can create a dividing line. And those divisions can sometimes make Jesus' command for us to love each other sometimes seem difficult. But, we are to love one another...as Christ loved each of us—sacrificially, unconditionally. There are supposed to be no divisions when it comes to love. And the greatest love, as Jesus tells us, is to be willing to sacrifice one's own life for another. This can be done in big ways—mortal ways—or it can be done in day-to-day choices where we sacrifice our wants for the good of another's needs. Good parents do it daily for their children. Good spouses do it daily for their spouses. Good friends do it for the sake of friendship, and strangers do it for strangers for the sake of justice, righteousness and mercy.

In **Defending David: Ittai's Journey**, the protagonist has made a choice that many think is foolish. He's chosen to follow a God that is not the god of his people, and he's chosen allegiance to a King of an opposing nation. But in being willing to lay down his life for what he believes is right, he finds peace and purpose for himself and those around him.

Have you ever wondered what the world would be like if there were no wars or prejudices? It seems almost unrealistic to think "world peace" could be anything but a cliché wished for by contest participants, but your choices can lead to world peace. Yes, one person can make a difference. When you love another person—either by open support or gentle correction, when you treat others with equity and respect; mercy and grace, you truly do take a step towards world peace. (Just think about if everybody did it!) So, the next time you're in a hurry and want to be rude to a cashier, stop and think about how tired he or she may be. The next time you want to spend your money on your frills when your children are hungry, forget the frills and feed your kids. The next time you witness an injustice, a person being harassed because of his race or one child bullying another, for example, make a stand. Love the downtrodden…and love the bigot and the bully, too. (Remember: love can be support, sacrifice or gentle correction). Your decisions have great impact—to those around you, to the world at large, and especially to God.

LORD, WHEN I CAN'T SEEM TO LOVE OTHERS THE WAY YOU LOVE ME, HELP ME TO SEE THEM AS YOU SEE THEM. HELP ME TO SHOW COMPASSION AND PATIENCE. HELP ME TO OFFER MERCY AND GRACE TO OTHERS, JUST AS YOU'VE SHOWN THEM TO ME. HELP ME ALWAYS TO CHOOSE THE RIGHT THING EVEN WHEN IT IS UNPOPULAR, AND GIVE ME PEACE AND PURPOSE IN ALL ASPECTS OF MY LIFE. IN JESUS' NAME I PRAY, AMEN.

A Note from Barbara

Thank you for spending time with Ittai and Rimona. I hope you enjoyed their story. You can find the story of Absalom's rebellion in the book of II Samuel in the Bible. I cover Chapters 15 through 19:8 in what would be relevant to Ittai the Gittite. Ittai is a historical person noted in God's Word.

Rimona is not mentioned in the Bible, but there is Scripture on Ittai's friendship with King David. Second Samuel, Chapter 15, tells of Ittai's arrival in Jerusalem and gives us his passionate speech of friendship and allegiance to David. Ittai arrives at a crucial time for King David, and I do not believe his arrival was a coincidence. God had a plan for Ittai and his exiled fighting men.

David must have had a bold trust in Ittai to place the Philistine over one-third of his army, an act that more than likely annoyed the king's nephews Joab and Abishai. Ittai is given his command in II Samuel 18:2.

We don't know what happened to Ittai after the battle against Absalom. Some commentators think he may have died, but since Scripture is silent, I believe Ittai survived. There is no mention of this faithful friend's death, and I believe such a loss would have been mourned in the text.

Scripture does not tell us how long David's flight from Jerusalem took or how long the battle against Absalom's forces raged. You'll find my story moves along at a quick pace.

How did Ittai come to have such a strong faith in

God and a strong allegiance to King David? We will never know this side of heaven. I make David's time in the Philistine territory of Ziklag the beginning of their friendship.

There is no Biblical record of Absalom meeting Ittai and his Philistine soldiers. How the two did not see each other when they traveled opposite directions to and from Jerusalem will remain a mystery.

Ittai and Rimona are fond of David's songs. Ittai and Lana recite Psalm 121 to Rimona's uncle. The talk of boundary lines is found in Psalm 16. David's song of praise about God being his rock is found in II Samuel 22.

Is King David playing matchmaker between Ittai and Rimona? David and his great-grandmother Ruth are in the lineage of Jesus Christ, and you can find them listed in the first chapter of the Gospel of Matthew. Ittai and Rimona have a son in the epilogue. Nathaniel means "Gift of God" in Hebrew.

With all the books on the market, I am blessed that you chose to read mine. I always say, God has the best storylines.

May the Lord bless you and keep you.
Barbara

Thank you...

for purchasing this Harbourlight title. For other inspirational stories, please visit our on-line bookstore at www.pelicanbookgroup.com.

For questions or more information, contact us at customer@pelicanbookgroup.com.

Harbourlight Books
The Beacon in Christian Fiction™
an imprint of Pelican Book Group
www.pelicanbookgroup.com

Connect with Us
www.facebook.com/Pelicanbookgroup
www.twitter.com/pelicanbookgrp

To receive news and specials, subscribe to our bulletin
http://pelink.us/bulletin

May God's glory shine through
this inspirational work of fiction.

AMDG

You Can Help!

At Pelican Book Group it is our mission to entertain readers with fiction that uplifts the Gospel. It is our privilege to spend time with you awhile as you read our stories.

We believe you can help us to bring Christ into the lives of people across the globe. And you don't have to open your wallet or even leave your house!

Here are 3 simple things you can do to help us bring illuminating fiction™ to people everywhere.

1) If you enjoyed this book, write a positive review. Post it at online retailers and websites where readers gather. And share your review with us at reviews@pelicanbookgroup.com (this does give us permission to reprint your review in whole or in part.)

2) If you enjoyed this book, recommend it to a friend in person, at a book club or on social media.

3) If you have suggestions on how we can improve or expand our selection, let us know. We value your opinion. Use the contact form on our web site or e-mail us at customer@pelicanbookgroup.com

God Can Help!

Are you in need? The Almighty can do great things for you. Holy is His Name! He has mercy in every generation. He can lift up the lowly and accomplish all things. Reach out today.

Do not fear: I am with you; do not be anxious: I am your God. I will strengthen you, I will help you, I will uphold you with my victorious right hand.

~Isaiah 41:10 (NAB)

We pray daily, and we especially pray for everyone connected to Pelican Book Group—that includes you! If you have a specific need, we welcome the opportunity to pray for you. Share your needs or praise reports at http://pelink.us/pray4us

Free eBook Offer

We're looking for booklovers like you to partner with us! Join our team of influencers today and periodically receive free eBooks!

For more information
Visit http://pelicanbookgroup.com/booklovers

How About Free Audiobooks?

We're looking for audiobook lovers, too! Partner with us as an audiobook lover and periodically receive free audiobooks!

For more information
Visit
http://pelicanbookgroup.com/booklovers/freeaudio.html

or e-mail
booklovers@pelicanbookgroup.com